A Presumptuous Hope

Daughters of the Gentry, Book Three

JENNIE GOUTET

Development edit by Jolene Perry at Waypoint Authors

Proof edit by Theresa Schultz at Marginalia Editing

Illustration by Sally Dunne

Cover Design by Shaela Odd at Blue Water Books

Dedicated to Louis-David Merhi, who was taken from us much too soon —and to the presumptuous hope we have of seeing him again.

CHAPTER ONE

"Christine, where in the *devil* did those mongrels come from?"

As soon as Christine Grey walked through the front door of Farlow Manor, her brother Gus's surly voice came from the kitchen amidst the sound of excited barking. She had expected this reaction from him when she'd discovered two starving, filthy puppies nosing around some cabbage rotting in the tenant fields near their estate and decided they certainly could not be left to fend for themselves. Guinea, her golden-colored pug, jumped off the little sofa and waddled over to greet her.

"You're a good little boy, aren't you?" she told him, bracing herself to deal with her brother. She didn't have much respite before Gus rounded the corridor into the drawing room.

"I thought I told you no more animals in this house," he said, in something of a growl. "You've already dumped three cats on me." As if on cue, her tabby, Ichabod, streaked across the floor and disappeared under the curtains.

With his dark curls, even features, and strong build, Gus had been blessed with fine looks and was frequently the object of admiring stares from the local young ladies. The brief flirtations never came to anything, though, for his character was not a conciliatory one. It would take a strong woman to put up with him. His marriage would save Christine from the brunt of his annoying traits, but she could hardly wish him on a lady she liked well enough to call sister.

"You did tell me, but I did not heed you," she replied in the pragmatic manner life had taught her to adopt with recalcitrant people. "You may not have the love of dogs that you have for your horses, but you could no more leave an abandoned foal to its fate than I could leave those dogs to theirs."

"They must be six months old if they're a day. They can survive on their own." Gus glowered at her in much the way their father had done; unlike their sire, he lacked the power to impose his will.

She picked Guinea up in her arms, comforting herself in the warm folds of the pug's neck. "I assure you, they were barely surviving when I found them, and they won't have to do so again while I have something to say. Besides, they are not mongrels. They're foxhounds and will make fine hunting dogs. Leave their care to me, and you shall be glad of them next autumn when they're old enough to hunt."

She brushed past him without giving him more attention than would be good for him. The more she argued with Gus, the more stubborn he became, she'd learned. It was better to simply remove the opportunity.

"We are not done talking about this," he called out from the drawing room.

"Of course not," Christine tossed over her shoulder as she entered the second pantry next to the kitchen, where the pups had their temporary bed. She set Guinea down and let him sniff along the sides of the wall as she went to the fenced-in area that kept the pups from exploring their new territory. There, she kneeled on the floor and patted her hand for Guinea to come and meet his new brother and sister. The pug would have none of it.

"You wish to remind them that you were here first. And you

2

are very right, Guinsey," she added, crooning the pug's nickname in a sing-song voice.

She turned her attention to the foxhounds, who had woken from a well-deserved nap after a copious meal of beef and barley and were now jumping up on the temporary gate she'd created. It would not serve for long, as these puppies would soon be big enough to leap over it. She reached down to caress each of them in turn.

"You see how much happier you are now that you're full of food? You look a great deal better already." She gave them a thorough examination, approving of the bright eyes and clamoring energy that was missing before but noticing the girl's watery nose augured a cold. They were the most delightful mix of caramel brown, black, and white. How Gus could think they were mongrels... But then, they did need a good wash.

"Miss, I didn't care to do so without your permission, but I thought I might give the pups a bath." Their footman came to stand at her side. "I've already filled the wooden tub in the garden and added some boiling water to take out the chill." Jimmy seemed to love animals as much as she did, which made it easy to trust him with them.

"Wonderful. Just make sure you rub them dry. There is a bite in the air, and the girl seems to have taken cold." She stood and smiled her thanks before leaning down to caress the pups' ears and speak a few more words of encouragement. Then, with Guinea's nails clicking faithfully behind at her heels, she left them to Jimmy's care. She'd not had time to think of names for her new dogs, but it would be fun to ponder while she baked something to serve with the tea.

SEVERAL DAYS later when the pups, now called Artemis and Hunter, were in excellent form and no longer content with the run of the house, Christine decided it was time to test their endurance on a longer walk. She would visit Philip and Honoria

3

Townsend, who lived a distance of under three miles, which should not prove too much exertion for two energetic hounds. They would have a good rest before returning home. And besides, she needed some company other than her brother.

The venture carried a risk that one of the pups would wander away. Hunter had that tendency. But she counted on Artemis for keeping her brother in order. Artemis never forgot who fed them. Christine set out with a jar of honey she knew Honoria would enjoy and followed the public road that bordered Philip's irrigated fields. After some distance—and with a glance at her dogs, who would quickly tire themselves out, running everywhere but on the road itself—she decided to leave the public road and cut through the private path that Philip had cleared after he and Honoria had married. This ran through the woods, along the border of the neighboring estate, the vacant Gracefield Park, and gave more direct access to the thermal spa they had developed on their property.

It was early October, and the air had turned crisp with the yellowed silver lime and gold-tinged oak leaves crunching under her feet. The dogs were in fine fettle, continuing to stray off the narrow path to sniff at delightful clumps of mystery, and Christine lifted her face to the weak autumn light that pierced the canopy of branches above to shine on the path. The woods smelled glorious. There was an ethereal silence around her except for the snuffling of the dogs, the wind that lifted the leaves, and the crunch of her boots. How she loved her home in Lincolnshire.

She was perfectly content. At age twenty-two, Christine had not had occasion to marry, and she was now resigned to not marrying. After all, it was unlikely she would meet someone eligible in Horncastle, and deep in her heart she wished to marry a Lincolnshire man who would never wish to leave it. It was even unlikelier that she would develop a sudden fondness for any local bachelor compelling enough to wish to bind her life to his. For all her brother was difficult to put up with, it was easier to bear with the failings one knew than court the risks of the unknown.

Those moments when she thought she might like to have children and a husband of her own were becoming less frequent. Her animals filled a good portion of her desire for affection. And the promised pleasures of some uncertain future paled before the contentment of her life at this precise moment.

There was a fallen log to her right, and a brief movement inside of it caught her eye. Curious, Christine went over to explore and spotted the large eyes and the cutest little ears of a hazel dormouse backing up farther into the log. As a girl, she used to search for and feed the wood creatures. Although the dormouse was not easy to find, her youth consisted of enough time spent outdoors that her patience was often rewarded with the discovery of one. In the three years since she'd moved back to Lincolnshire following her mother's death, she hadn't seen even one.

"Oh, you are looking for a nice place to settle down for the winter, aren't you?" she said, her smile sounding in her voice at this window of nostalgia the day had brought her. Were there hazelnut trees nearby to add to the creature's winter store? She couldn't be sure.

The distant sound of hooves beating down the path caused her to stand, and the mouse scurried out of the log and out of view. She wondered who could be riding through the woods at such a pace. Philip wouldn't do that unless there was something wrong. Christine came to the edge of the path with the intention of signaling her presence and wondered how to do so without startling him.

The horse that came into view was a black stallion she did not recognize. Its rider wore a voluminous cape, but he was not any more familiar to her than the horse, though he appeared to be a gentleman. She slipped back into the woods behind a tree, prepared to conceal herself until he went by. He should not be on a private road, and she must tell Philip and Honoria about him when she arrived.

Where are Artemis and Hunter?

The thought seized her and filled her with terror. She had

5

not seen or heard the pups since she veered off the path. They would surely be frightened by the noise and movement, and if they were frightened, they would not act predictably. She hesitated and stepped away from the tree, judging what best to do.

The rider approached in a cloud of dust at the same time the sound of barking reached her from the opposite side of the path. The yaps grew louder as the pups raced toward her, and suddenly she could not stay still.

"No!" Christine yelled, jumping onto the path as the rider drew level.

He swore an oath as both dogs converged on the road in a mass of noisy confusion. Christine froze at first, her blood turning to ice, as her eyes fixed on the terrible sight of both dogs running through the legs of the stallion, which immediately reared. She couldn't bear it anymore and ran forward to catch hold of the nearest dog just as the horse brought his legs down and reared again. The rider held the horse with an iron grip and was not thrown, but the horse came down a third time and broke into a run as Christine pushed the dogs to safety.

Her heart pattered as she examined them, and she nearly dropped from relief at the knowledge that neither dog was injured. Some distance ahead, the rider slowed and was bringing the stallion to a halt in less time than even Gus could have done.

Artemis and Hunter jumped up on her skirt, continuing to bark, then circled around her, skittish and excited after the beast had nearly trampled them to death. Christine trembled still and heard rather than saw the rider bringing the horse back to where she bent over her dogs. He had been irresponsible to ride at such a pace, but at least he had the decency to return to apologize and see to her well-being.

"Miss!" The man's voice snapped out an authoritative command. "Whatever possessed you to charge in front of a horse like that?"

He leapt down from the stallion and led him forward, causing the dogs to begin barking again. His riding cape swirled around his legs as he strode forward, his riding crop gripped in a tight, gloved hand. The fear and agitation that had shot through Christine now turned to fury as she faced him.

"Are you mad? What man of sense comes thundering down an unknown path through the woods at such a furious pace? A private road, I might add!"

He ate up the remaining distance toward her, her dogs barking madly around him, and with difficulty kept his horse from rearing up again. Hunter darted forward, and the rider tossed out his boot at the dog. It was more defensive than unkind, but it raised her wrath to the degree that her vision was clouded.

"Do not touch my dog," she snapped, her chest heaving. "How dare you add to the sins of your reckless behavior by kicking at him like that?"

The stranger had strong cheekbones and the kind of wavy brown hair she privately admitted a weakness for. Well, the kind she might admire if the man in question behaved as a gentleman should. He was much taller than she was, but it didn't stop her from lifting her chin and facing him, arms akimbo, as she challenged him with her gaze. He stared down at her, his expression no more amiable as he continued to control his horse, who fretted and pulled against his hold.

"I, reckless? What do you call it when you allow your dogs to run headlong into the path of an oncoming horse? And then compound the folly by leaping onto the path yourself just as the horse is rearing up to bolt! Do you have a death wish?"

The vague thought that he had a point, and that her dogs should be better trained, penetrated her cloud of anger, but what could she do? They were mere pups and had only joined her household days ago. Just now, they were making a great racket and running in between the horse's legs, then circling around to the stranger in excitement. That he might be even a little bit right only served to make her angrier.

"What do you expect, sir? This is not a racetrack, nor is it a public road. You should not even be on it."

Her eyes betrayed her as they traveled to the handsome coat

7

underneath his cape, noticing the strength that was visible through the tight sleeves as he held the horse still. The gentleman was white around his lips, but when he turned over his shoulder, his voice was gentle.

"Quiet, Gypsy." He shushed the stallion, who grew calm, despite the barking chaos that persisted. After a few seconds, he spared her a glance. "Call off your dogs."

Christine knew it was difficult for him to maintain his stallion in place with such distractions as barking, racing pups, but she did not care for his tone. He should see she would not hurry to do his bidding.

"First, tell me who gave you permission to be here."

The reins now loosened in his hand, he dropped on his haunches and made a sign for the dogs to come. Traitors that they were, the hounds began jumping on him instead of the horse, their barks turning to panting and squeals of pleasure as he petted them.

While he was engaged in pilfering her dogs' loyalty, he lifted his head. "I am aware that this road is private, as it is on my own property."

"Artemis! Hunter! Come here," Christine ordered her dogs, who completely ignored her. The indignity of this prevented his words from reaching her right away. At last they penetrated, and she turned a startled gaze to him. "This cannot be your road. Philip Townsend had it cleared. It is on *his* property."

"You are wrong, miss." He raised his set of thick eyebrows. "The road was meant to be on his side of the border between our properties, but he did not calculate correctly. He cleared the path on mine, as he was brought to see when I paid him a visit carrying proof." The stranger broke her gaze and stood, stroking his horse's nose who now waited patiently. Her pups lost interest and went off to sniff in the leaves.

"Therefore, you are trespassing on *my* property"—he glanced at Artemis and Hunter with something like a smirk—"and your dogs are, too."

"Artemis! Hunter!" she called again, ignoring his smug look.

Insufferable boor. The strange gentleman unsettled her. She did not fear him or fear for her safety, though they were alone in the woods. And with those caramel locks and angled green eyes, he was better looking than he had any right to be. But the fact that he was mostly in the right over their confrontation did nothing to soften her temper. Her dogs continued to ignore her and began exploring the woods again, crossing over on both sides of the path.

"Good day, sir."

She curtsied before turning to continue her walk to the Townsends', giving a sharp whistle for her dogs to come. It was oddly satisfying. Behind her, she heard at first nothing, then before long came the sounds of him mounting and turning his horse before continuing along the path, this time at a trot.

Christine had not succeeded in calming her agitation by the time she reached Boden House, but she kept it concealed, an effort to which she was no stranger. Therefore, when a servant brought her to Honoria, she was able to greet her friend with complacency, handing her the honey and admiring the new sofas and chairs which had arrived since her last visit.

"I've brought my new pups with me," she announced. "I left them with your gardener, who said they won't bother him any."

Honoria's affectionate eyes followed her son as he toddled over to Christine. "Pups? As in more than one?"

Christine picked Matthew up and held him, kissing his stomach to make him laugh. "Yes, there are two. I couldn't leave them. They were poking about in the tenants' fields, trying to survive off rotten cabbage. They are adorable." She turned her attention to the child in her arms. "Just as you are."

"Are you comparing my son to a dog?" Honoria asked, entirely without rancor.

"It would be a flattering comparison, wouldn't it?" Christine asked the baby boy before giving him a kiss on his cheek. "Oh yes, it would. Dogs are lovely creatures. Just as babies are."

"I am glad to hear you say so, because I have news." Honoria's broad smile gave a hint of what was to come. "I am increasing. Again."

Christine had no hesitation in going over to hug her and wish her all the happiness, handing Matthew back to his mother when he reached for her. "That is wonderful news. Your baby will be less than a year in age to Arabella and Theo's then. When are you due?"

"In March, I think. Or early April. In any case, soon enough that the dress I had made for the Stuff Ball will likely be too tight by the time the ball comes around. I am not sure I can have it taken out either, because I cut the cloth so close."

Christine hid the tiny pang of jealousy that sprang up. Envy was a sentiment she refused to allow in her friendships. It was only that in moments like these, it was slightly harder to reconcile herself to remaining single—when she contemplated the idea of being only an aunt to her beloved friends' children and never a mother herself. The longing always arose at inconvenient times, just when she had decided she was satisfied with her current status. To distract herself from these undesirable thoughts, she offered to look at the gown and see what might be done.

As Christine studied the stitches in the dark purple cloth and judged how to add panels, Honoria recounted the most recent changes in the nursery and how news of their mineral bath had traveled as far as Leicestershire. The thermal spa had sprung up naturally in the abandoned mine on their property, and its discovery had helped in restoring Philip's fortune. They were undergoing more recent renovations to modernize it, and Honoria said Philip was speculating on whether it might not be expanded. Christine listened quietly, and when the conversation had continued long enough in these comforting lines for her to trust herself, she brought up the topic that was on her mind.

"Do you have a new neighbor? I'd heard that someone purchased the baron's old estate, but that was a year ago and no one has moved in since."

"Oh, yes." Honoria smiled and glanced at her, forehead knit.

"But how do you know? Don't tell me Gus went to pay a call on him?"

"No." Christine gave an unladylike snort. "I believe I encountered the gentleman in the woods on your private road, which he says is his, by the way. Is that true?"

Honoria leveled her gaze at Christine without returning an immediate answer. She knew her better than anyone. Even better than Gus did, although that didn't say much since he wasn't particularly observant.

"He bothered you. What happened?"

Christine shrugged. "Nothing, really. It was fine. He merely galloped his horse down the path at such a pace as to endanger man and beast."

"Or Christine and pups?" Honoria suggested. "Is that all?"

"He was truly a most unpleasant gentleman." Christine pressed her lips together, remembering the way her dogs leapt all over him—the enemy—as though he were their favorite friend. "Even if he did handle the reins well."

"Unpleasant? That surprises me. Sir Alexander Thorne paid a call on us to introduce himself and discuss the mistaken property lines, but he could not have been more conciliatory. I thought him most gentlemanly." Honoria gave an impish smile. "I even thought he might be a good match for my dear friend, Christine."

The wavy head of hair, green eyes, and mouth turned down in irritation passed through Christine's vision, causing her to reply with uncharacteristic bitterness.

"Oh, yes. 'Tis all I need to achieve bliss. Tie myself to someone who can barely keep a civil tongue in his head, when I already have Gus to fulfill that role."

Honoria lifted her hands in surrender and laughed. "Very well. I shall abandon the idea—*for now*. Come and try my cook's Shrewsbury cakes. You look in need of a hot cup of tea."

CHAPTER TWO

Sir Alexander Thorne set out for his second visit to Horncastle, this time riding Gypsy at a proper, sedate pace. There had been no callers in the week since he'd at last taken up residence at Gracefield Park, after purchasing it a full year ago, and he could only assume the news of his arrival had not yet spread to local society. It was time he took matters into his own hands.

His ride through the woods brought to mind his disagreeable encounter with the woman from the day before. His object *then* had been to exercise his stallion who was badly in need of it; however, he had not ridden as a sensible man would. When the shady path in the woods appeared before him, he had raced along it as if being chased by demons. It was as though the anxieties and desires that kept him up at night had taken physical form and chased him across the shire.

For a brief time, that gallop had brought his ambitions and reality into harmony again, although such harmony never lasted long. It was a heady thing to come close to achieving one's goals at the young age of thirty-two, and there was no guarantee Fortune would continue to favor him in a world belonging to the nobility and gentry. His own family's origins were in trade, but now with the purchase of his estate, he was a landed gentleman.

All was well, was it not? There had been no need to gallop through the woods of Lincolnshire as though the hounds of hell were at his heels.

The result of his lapse was that he'd nearly run down a woman mad enough to step onto his path. The image of the dark-haired maiden appearing suddenly in a flash of blue caused a shudder to go through him. There was the surprise and fear from the harm he'd almost caused. Then there was the way she'd yelled at him, going on about how irresponsible he was to ride on his *own* path. He tried to put the episode out of his mind, but that was not an easy thing to do when he had few acquaintances in his new home to distract his thoughts.

Alex slowed his horse to cross the short bridge over the River Waring that led into town, still prey to the same futile thoughts about the unknown woman. Even now, the memory of their near run caused him to clench his teeth in irritation—at her for yelling at him like a shrew? At himself for being careless? He could not say. If he was being fair, she certainly hadn't resembled a shrew in their flash encounter. With dainty features, a slight build, and rich dark hair, she was nothing if not attractive. And her accent and clothing seemed refined, although the circumstances of their meeting left those details hazy. In different circumstances, she might be a woman he sought to gain an introduction to at Almack's.

He entered the quiet street that led to the mews and tipped his hat to a handsome couple driving in the opposite direction. They nodded a greeting in turn. The cordial exchange was just the thing to turn his thoughts in a more suitable direction—to his future position in Horncastle. Alex knew he had been particularly blessed with wealth and connections, despite coming from modest beginnings. His father had built the largest iron ore mill in Derbyshire, along with an adjoining forge to turn it to steel, and the family business was thriving under the care of Alex's older brother, Leonard.

As if his family wealth were not enough, Alex had also come under the notice of a baron hailing from Lincolnshire, Sir

William Winton, and his wife. Their only grandson had been Alex's friend in the short years before a childhood illness took him. Filled with nostalgia, the baron and his wife continued to visit the bereaved parents in Derbyshire each year, inviting Alex to come to the house so they might talk with him and imagine what their grandson might have become had he lived.

His father encouraged the relationship to continue through letters as soon as Alex learned to write. This resulted in Sir William and Lady Winton using their connections to obtain Alex a place at Eton, where his first education lay in refining his speech and imitating the mannerisms of the young gentlemen. It was not until later at Oxford that Alex began to grow more secure in his worth as he discovered in himself a talent for engineering and took pride in a skill that he had fostered entirely on his own. In the years following university, he put his talent to good use at the family mill by developing an effective prototype of a steam pump that could be reproduced and sold.

Mr. Thorne senior had always been impressed with both his sons but declared, before his death, that Alex would be the one to bring the Thorne name into the sphere of the gentry within the space of one generation. His brother did not cease to remind him of this duty—or that Alex must sponsor his nieces in London when they came of age. Even if Leonard had taken a genteel bride, his wife Martha could not boast of connections in fashionable London society, so it would be up to Alex's future bride. The pressure of all these expectations and ambitions would cause any sane man to gallop across the countryside in an effort to restore his peace of mind.

Alex dismounted in front of the mews and led the stallion inside, signaling to one of the men there to take his horse. "Rub him down and give him some water and feed."

He tossed the stable hand a coin, and the man brought Gypsy into one of the stalls. Alex exited the chilly interior of the stable into the October sun and looked around him at the simple brick buildings with thatched or slate roofs, not unlike the ones in his home in Derbyshire.

He turned onto High Street with its row of shops, still alert and fresh from the exercise of riding—and conscious of his desire to make a good impression on his future constituents, if all went as he had planned. Streams of people entered the shops or hurried to another destination, some stopping to greet a familiar face. His gaze sought out the ones who appeared to be of the gentry class, and he was gratified to see a number of them amidst the tradespeople. One day, he would be one of those people others sought out, particularly when they learned he had been given a seat in Parliament and owned one of the largest estates nearby. At least, he hoped it would be so. He nodded at a gentleman in passing and it was returned.

The door to the apothecary was open, and he entered it. The man behind the counter could not have been many more years than Alex, but he had a deliberate way about him that made him seem older than his years.

"Welcome, sir. How may I help you?"

"I am in need of tooth powder." It was nothing urgent, but Alex had to start somewhere, and making the acquaintance of the shop owners was a place to begin.

After rummaging around on the shelves behind him, the man handed a small jar to Alex. "Here you are, sir. That will be two shillings and five pence, if you please."

A young woman with a thin nose and pale lips came out carrying labeled jars, which she set on the shelf behind the apothecary. She examined him curiously, then turned to her husband, communicating to him with a nudge.

The apothecary asked what she had not. "Have we seen you in Horncastle before?"

"I have acquired an estate here but have only recently taken up residency. Perhaps you have heard of Gracefield Park?" Alex abhorred boasting, but he knew not how else to let people know who he was.

"You must be Sir Alexander Thorne." The woman had found her voice. "The vicar's housekeeper told us of your arrival."

"I am he," Alex said with a bow. He'd had the notion to introduce himself to the vicar upon his arrival, although it had not as yet produced any visits to his estate.

He went on, knowing he must mention his bid for the parliamentary seat as well. It would take some time for word to spread. "I am currently a member of Parliament, but I hope to transfer my representation to South Lindsey. I will be running for election here next year and am sure we will be meeting again in the future."

"We'll look forward to it." The apothecary glanced at the woman at his side before saying, "I am Martin Pasley, and this is my wife, Helen Pasley. Allow me to wish you success in your venture."

"You are very kind." Alex bowed again with a smile and tucked the jar of tooth powder into his pocket.

He left the apothecary and headed for Mrs. Reid's creamery. In addition to the dairy products she supplied to the town, which his cook had told him were the only ones she used, Mrs. Reid made cream cakes that he had bought and liked on his last visit. She had been very cordial to him as well, which made this second visit an easy choice. As he cut across the street toward the creamery, he noticed that more than one set of young women directed admiring looks his way.

Those he firmly avoided, for his aim must be higher. His goal was to secure a wife, issued of a good family, and at ease in society from birth. With a woman like that at his side, Alex's political success would be assured, and he could fulfill his promise to elevate the family name and launch his nieces into society. He would finally have everything a man could aspire to. It was time.

He paused outside of the creamery, allowing his eyes to roam in both directions on High Street as he turned the signet ring on the little finger of his left hand. His life, it seemed, was destined to follow the path of an ascending star. Roger Garrick, nephew of a duke, was his closest friend at Oxford, and it was Roger who'd put Alex in the way of the Prince Regent which had led to his eventual knighthood.

Even his severest critics could not object to this distinction, for the Thornes had put their steel into fabricating the Baker rifles used in the Peninsular War to defend England. Besides that, Alex, himself, had contributed his engineering knowledge and the family's steel to the construction of Brighton Palace. It was not surprising that Prinny should be pleased with him. Truly, he must cease to fret about his standing. Nothing would hinder his plans, when he had worked so hard to achieve them. The hunt for the perfect wife would begin when Parliament opened in the spring.

"Good day, Mrs. Reid," he said, upon entering.

"Sir Alexander." She curtsied before turning to reach behind her on the shelf and pull down the tray of cream cakes. "If I am not mistaken, you have come for more of these? You said you would."

"You have guessed correctly," he replied. "I will take four, if you please."

Mrs. Reid carried on a steady stream of conversation, specu-lating about the potential effect of his arrival in a way he was thankfully not required to answer as she wrapped up the cakes. He stayed for a minute longer, knowing how important these simple exchanges were. If he were to reach his goal of exchanging his meager influence in Parliament from the "pocket" borough of Grimsby that Sir William had gifted to him for that of South Lindsey—which had a real constituency and could only be won by fair election—it was essential that Alex begin fostering local connections without delay. After all, now that he'd tasted the pleasure of having a say in the country's future, his greatest wish was to establish himself more credibly.

After a few more of these pleasantries, he took leave of Mrs. Reid and decided to visit the draper's to see what kind of cloth was available if he needed to have something made in a fix. Alex stepped out of the creamery and squinted at the shops across the street, trying to remember which of the buildings housed the draper. While he was thus engaged, he heard a female voice calling out his name. He turned to find Mrs. Honoria Townsend smiling up at him. The pleasure of being addressed—of being known in his new town—brought a smile to his face, and he bowed and returned the greeting.

"I see you have discovered the delicious cakes that Mrs. Reid offers," she said with a knowing look at the package he was holding.

"You might say so, as this is my second time purchasing them." He glanced down at her basket, which appeared heavy. "Might I carry your basket for you?"

"That is most kind of you," she said, easily giving up her burden. "I was returning to the mews as my errands here are finished."

"Now that I have my cakes and tooth powder, there is nothing else I need," Alex replied, easily giving up his plan to visit the draper's that day. The errand could wait.

They began to walk forward, and Mrs. Townsend glanced around at the other pedestrians before returning her attention to him. "Are you partial to cakes?"

It seemed a strange question until he remembered the cream cakes he held in his hand. "I am, I confess. It is not something I ate much of growing up since my father did not approve of indulging one's sweet tooth."

She nodded, a smile hovering on her lips. "I have a friend who is very skilled at baking cakes. Perhaps one day you will try one of hers."

He sent her a furtive glance, wondering if this was a prelude to attempting to set him up. He did not want to hurt their fledgling acquaintance by telling her she would catch cold at it.

"Perhaps one day I will," he said, noncommittally.

To his relief, Mrs. Townsend said no more on the subject. "Gracefield House has been vacant for so many years. Do you have much to do in the way of repairs and renovation?"

"Much to do, and I am quickly coming to realize what a daunting project it is," he answered. "I know very little about decorating and such things."

"*Hm!*" She furrowed her brows. "Would you take it amiss if

Mr. Townsend and I came to call with the aim of walking through your house and offering suggestions? We have been renovating our own home since we married and our experience might be of some use to you. At the very least, we will have names of local tradesmen and workers who can provide a variety of services should you need them."

They had arrived at the mews, and the look he sent her was one of pure relief. "Far from taking it amiss, I would be much indebted to you."

"Well then, I will speak to my husband about it." Mrs. Townsend reached out for her basket and he handed it over to her. "He will be busy this week, but I am sure we will be free to come the week after if that is agreeable to you."

"Most agreeable," Alex replied, bidding her farewell with a bow.

He could hardly believe his luck at this chance meeting and her generous offer. If he needed any sign to convince him he had done right in settling in Horncastle, this was it. All he needed now were more calls and invitations—more entry into local society—and he would be well on his way to winning over the hearts of his future constituents.

CHAPTER THREE

The next morning held another leisurely examination of his property lines after breakfast, which Alex could scarcely grow weary of. At the end of it, he arrived at the large house and swung down from Gypsy, handing his groom the reins. "It was another long ride today."

Quinn brought the horse around to his right side and patted the stallion's neck. "He's young enough. He'll do."

Alex nodded and left to approach the front entrance to his home. Gracefield House, simply called, was more like a castle and grander than anything he had ever known. Made of brick, its three floors of windows stretched nine across and even the farthest ends jutted forward like—and it was the most ridiculous notion he'd ever had, but he could not shake it—like a person holding out his arms for a hug.

His initial reason for settling in Lincolnshire was to take Sir William up on his offer to enter Parliament by representing Grimsby, which was small enough for Sir William to use his influence to elect whom he liked. It did not take long for Alex to admire this part of England for its diversity and beauty, from the fens near the coast to the rolling hills of the wolds and all the beautiful countryside in between.

He found a way to put his steam pump to use on the coast

near Boston, using it to drain some of the remaining fens there, so that they might be turned into land for growing crops. The project was easy to oversee and left him with time on his hands, and he began to aspire to be elected to a seat based on merit rather than favor. That was when he had his solicitor look into properties for sale in the area of South Lindsey. After examining the possibilities, Smithson said that Gracefield Park near Horncastle might suit his needs, and Alex was immediately taken with it. Every time he lifted his eyes to the magnificent structure he owned, he felt the change in his circumstances with a degree of wonder not unmixed with pride.

The main entryway of the house had been repainted, and as Alex entered it, the clean walls and polished floors gave him a taste of what the rest would look like once he'd had everything redone. The problem, he had already admitted to himself, was that he had little sense of how to decorate each room. What colors should he use? What materials? How would he begin to pick out furniture or artwork? This was well beyond the scope of his talents, and he was looking forward to the promised visit of the Townsends. Smithson had hired men from Lincoln to do the job, but they would do nothing without guidance from him—the very last man equipped to give it.

If the house had not been in such a sad state, he could have left its complete renovation to the wife he would select in the spring. As it stood, it was impossible to bring a woman with any degree of sensibility to this home without at least setting *some* things to right before a wedding could occur.

A footman came to take his riding crop and hat, and he handed the items over. "Have a bath prepared and see that Mrs. Mulhouse sets out something in the way of tea."

"Yes, sir," the footman said, hurrying away to carry out his orders.

It pleased Alex to be quickly obeyed. Although it was his first time hiring servants accustomed to serving a gentleman, they were behaving as they ought. In Derbyshire, the family servants were more accustomed to serving a merchant and somehow managed to be familiar without giving offense. It was impossible to put them back in their place. Engaging servants was quite a different matter, he'd learned, when attempting to set up a home in the fashionable part of London. He discovered they could be high in the instep, and he didn't like being laughed at in his own home.

In a short time, Alex was bathed, dressed, and sitting in his study, ready to go through his correspondence. The tray of tea and refreshments sat untouched at his elbow. His first order of business was to reply to another member of Parliament about sitting in on a committee for the Mutiny Acts. He would not do it, as his interest lay in promoting the Corn Laws. They must not allow foreign grain to be imported, thereby weakening the income of English farmers. And now with his steam pumps at work on the fens, landowners there would be able to grow crops and increase their wealth, which would put them in favor of the Corn Laws, too. That must be where his focus lay if he were to be elected—to make himself valuable to local wealthy landowners.

Of course, he would have to word his refusal delicately, as his place in the Commons was not assured, representing a mere pocket borough. He took out a piece of paper and began scratching out polite courtesies but had not got far before he realized this would have to serve as a draft, never mind the waste of paper. His reply must be nothing short of perfect.

There was a knock on the front door, and Alex paused in his work at the novelty. At last, someone had come to pay a call on him. His one and only visit with the Townsends had occurred only because of the confusion over the property border. Apparently, his neighbor had been working from an old map—at least Alex did not think Townsend was attempting to carve out some of the land from Gracefield Park. He had not pegged him as the type. He was even more convinced of his innocence after Mrs. Townsend's kind offer in town the day before.

A tap on the study door sounded next, and when Alex called for him to enter, his butler carried in the two cards of the visitors. They belonged to a Mr. Theodore Dawson of Penwood Estate and Mr. Augustus Grey of Farlow Manor.

"Show them into the drawing room," he said, glancing at the tea, which he had scarcely touched. "And see that a tray of refreshments is brought to the visitors in case they should wish for something."

"Yes, sir." The butler left to do as he was bid.

Alex wasted no time in entering the drawing room, where he was pleased to find two gentlemen who looked to be about his age. If he had harbored a secret fear that purchasing an estate near Horncastle would be condemning himself to a life of older, sedate society, this visit, coming on the heels of the Townsends', relieved that fear at least.

It looked as though one of the gentlemen could have been related to him, although such a thing was not possible when he knew every relative right down to the most distant. It was not in the hair color, either, for both men had darker hair; but with one of them, he seemed to share some regularity of features and they were of the same build. It was only when the man smiled that he saw the difference. His smile was friendlier and more natural than Alex's would ever be. The other had a lanky grace and moved with a casual lassitude. In a flash judgment, Alex decided that nothing likely ever ruffled these men. Neither would have faced the precariousness of fitting into society that he had faced at Eton.

"Mr. Dawson," he said with a bow, "Mr. Grey, a pleasure to make your acquaintance."

"I am Theo Dawson," the one with a familial likeness said as he returned the bow. "Allow me to say the same. I heard about your arrival from Philip Townsend, who is my cousin. I brought our neighbor Gus along to see how you are settling in. That way you will feel free to return the visits should you wish to."

"Most kind of you." Alex smiled and gestured forward. "Have a seat, if you will. I ordered my servant to bring us something in the way of refreshments." The men sat, and a puff of dust erupted from the sofa cushions, causing Alex to grimace. "My arrival is recent. I am attempting to get the house and land in order, but it is a monumental task."

"I understand it has been vacant for some time," Mr. Dawson said. "Gus here says everyone has been waiting for either a long-lost heir to show up or for someone to purchase it." Alex gleaned from the comment that Mr. Dawson was a newer addition to Horncastle. Another reason to like the man. They had something in common besides an air of family.

He explained that he had been one of the first visitors to Gracefield after the house had been put on the market, which could not be done until the solicitors had proven there was no living heir. He then described what little he knew about their efforts and answered their questions about the property.

The servants were not slow in bringing in a tray with the tea, along with cakes and fruit that would be more appropriate for a social call than the meat and bread he'd initially wished for. Once he'd received the assurance that his guests preferred tea to claret, he waited until everything was set out and the maid had poured the tea—it would have to do in the absence of a female relation to perform the task—before turning his attention back to his visitors and the question Mr. Dawson had asked about the renovations.

"My objective is to do as much as I can to the estate before the parliamentary sessions open in the spring. Then I will need to go to London." Alex drank his tea and indicated for the men to help themselves to something from the tray.

"Do you serve in Parliament? The Commons, I suppose." Mr. Dawson appeared to be the more friendly of the two and had taken up the bulk of the guests' share of the conversation.

"Yes. I will also be running for election here in hope of switching seats. I stand at least some chance of winning since the incumbent is stepping down." Alex rubbed his fingers free of crumbs from the cake he had set on his plate. "Therefore, I must reside in London in the spring. Do you have a house there?" His guests both sported the attire of country gentlemen. Perhaps they had no higher aspirations than to remain in Lincolnshire.

"Not I." Mr. Grey focused on eating his cake, adding between mouthfuls, "I spent enough years living in rented rooms in the city of Bath, with never enough time for sport. Now, I have no ambition to do anything outside of Lincolnshire and hope I may never have to leave it again."

"I am originally from Nottinghamshire," Mr. Dawson said, confirming Alex's suspicion about him being a newer addition to Horncastle. "But I confess to a similar desire. I prefer to stay on the estate with my wife and child. My last trip to London was fraught with more excitement than I needed, and I have no immediate wish to return."

His enigmatic smile did not encourage Alex to ask him to elaborate. Instead he turned to Mr. Grey. "And you, sir, are you married?"

The man in question helped himself to another cake, needing no invitation to do so, and shook his head. "No, I live with my sister. She runs the home to perfection. I suppose I shall find a wife soon enough, but it is not my most urgent preoccupation."

Alex returned no answer as he sipped his tea, quite easily picturing Mr. Grey's older, spinster sister. He wouldn't mind having such a relation to see to his home and help with the decorating, although not even the convenience of a spinster relation would have stopped him from seeking a bride.

He had always wanted to be married—and not just to have a well-born wife to elevate his position. He hoped for conversation by the firelight and even affection. His memories of his own mother were elusive, but from what he'd witnessed of the Baron Winton and his wife, he assumed such a thing must be possible. He could quite easily picture them sitting by the fireside of an evening and sharing news about their day.

"Where are you from, Sir Alexander?" Mr. Dawson inquired, bringing him out of his reverie.

"I'm from Derbyshire, near Butterley." He clamped his mouth shut before inadvertently hinting at the fact he came from trade. It was not that he was ashamed of it, but he generally judged whether to disclose it after further acquaintance.

Experience had taught him that the news did not usually serve to raise him in the esteem of the people he spoke to.

"So not from Lincolnshire at any rate," Mr. Dawson said with another friendly smile. "I hope you are pleased with it so far."

Alex nodded and said he was.

"Did you attend Oxford or Cambridge?" Mr. Grey asked, which at least showed they thought him enough of a gentleman that the question of his education was an obvious one.

"Eton. Then Oxford. And you both?"

"We met in Harrow." Mr. Grey flashed him a grin. "I introduced Theo here to his own cousin. He and Philip had been estranged growing up."

"You are all connected through childhood ties, then."

This was just as it had been in Eton. His classmates had had these sorts of relationships that went back through the years; they did not have to learn how to speak and behave in order to fit in. Somehow, he had never managed to break into those circles in his first school. The only reason he had been given admittance to Eton was due to Sir William, and he had not found his footing until he was at Oxford.

"Nearly," Mr. Dawson replied with a smile. "As my mother married beneath her—my father was a cloth merchant—my uncle, Philip's father, did not acknowledge the connection. We nearly missed our childhood years altogether before being acquainted."

Alex was surprised by the admission and felt an immediate kinship with his guest. So Mr. Dawson was not a gentleman by birth either—at least not through his father—and yet he seemed to have found his place here. Perhaps they would soon be on a first-name basis.

He was not able to open up more about his own past before Mr. Dawson asked, "Have you thought about how you plan to restore the walled garden?"

The question pleased him because it was his desire to plant an orchard where new species could be grafted in. He launched into this topic and found an attentive listener in Mr. Dawson and a distracted one in Mr. Grey. As they followed that conversation thread, he didn't notice the time pass until Mr. Grey nudged him back to the present.

"We should be taking our leave." Mr. Grey stood, and Alex and Mr. Dawson did the same. "You have my card, and I hope you will come to visit us. I am sure my sister will be glad for a visitor. Just don't let her cats rub their fur all over you. You will never get it to come off."

Alex laughed, for Mr. Grey had completed his mental image of the spinster sister. Mr. Dawson gave a weak smile before adding, "Don't listen to Gus. His sister is a most genial woman, besides being a fine baker. I am persuaded that whatever dainty cakes Miss Grey provides will melt in your mouth. And I hope you will also consider coming to visit us, as well. My wife and I will be happy to receive you."

Alex thanked them and showed them to the door, promising to visit that week if they were not opposed.

"Come Thursday," Mr. Grey said as he stepped outside.

"Any time is fine for us," Mr. Dawson added with a lift of his hand.

Alex promised he would do so. He would visit Mr. Dawson first, though. He was a much easier man to get along with. Besides, he didn't have a spinster sister who would only make sheep eyes at him over the heads of the cats perched on her lap.

CHAPTER FOUR

C hristine opened the cellar door, which fell to the ground with a *whack*, revealing a few stone steps that led into obscurity. It was time to tackle the root cellar near the shed opposite their back door, which had not been cleaned since she and Gus had returned from Bath. The gardener had begun to dig up the remaining carrots and potatoes, anticipating a freeze, and she did not wish to store them in the cellar until the space had been cleaned out. A good mistress must oversee such tasks herself, even if it meant wearing a bit of dirt.

Gathering her courage, she went down into the cellar and began making trips with all the remaining root vegetables from last autumn. The sorting she wanted to do herself, then the servants could begin cleaning. She did not love the spiders that hid in the dank cave, but one could not put off responsibility just because of one's distaste of sly creatures of the eight-legged variety.

Artemis and Hunter chased each other around the walled garden, and even Guinea had resigned himself to their presence and begun to tag along, although he could not come close to keeping up with his brother and sister. It did not stop him from hustling forward when the pups took off, then skidding around and moving as fast as his little legs would carry him when they shifted in another direction.

Standing by the cellar with another basket of roots, Christine stopped to enjoy the sight, laughing as she watched them. The foxhounds' coats looked healthy now. Even Gus had grown accustomed to their presence and had begun testing the dogs' ability to respond to commands. They were now a permanent part of the household, just as she had known they would be.

Petunia, the most affectionate of her cats, slunk between her legs, causing her to glance down—where she got an unwelcome glimpse of her own appearance. The dirt from the cellar had spread from the apron to her dress. It was a good thing she had worn her oldest clothes for the task, but she would have to change before Sarah Pasley, the apothecary's sister, stopped by. It could not be said that she and Sarah were close, but they had developed something like a friendship in the last few months. And Christine had promised to give some of their hyssop and echinacea plants to Sarah, along with tea and cakes when she came for a visit.

It was too early in the day to be receiving visitors, however, and there was work yet to be done. She sorted the good vegetables from the bad, tossing the latter into a pile meant for the compost. Now it was time to bring the vegetables she planned to salvage into the kitchen and allow the maids and footman to continue the work in preparing the cellar for the late autumn harvest.

"Jimmy, I am finished with my part. Go and find Mary and Beatrice, who by now should be done washing windows on the south side of the house."

Christine entered the house, cradling the vegetables in her apron. She had chosen this day for her messy project when Mrs. Bunting was away for the day visiting her sick mother. Their cook would have fretted over the disorder and would only have been in the way besides.

A knock at the front entrance heralded the presence of one who, at the very least, could not be a tradesman, for they knew to use the side door. Although the visitor could be Sarah, if she'd come early, it was more likely Arabella or Honoria. Her closest friends sometimes came at an earlier hour for uninterrupted conversation. She unloaded the vegetables onto the kitchen table. Then, wiping her dirty hands on her slightly less dirty apron, Christine went to open the door.

The gentleman outside turned from surveying the courtyard to her, and when she caught sight of his face, her mouth went slack. It was the stranger—the rider from the Townsends' woods. For a stunned moment, they both stared, she at the shock of seeing *him* at her front door rather than finding one of her close friends, and he...well, since there had been a flash of recognition, she supposed he must be staring at her appearance. She swiped at a strand of hair that had fallen onto her cheek and tucked it behind her ear, then tried to clasp her hands in front of her to mask the discomfort she felt. It did not seem possible, however, to summon the words necessary for a greeting.

"Excuse me, miss," he began, before tightening his lips into a straight line. She could not tell if it was in disapproval or whether he was hiding amusement. Neither reaction was welcome.

Sir Alexander, Honoria had said his name was. His riding cape was thrown over his shoulders, and if she had thought him well built at that hasty encounter on the road, exposing more of his person did nothing to change her mind. Despite herself, the lingering irritation she'd felt over the memory of their encounter softened in the face of his attractiveness.

"Would you inform your master that Sir Alexander Thorne is returning his visit?" He paused for an imperious moment before adding, "He said I might call on Thursday."

This opened Christine's lips, although she could feel the flush that raced up her cheeks from embarrassment—and from the return of her ire in full force.

She responded in a clipped voice. "You are speaking with the *mistress* of Farlow Manor. I will tell my brother that you are here."

He flicked a glance at her clothing, then up to her face. "My apologies."

The apology, such as it was, only caused her lips to press together more severely. She was fully tempted to make him wait outdoors, but that would be ill-mannered. "Please. Come in."

Abandoning him in the entryway, she marched forth to find Gus. Where was he? She would wring his neck. Christine finally tracked him down in the study, and he glanced up when he saw her, merely raising his brow at her unusual appearance.

"You have a visitor," she said, spitting out the words. "A Sir Alexander Thorne. He said *you* told him he might call on Thursday. I would not wish to accuse the gentleman of telling an untruth, but did you indeed do so? And not inform *me* of the visit?"

Gus gave a crack of laughter, then upon seeing her murderous gaze, fixed his expression into something more conciliatory.

"I am terribly sorry. I did indeed invite him and forgot to tell you of it. In my defense, you are usually perfectly put together and ready to welcome a visitor, even without having prior warning. But this..." He gestured to her appearance. "Were you gardening, perchance?"

"I was cleaning the cellar." Christine started tapping her foot and continued in a lowered hiss. "What is he even doing here at this hour? It is not yet noon."

"Is that so, missy? If you were more presentable, the hour would not matter. How many times do I need to tell you to stop doing the work of the servants? It is not conduct befitting a lady." Gus glanced at his timepiece. "And I regret to inform you that it is nearly two o'clock."

Christine groaned. The time had flown by, and Sarah would arrive soon as well. "You go and entertain him. I will clean up, then see to a tray of tea. And next time," she said, rounding on him, "you *tell* me if you invite someone to call on a specific day. *Especially* if it's when Cook has a day off."

"I will," he replied meekly. When she turned to go, he added,

"You might want to see about washing your face. You have a streak of dirt across your cheek."

With the unhelpful comment chasing her out of the room and reminding her of what a fright she looked, she went upstairs to clean, brush and repin her hair, and change her dress. She did this as quickly as she could, not because she wanted to rush back and see Sir Alexander. Oh no! If she never saw him again, she would be all too pleased. Gus could see to his own guest. But she was proud of her reputation for the tea platter she set out. She wanted it to remain intact and hoped the refreshments would erase the visitor's poor opinion of her—*not* that she cared about that. With any luck, he would feel no desire to stay and would be on his way before Sarah arrived. That way, they wouldn't all need to sit in a cozy circle over tea and cake.

This hope proved too optimistic, for as soon as she reached the bottom of the stairs, the sounds of Gus and Sir Alexander's voices poured from the drawing room, and beyond it, another knock came on the front door. As the drawing room was situated right by the entrance, Christine was required to walk past the men in order to answer it. Wearing her finest day gown of bronze linen with yellow trim, she threw her shoulders back, lifted her chin and gave a queenly nod as she crossed in front of them.

Both gentlemen leapt to their feet as she went to answer the door and usher Sarah in. Gus gave Christine a look of pique at discovering the identity of the second visitor. He and Sarah bumped heads whenever they met. Christine ignored him—it would serve him right to feel a bit of discomfort himself for once. Sarah removed her cloak, bonnet, and gloves with an efficiency that matched Christine's own, then turned to curtsy before the gentlemen. She was petite with light brown hair that shone but was often out of place as a consequence of her love of riding and hunting.

"Sir Alexander," Gus said. "Allow me to make the introductions. This is Miss Sarah Pasley, sister to the apothecary in town."

"I am pleased to make your acquaintance, Miss Pasley. As a

matter of fact, I met your brother and his wife on my last visit into town."

With something like a smirk, Gus looked Christine's way, adding, "I don't believe you were properly introduced earlier, so please allow me to present my sister to you, Miss Christine Grey."

She brought her skewering gaze from her brother to Sir Alexander and dipped into a curtsy. "A pleasure, sir."

Even she could hear from her own dry tone how little a pleasure it was. First he tore through the countryside posing a danger to everyone around him, and then he leapt to the assumption that she was a servant, simply because she liked to have a personal hand in how her home was run. He was clearly a stranger to what it meant to value one's possessions.

Sarah selected a chair in the drawing room circle while Christine went to fetch the tea. She heard her asking Sir Alexander if he was new to the shire but did not stay to hear his reply. Placing the seed cakes she had made first thing in the morning onto a platter, she set out her patterned blue Spode china. In one dish went the jam, and in a matching jar went the cut dahlias that formed a tidy bouquet. The dishes belonged to her finest tea set. Nobody would have cause to say she was not every inch a lady when she set a tray out like this.

The maid entered the kitchen, now covered with dirt as Christine had been. "Would you like me to take the tray in, miss?"

Christine shook her head. "I will do it. Are you finished with the cellar?"

"Ay, miss. It's clean and ready for the carrots."

"Good. You may clean up and begin preparing dinner since Cook is not here." Christine smiled her thanks, then carried the tray into the drawing room.

As the men got to their feet once again, Sir Alexander glanced at her before turning to Gus with an air of bewilderment. "Do you not keep servants?"

Gus laughed rather than take offense, and even Sarah covered the chuckle that erupted from her lips. With the apparent sincerity of their visitor's question, Christine's opinion of him was fixed. Did he only deign to visit households whose occupants sat by idly while their servants ran the household? Maybe this was done in London, but not so in Lincolnshire. Perhaps her lapse, as he saw it, was a way to ensure he never came again. Since Gus did not answer, she was required to do so.

"Our servants are busy preparing the cellar for the winter. Some of us like to see that our homes are run efficiently without any hidden corners of dust or decay. At times, that requires getting one's hands a little dirty."

Christine caught sight of her own hands as she set the tray on the small table and quickly hid them from view. With no time to spare, she had not been as diligent as she ought to have been in cleaning her nails, for there was still dirt visible underneath.

While the tea was steeping, she sat and drew Sarah into conversation. "I have the herbs I've promised you set aside in the kitchen."

"That is kind of you." Sarah's eyes wandered to Gus, who had leaned forward to heap his plate with cakes. "My brother will be glad of them, as he won't be able to restore his flooded herb bed until next spring."

"Do you hunt?" Gus asked Sir Alexander as though the women weren't speaking. He balanced his plate on his lap, and Christine handed plates to Sarah and Sir Alexander before beginning to pour the tea. There was a moment's silence as she served cake to their guests.

"I've not had much opportunity in the last couple of years, but I do enjoy it." Sir Alexander bit into the cake and jam she'd served him, and she caught his look of surprised pleasure. That gave her private satisfaction. He might think her no better than a servant, but he would have to own she was a talented baker. He savored another bite before adding, "Are there good runs in this part of the county?"

It was Sarah who answered. "Oh yes. The Burton hunt near Lincoln is the best in all of north England. You might run over twenty-five miles if it's good sport. And Burton is certainly famous for that. It could rival the Quorn, *I* think." Her eyes brightened as they always did when she was speaking of hunting.

"Miss Pasley is right," Gus said. "But as she is already aware, my opinion is that there is no room for women on the hunt. They only get in the way."

"Oh yes, very true." Sarah calmly stirred the sugar in her tea. "Especially when the lady's horse is faster and able to leap over the stile before the other gentlemen are even in view." She lifted her cup to her lips, her eyes twinkling at Christine.

"That was once, and you had a more direct access to it," Gus grumbled. "It does not make you a superior rider."

Aster, Christine's cat with white paws, jumped onto her lap, and she started petting him absentmindedly. The rumble of its soft purrs soothed her as Christine looked up to follow the discussion. Sir Alexander's eyes were on her, and his expression revealed a cross between surprise and humor which puzzled her. What could possibly be funny about her petting a cat? Unless it was only that he found it odd that she liked animals.

It must be that, disagreeable man that he was. Although...he had done well with his horse and even her dogs, she grudgingly had to admit. So he must have some affection for animals. She dropped her gaze to her cat.

As Sarah and Gus's banter continued back and forth, she glanced up again, curious as to what the visitor made of it. His lips turned downward as he watched Sarah's animated countenance, which likely meant he agreed with Gus. Women were apparently not capable of any accomplishments besides what rendered a man's life comfortable. It reinforced her idea that Sir Alexander was a proud man, one who thought only of his consequence.

Sarah seemed to remember the plate in front of her, and after biting into the seed cake, dusted her fingers. "Perhaps you think a woman will hinder you on the hunting field, Gus. You might think it of me, even when I've proven to the contrary. But you

35

cannot deny that I've been able to shoot and bag more birds than you the one time we set up against each other."

"I don't know what came over me to agree to it. Women should not be shooting birds. I've told you that before, and I will not change my mind on the matter."

Gus's face had gone mulish again, and Christine alternated between embarrassment for her brother's weaknesses so openly displayed and enjoyment of Sarah's ability to poke at him in ways other people could not. More than once she wondered what Sarah truly thought of him. She had never brought herself to ask.

Sir Alexander's eyes flitted between the two of them with an impossible-to-read expression. It was not in Christine's nature to put herself forward in a conversation, even when she knew the participants. But in this case her resistance to contributing her mite was increased by the fact that she did not want Sir Alexander to have anything of her conversation without having to work for it. She could only guess that he was of the same mindset because neither of them said much in the short time they all sat over tea. Rather, they listened to Sarah and Gus carry on their dialogue, interspersed with little jibes. It would have been entertaining were she watching it on the stage. It was less so when she was an unwilling actor in the comedy.

At last Sir Alexander got to his feet. "I am afraid I must be going. It has been a pleasure to make your acquaintance, both of you." He bowed to Sarah, then her, but did not look in her direction when he did so. Sarah also jumped to her feet.

"Oh my goodness, I had almost forgotten. I promised Martin I would be home quickly with the herbs, for he needs them this very afternoon, and I have allowed my mouth to run away with me. Christine, do you mind very much? We shall have to talk another time."

"Think nothing of it." Christine left the tea tray in place and went to the kitchen to retrieve the bundle of herbs.

She brought them out and handed them to Sarah, who had already put on her bonnet and cloak. Sir Alexander was standing awkwardly by the door, and Christine realized it was because there was no footman to open it. Jimmy must still be with the gardener—or getting cleaned up. Gus, of course, was still haranguing Sarah on the ineptitude of women and had not noticed. Christine handed the bouquet to Sarah and went to open the door.

Their visitor bowed to her. "Good afternoon, Miss Grey." He glanced at Gus and Sarah, who ignored him still, then turned to leave without offering anything further. Christine did not have to wonder at what he thought of their ramshackle household. It was written all over his face.

Sarah took advantage of the open door to extricate herself from Gus and came and touched Christine on the arm. "Thank you. Again, I am terribly sorry to rush out when we had planned to spend more time together. Next time I promise to stay longer."

Gus gave an ill-natured grunt behind them, and Sarah winked at Christine before stepping outside, where Sir Alexander waited for the groom to bring his horse to him.

"Good. They're leaving together," Gus said when the door was shut, their guests' figures were still visible through the side-light. "Perhaps they will decide to marry, and Sarah will be too busy to haunt our doorstep." He went over and grabbed the last cake, then snapped his fingers at Hunter and Artemis, who followed him out the door.

Hidden from view, Christine watched their guests talking briefly before parting ways, Sarah to the carriage being held by her footman, and he to climb up and turn his horse in the direction of his home. They did not look like two people who had developed a sudden interest in each other. Then again, Sir Alexander did not look as though he was capable of such a thing with any woman. His enigmatic face could not have been more unfriendly.

As for Sarah, Christine mused...she could not be entirely certain that Sarah did not have some unaccountable attraction to Gus—and, even more inexplicably, one that was returned. Could Sarah truly enjoy Gus's company enough to feel a *tendre* for him and not just the simple joy of baiting him? Could Gus actually like her back, despite his curmudgeonly reaction when she was around? He acted the opposite of what he was usually like when he flirted—but then, his flirtations always came to nothing. She hoped Sarah would not end up hurt.

Christine turned from the window and returned to the sitting room. The fatigue of the day came upon her, and she sat and poured herself more tea. It was the dregs of the pot, with little broken tea leaves swirling at the bottom of her cup.

Perhaps she ought to ask Gus outright about Sarah.

CHAPTER FIVE

T he friendly knock on the door to the downstairs pantry at the Greys' house was followed by Honoria stepping through it without waiting for anyone to answer. Christine stood, bent over her small worktable, upon which rested one of the family paintings—of little value but much sentiment—and she was applying gold paint to its frame. The ornamentation on the wooden frame was of molded plaster rather than carved wood, and she had already glued the missing swirl that had broken off due to the heat of the chimney. She would be placing the painting in a different part of the room to avoid a repeat of the misadventure.

"You only just noticed the missing piece this week, and you are already repairing it," Honoria observed. She leaned over the painting, studying it. "The brightened frame improves it."

Christine was pleased at her friend's praise and set down her brush. "I am finished. I will decide when it is dry whether I should paint a second coat. Would you like some tea?"

Honoria shook her head and patted the small bump at her midsection. "I seem to have lost my taste for it, which is a shame because I so clearly remember the *enjoyment* of it."

"Let us go outdoors, then, if you are not too tired. I have been immobile for too long." Christine led Honoria to the back of the house and into the garden. It was good to be out of doors, although it would be too cold to stay out for long without going for a brisk walk.

"I am come with a purpose," Honoria said, slipping her arm through Christine's. "Philip and I are to visit Gracefield Park on Wednesday and assist Sir Alexander Thorne by giving ideas for renovating his house. I thought you might wish to come with us, since this is a particular skill of yours."

Unaccountably, Christine's breath stilled at the mention of Sir Alexander's name and even more at the idea of deliberately putting herself in his presence. She had thought of him more than once since he had come to call at Farlow, the memory sparking indignation each time at his having mistaken her for a servant. Whenever she thought of it, she always imagined a different ending in which she came out of the encounter the victor.

In great confusion, he would beg her forgiveness for having made such an error, assuring her that her status as a lady was unmistakable. Or he would stare at her as though enraptured—the scales suddenly falling from his eyes to see a woman who was not only beautiful but also capable and industrious. He would beg to know her name. The wayward direction of her thoughts was foolish beyond permission. And this particular fantasy resulted in a telltale blush and a severe scolding delivered to her fanciful, not to mention pathetic, imagination.

Honoria took her sudden silence in stride. "I know you will say you have no business in going there, but surely you wish to see Gracefield House with your own eyes after we grew up hearing about it. I have never even seen the *outside* of it. Have you?" She looked to Christine for confirmation, who shook her head. "You cannot deny your curiosity. Say you will come."

Christine must decline, of course. After Sir Alexander had looked down on her in her own home, she would not give him cause to look down on her in his. But Honoria was right about one thing, at least. The desire to see the inside of the house in its unfinished state was nearly impossible to resist. There was nothing more enjoyable than to solve the puzzle of how long it would take to restore the house to its finished state and exactly what was required to bring it there. Certainly, Sir Alexander's wife would be the one doing such a thing one day, but she could pretend that the project was hers to enjoy afterwards. Rather than renovating a stranger's home to turn over to his future wife, she would decorate each room in her mind and imagine living there afterwards.

The sound of a twig breaking underneath her feet caused Christine to snap out of that pleasant little delusion. She must have been quiet for longer than even Honoria could put up with, for her friend tugged her to a stop and shook her arm playfully.

"Oh, do come. Philip has no taste for such a thing. It won't be half as fun unless you come too."

Christine allowed a little smile to settle on her lips. Although the idea lacked sense, she still wanted to go. Perhaps it would not be as horrid as she pictured, with Sir Alexander looking down upon her, a mere woman. Perhaps she might impress him with her ideas and turn his opinion of her on its head. After all, this was the only area in which she truly excelled. It might cause him to regret his former judgment. She knew she should say no. But...

"I will go."

"Excellent." Honoria released her arm to clap her gloved hands together. Her laughter made up for the lack of sound. "Now we shall have some fun."

ON THE DAY of their scheduled visit to Gracefield Park, Honoria was alone when she came to fetch Christine. "There has been a crack in the side of the bath that has caused water to soak the ground. The leak worries him," Honoria explained. "Philip would not be easy unless he stayed behind to manage the situation."

"I am sorry to hear it. I hope it will be simple to repair."

41

Christine paused in her steps toward the waiting carriage. "Should you be there with him rather than visiting neighbors?"

Honoria shook her head decisively. "I think in this I will only be in the way. He has called his engineer to come and see what might be done. Besides, I did not wish to put off this visit."

Nor did Christine. She could not deceive herself about this, as the embarrassing fantasies—which she would never admit to anyone—had only gained in strength.

In all of them, she appeared in her most capable light before Sir Alexander, no matter that it was far from the truth. In their short acquaintance, she had only managed to yell at him—even if it was mostly his fault—and inspire him to call into question whether she was a lady. She had thought over the second incident, and as much as she liked to believe she ought to have no shame in being involved in the deep cleaning, a secret doubt had overtaken her that she had carried her enthusiasm too far. She did not know any lady, friend or otherwise, who would willingly take on a role more suited to a scullery maid.

"Let us go, then."

She shoved these thoughts aside, following Honoria to where the Townsends' groom held the door to the coach for them. The carriage started forward, and they spent the short distance to Gracefield Park speculating on what the house must be like. They had heard it described as massive, but they could not imagine it could be all that large, hidden away as it was in the countryside.

When they turned from the public road onto the private one, Christine peered through the window and stared as they drove through the iron gates cut into the stone wall. The alley was flanked by trees, and they rode on for another five minutes before exiting into a clearing where the road turned to gravel. That was when they were given their first glimpse of the house.

"Why...it is grand!" Christine exclaimed. She turned to look at Honoria, who pulled her head back into the carriage and smiled at her.

"Grander than I had imagined, and he is yet single. Now you

see why I thought of you when Sir Alexander came to call on us?" She raised her eyebrow with a significance that was difficult to miss.

Christine pursed her lips in disapproval. "I hope you did not have any such schemes in inviting me to come today. I daresay you will be disappointed."

"No, no." Honoria was not quite convincing as she demurred. "He will truly benefit from your advice in the area of decoration. He led me to believe it is a daunting project."

Christine was only partially mollified and sincerely hoped her generous but misguided friend had not spoken of her eligibility —or worse, that she had not hinted at Christine's expectations of receiving an offer. That would be mortifying. The carriage came to a stop in front of the main entrance and they alighted, moving forward to the shallow stone steps underneath the portico. Honoria knocked, and the butler admitted them into the entryway. This, and the corridor leading to the rest of the house, was freshly painted, if bare of decorations.

The butler brought them to the drawing room. This was of a stately size, but its rugs and upholstery were threadbare, and the somber curtains and stained wall hangings seemed to cast dark shadows on the room.

Christine turned slowly to look at the size and layout of the room and its windows, appreciating its potential. There was dado and skirting board already in place around the room, although it was difficult to distinguish from the wall hangings, since they were of a similar color. It appeared to have once been a dark olive green but was hard to tell with age and dirt.

"What a light green wall color with a cream paneling and skirting board wouldn't do for this room," she sighed, imagining it in its finished state.

"Is that what you think the drawing room needs?" Sir Alexander had come in behind them, and Christine turned and dipped into a curtsy.

She hadn't expected him to arrive so soon and had certainly not heard his entrance. If she had, she would have kept her observation to herself, for it flustered her to be overheard speaking words she had meant only for a friend to hear.

"I think it is a possible solution for decorating," she answered carefully, "especially if you are to order fabric in a gold and cream color for the chairs and sofas."

"Shall I not just replace the whole lot with new furniture?" Sir Alexander replied as if such a solution was natural.

She frowned at him in surprise. "Not this furniture. It is modern enough. Sheraton, some of it. And Chippendale. They only need to be polished and reupholstered."

Sir Alexander considered this for a moment before turning to Honoria abruptly. "I am forgetting my manners. Welcome, Mrs. Townsend. And welcome, Miss Grey."

Honoria smiled and curtsied. "Please excuse my husband's absence. He had intended to come as promised but encountered a problem at the thermal bath that needed his urgent attention."

"I hope it is not serious."

"I am sure it is nothing to worry about." She gestured to the furniture he and Christine had just been discussing. "I agree that the frames of the sofas and chairs are elegant and need only reupholstering and perhaps some polish. But I am glad you can hear Christine say it, as well. She has a gift for decorating, and you may rely upon her good sense when she makes a suggestion."

Christine was embarrassed by her friend's praise, and she hoped he wouldn't think she had come in hopes of becoming mistress of Gracefield one day and begged for her friend to put in a good word.

He acknowledged this with a grave nod. "I will gratefully listen to whatever you both propose. Shall we visit the parlor adjacent to the dining room?" Without waiting for an answer, he led them across the drawing room toward it.

The parlor was a fraction of the size of the drawing room, but equally as shabby. She turned and lifted her gaze to the ceilings, whose paint was peeling and attracting dust, especially above the chimney where soot had collected and left a darker ring around it. She went over and fingered the frayed cloth on a sofa that had been placed to one side of the chimney. The room would likely be used to entertain a smaller set of guests before dinner was served, and if the party were larger, it would be a simple matter to cross it to reach the dining room.

"Who are you using for your renovations?" Christine asked. "I noticed that the hallway has already been redone." She made no mention of its bare state, for fear of how their host might take it.

"My solicitor hired a team of workers from Lincoln. They work under a man by the name of Gerry Banks, although he was hired primarily to repair parts of the roof that are rotten. The entryway was done at my solicitor's instigation before I moved in, and I suppose Banks was the one to do it, although I did not inquire."

Sir Alexander looked around the room as if seeing it for the first time. "I have not been able to decide where next to begin."

"Have they been given orders to make over anything else indoors?" Honoria asked curiously. "Or do they wait for your instructions?"

"It is partly that, and partly that they are not able to find the materials locally. Banks tells me they have to send away to Lincoln for them," he answered.

Honoria and Christine exchanged a glance, and Christine allowed a fleeting smile to appear before she spoke.

"It is possible that they are giving privilege to the merchants in Lincoln. If you had hired a team from Horncastle, they would have done the same, but in this case it would have benefited you, for you would have had it quickly."

"I see."

Sir Alexander appeared to have nothing more to say to this because he gestured forward, leading the way into the dining room. Christine followed, wondering if she had stepped out of line. She didn't think she could have, for it was common sense to anyone who had grown up in a small town. But perhaps he had not liked being shown the error of his ways.

In the dining room, she remained silent out of caution,

allowing Honoria to carry the conversation, praising of the tableware, sideboard, and the long wooden table with its elegant, matching chairs. This room would be simple to refurbish, needing only to have the floors sanded and varnished, some artwork added, and a fresh coat of paint, perhaps.

They had reached one end of the house, and it was in this breakfast room that Christine found her voice again. Stacked on the sideboard in three rows were beautiful engravings of horses. The three visible in front were compelling in their movement and details, and she stood in front of the stacks to admire them.

"These are magnificent." She flipped the first engraving toward her to examine the second. She looked at each one in turn before moving to the second stack and then the third. "These should not be hidden away here. Such a collection deserves a more prominent place to be displayed."

She glanced at Sir Alexander, aware that she had spoken again without thought. For the first time, he met her regard with an open, pleased expression.

"It is my own collection. These are all done by Mathias Merian, and I purchase one whenever I can find it. I thought I should replace the frames with something grander before finding an appropriate place to hang them."

There was a hesitation, a question in his voice that gave her courage to respond with more warmth. "You have collected a very fine set of engravings. They are not stipple engravings?"

He shook his head. "Before that."

She examined a few more to give herself time to think before risking her honest opinion. "I am not sure you need to have anything better than these simple frames, although they must be made uniform. And because these engravings portray the horse's movement, I think you might put them in a place such as the corridor, where people are also moving. Or better yet, the main stairwell. That way, everyone who walks by it or climbs up it might admire your 'wall of happiness' as my mother used to call her collection of favorite portraits."

"Wall of happiness," he repeated before she could recall her

46

impetuous words. "I like that. And I like the idea of creating movement with them as you suggested. I am much obliged to you."

Christine went still at his praise and almost smiled at him until she caught Honoria watching her. She would have to be careful not to give her friend any encouragement in her match-making. Honoria must not imagine her to be a case for charity. Christine cleared her throat and pointed to the larger, framed paintings that were stacked on the floor on the opposite side of the room.

"Let us look at these paintings here, for I noticed there might be room for them in the dining room."

Without waiting for an answer, she went over to where the stacks of paintings with gilded frames leaned against one wall. In front of one of the middle stack was a newer painting with an elaborate gold frame that did not at all match the painting.

She stared at it for a minute, then began flipping through the other stacks of paintings leaning upright against the wall. These were much better. While these paintings showed the traditional hunting scenes, portraits of unknown people of the past, or meadows with blue skies and gray, the newer painting was a poor example of a modern painter attempting to imitate the past. The subject was a young woman, who was lovely enough, but she had been placed against the background of a Grecian temple with winged cherubs floating around her like clouds carrying stringed instruments. It was done in incredibly poor taste.

"The less gruesome hunting scenes would do for the dining room, as would most of these portraits. I can't think why they would have been taken down." She glanced at Sir Alexander. "The scenes of meadow and countryside might grace the walls in here or in the drawing room or morning room."

"This one," she said, indicating the Grecian travesty and biting her lips to keep a smirk from forming, "might have its place in the pantry, or somewhere where it will be well hidden, only you will have to remove the frame so it fits."

She made the mistake of looking up to see if he shared her

47

humor and was taken aback to see what looked like a thunder-cloud forming on his face instead. Could he truly like the painting? Had he selected it himself, rather than inherited it with the house like he had done with the engravings? But those were in such *good* taste.

"I will find a place for this one," he said coldly, "but perhaps in a private room more frequented by myself than the pantry. It is a portrait of my late mother."

Christine shot a look at Honoria, whose visage of horror matched her own. She brought her regard back to Sir Alexander and managed, through her constricted throat, to say, "I am sorry for my comment."

"Yes, well." Sir Alexander stood frozen for a moment as though unsure of what to do next. The weighted silence was awful. "I must thank you both for the time you have generously accorded me. I beg you will excuse me now, for I am expecting my solicitor to call. And I should not wish to trespass upon your time any longer."

"Of course," Honoria said, coming forward to sweep Christine into her arm as she led the way to the door. "It has been a pleasure to visit Gracefield for the first time, and we are honored to have been given the opportunity to do so."

Christine could barely put one foot in front of the other as she walked numbly at Honoria's side. Sir Alexander had taken the lead and was bringing them to the front door at a pace that showed how desirous he was of putting them on the other side of it. She curtsied and bid farewell without looking at him and scarcely dared even meet Honoria's eyes when they were in the carriage heading back to Farlow Manor.

"Well, I do think you gave him some things to think about," Honoria said. And then, as though realizing what her words might mean, she added hastily, "That is, you did give him some very good ideas. He might easily begin the renovations with the suggestions you made."

Christine sent her friend a dry look that said she was not deceived about the magnitude of her gaffe before turning to look back out the window. In her entire life, she could not remember a time when she wished so fervently that the ground would swallow her up.

She hoped her face would return to its normal color before she arrived at home.

CHAPTER SIX

mong the pile of letters that had been left for Alex on the breakfast table was one from his brother, and he poured himself some coffee and broke the seal. He may as well get this over with first and then enjoy his breakfast. Leonard had a particular way of getting under his skin. He did not mean to do it. However, added to the sibling rivalry Leonard could not seem to refrain from was an elder-brother superiority that had only inflated over the years after having married a woman above him in station. Both the rivalry and the superiority, Alex could heartily do without.

The beginning of the letter was all the usual prattle. Through his wife's connections, Leonard had gained so many orders his only preoccupation now was how to fulfill them all. He followed this with usual boast about his wife's genteel nature—whatever Martha had seen in Leonard, Alex had yet to discern—and he was daily witnessing Martha's beauty and charm unfold in Anna and Clara, who would one day take the town by storm.

Then came the part Alex dreaded: the reminder. He owed a debt to his brother for all he had done to increase the profit of his share in the mill, so he must not think to settle down in some forgotten corner of Lincolnshire and concern himself with only his own affairs. Nor should he forget his promise to seek out a

London society woman for a wife, who could actively promote his nieces when it came time for their season in four years.

Alex threw down the letter impatiently. It had always been his intention to do so; he had given his word. If only Leonard would learn that his nagging was not going to make Alex keener to do it.

He lifted his eyes to the painting of his mother that Miss Grey had disparaged in that haughty way of hers. He had placed it where he could see it next to the engravings and now studied it with a more sober eye. He had always loved the portrait of the beautiful woman he could scarcely remember—his mother. She may not have been genteel, but despite the artificial background of the painting, she appeared every inch the daughter of a gentleman that Miss Grey was.

Of course, he knew the portrait was done in poor taste, although his father had been inordinately proud of it, but what mattered was its sentimental value. Leonard had chosen to keep the only other portrait that existed of their mother because it had always hung in the office at the mill, and he did not like change.

Alex stood and walked over to the painting, taking it in his hands. He stared at it with an artistic, rather than sentimental, eye and came to the conclusion that Miss Grey had been right, despite how little he liked to admit it. If he was going to have a home he was proud of, he could not display this in any room where it might be seen. What if his future wife took one look at it and was horrified at the discovery of where he came from? He bent down and slipped it to the back of one of the stacks of paintings, then swept up his correspondence and left for the study.

One of the local gentlemen, Mr. Mercer, had come to call on him earlier that week, and he brought an invitation from Mrs. Mercer to dine at their home this evening. In truth, Alex was growing tired of dining alone. He would be fixed in place for some time if he wanted to have some of the rooms in Gracefield set to rights before he left for the parliamentary season in

London. He had already sent away to implore his friend Roger Garrick to join him for a fortnight and relieve his boredom and had yet to receive his response. Despite being a friend one could rely upon in most things, Roger was not faithful at all in his correspondence.

At least tonight, Alex would be dining in company.

IT HAD GROWN dark at an early hour, and the cold air whipped the leaves around the bottom of his cape. The Mercers' servant opened the front door, revealing an interior, inviting in its warmth and softly lit with candles. The smells of some sort of ragout greeted him at the door, and for the first time in weeks, a sense of well-being pervaded. He was building relationships with local society as a fellow landowner and was the guest of someone who apparently possessed a superior cook. He would be making connections that would land him the seat in Parliament he aspired to. His future was promising.

"Sir Alexander, a pleasure to welcome you here. My wife, Mrs. Mercer."

Mr. Mercer stepped forward to shake his hand as an older woman followed behind and dipped into a curtsy. She possessed a kindly air and a head of thick gray curls—the sort of woman his mother might have become had she lived.

"Thank you for your invitation," he said, bowing. "You have saved me from having to dine in my own company again." Alex smiled, surprising himself with this unusual display of bonhomie which was not natural to his character. It must have been the warm welcome, not only from the Mercers but the house itself.

The couple led him into the drawing room, where four faces turned to look at him. The Greys and the Townsends had already arrived. He paused on the threshold at the unexpected sight, for he'd thought he would be the Mercers' sole visitor. It was not an unwelcome development, though, as it would allow conversation to flow more smoothly among them, where he could observe rather than contribute. And he was glad to see the Townsends again.

Something about the Greys made him pause, however. Upon first impression, Mr. Grey did not seem someone he could be friends with. He had a taciturn air about him and did not appear the type to go out of his way to make another feel welcome. Since Alex did not possess this talent either, it seemed an acquaintance doomed to failure. As for Miss Grey, she unsettled him.

He could not read her character as he would like to. He owed much of his success in politics and in society to being able to read people. But with Miss Grey, he was still in the dark. First, she traipsed around the woods alone with an uncontrollable set of pups. Then she answered the door looking like a scullery maid and seemed hardly abashed at presenting such an unusual appearance. And she'd scarcely said two words when they sat over tea. Although, he had to admit in her favor that he had never tasted anything quite like her cakes. They were airy and flavorful, and he could happily eat them every day for the rest of his life. But then she had come to Gracefield, and although she had admired the house itself—which he could not help but be gratified by—she had given him a taste of her hauteur with that snide comment about his mother's painting. It had hurt as much as it irritated him—even if she had not been entirely wrong from an artistic standpoint.

His first glance at her appearance tonight revealed a very pretty picture, although he would rather bang his shin on a low table than admit it. Her dark brown curls were pulled back with beads like little pearls that made a pretty contrast with her hair and matched her white teeth. Her carmine-colored gown was of the first elegance despite its simplicity, and was fitted to reveal every curve—

"You remember my wife, Honoria."

Alex pulled his eyes away from Miss Grey as Mr. Townsend came forward to greet him.

"A pleasure," he said, bowing. *Honoria?* Did Townsend intend for him to use her first name after just three meetings? He could not do so.

"How do you do," Mr. Grey said, coming forward to shake his hand. His sister had stood up but remained in place as though hoping to avoid having to greet him. When he glanced at her, she turned her face from him.

Alex shook Mr. Grey's hand, and Mr. Mercer opened his arm to include the room at large. "I believe you know Miss Grey," he added. Alex gave a stiff bow in her direction, and she dropped into a simple curtsy, unsmiling.

Another knock sounded on the door, and the Mercers went to answer it. Conversation ensued from the entryway, and he was startled by Mr. Grey's appearing at his side with a touch on his elbow.

"Just what we need to complete the happy party. Sarah Pasley."

The sarcasm in his voice caused Alex to turn in surprise, and Mr. Grey elaborated. "She is not of our class. Well, I suppose their uncle left them a bit of a fortune and technically her brother is educated, but their father was a blacksmith."

He clearly expected Alex to respond to this, and he did with a wordless nod. Of course a man like Grey, who had never had to fight for his standing in society, would be unimpressed by Miss Pasley. It was no small wonder Miss Grey had revealed that bit of snobbery at his house, for that was the type of people they were. He would have to be on guard lest they try to snub *him*.

Miss Pasley was ushered into the drawing room. "Once we learned that Martin and his wife had gone to Grantham, we invited Sarah Pasley to join us." Mrs. Mercer smiled at him as though she had done it for his sake. "It keeps our numbers even. I do wish the Dawsons had been able to attend, but Arabella has been feeling under the weather. Sir Alexander, may I present—"

"They've met." Mr. Grey said shortly, coming over. "I can save you the trouble, Mrs. Mercer."

"Ah." Mrs. Mercer looked disappointed at having lost the element of surprise as she turned her gaze to Miss Pasley. "Well, this evening you will have a chance to further your acquaintance."

"If you want to talk about hunting all evening," Mr. Grey grumbled.

"Gus, you know you would like nothing better than to talk about hunting all evening, so I don't know what you are complaining about." Miss Pasley perched a hand on her hip, her lips turned up. She was a fair-looking lady but a bit too boyish for Alex's taste.

His gaze slid over to Miss Grey who—after stopping to greet Miss Pasley—was listening to Honoria Townsend recount something in animated conversation. Miss Grey held herself very still, her eyes intent on her friend, and her posture queenly. He wished he didn't find her so attractive. She could be the epitome of grace when she wasn't running over the countryside or covered in dirt.

"Please join us in the dining room," Mr. Mercer called to the room at large. "We don't want the food to grow cold and have our cook leave us for a better situation." This was followed by light laughter as everyone filed into the adjoining room.

"Sir Alexander, you are seated at Mrs. Mercer's right as the newest addition to Horncastle and our guest of honor. Christine, we have put you next to Sir Alexander." Mr. Mercer laid out the seating placements of the small table so that everyone alternated, male and female, and no one was placed next to spouse or sibling.

The meal began with lively conversation as the dishes were brought, then passed around in an informal manner. The style of the dinner reminded Alexander of what he had grown up with, although the conversation then was not as elevated nor the food nearly as abundant or rich. In contrast, the atmosphere here was not at all like what he knew in London. There, the crowds he mixed with were either gentlemen higher than he in station and at pains to let him know it, or men and women like him attempting to get ahead and therefore stepping on each other to be seen.

As much as he longed to bring the Thorne name into more elevated circles, he had no wish to become high in the instep, and neither could he abide people who clamored to establish themselves. It would have to be his character and achievements that brought him into the place he sought in society, never mind what his brother pushed him to. Alex had a glimpse in this room of what that would be like.

The cod melted in his mouth, and after he had taken the edge off his hunger, he glanced to his right at Miss Grey, knowing he should begin a conversation but reluctant to start. The glimpse afforded him a view of her elegant neck and profile. She held her fork with slender fingers, but he did not recall having seen her smile that evening, not even when she was speaking to the people she knew well. Perhaps she was simply a cold one. It would not surprise him.

Miss Grey turned to meet his regard, and he flushed upon realizing he had been staring. She sat up straighter and turned away. The rebuff caused him to flatten his lips. She should not think him so far beneath her.

"Tell me a little about yourself, Sir Alexander."

The question came from Mrs. Mercer, his hostess, who continued to meet his gaze with an expression of interest. He could not repay such kindness with his usual reserve. It would not be right.

"I come from Butterley in Derbyshire, where my father had an iron ore mill. Now my brother runs it, along with the forge to turn the iron into steel." The interested light in her eyes had not dimmed at his revelation, so he was encouraged to continue. "I had a sponsor in the Baron Winton and his wife, who reside in Grimsby and who sent me to Eton and then Oxford. That is where I discovered an interest in engineering."

"Is that so?" Mrs. Mercer ate some of her dinner, and he thought the conversation must naturally turn to a topic she could participate in, but she surprised him. "Have you been able to use your field of study?"

Her unexpected interest in a topic he thought must bore her raised Mrs. Mercer in his esteem.

"Actually, I have. I developed a steam pump that is currently being used to drain the fens on the Lincolnshire coast near Boston. That is one reason I purchased Gracefield, besides being hopeful of being elected to represent South Lindsey in Parliament. It's near enough to my project to make it easy to visit, but allows me to live on an estate that suits me."

Mrs. Mercer served herself some of the asparagus and passed the dish to him. "Have you spoken about your pump to Mr. Mercer? It would be of great interest to him."

"I have not," he replied, pleased to hear it. "His visit to Gracefield Park was cut short, unfortunately, by the arrival of my solicitor, so I did not have the chance to welcome him as I would have liked. Otherwise, I am sure the subject must have come up."

"You must certainly tell him of it over port. So you mean to make your permanent home in Lincolnshire? That is good news." She patted his hand in a motherly fashion that only a cold-hearted person could take offense to.

"Yes. That is...I will be here part of the year at least. I must be in London when Parliament is in session."

"Of course," Mrs. Mercer replied. "You have a seat in the Commons, I am to understand."

"'Tis so, madam." He drank some of his wine and thought how he might contribute to the conversation. "And how did you and Mr. Mercer meet?"

"Mr. Mercer and I have known each other all of our lives, as our families are both from the area surrounding Horncastle. Ours was a simple match, set up by our parents, but desired by us both." She smiled at him. "Do you have plans for marriage, Sir Alexander?"

Why had he chosen marriage as a topic? It had been as sure as anything to lead to the very question she had asked him, and that was one he did not wish to answer. Neither could he imagine snubbing his hostess.

"I must marry eventually. Perhaps I will see to it when I am in London." *See to it? Oh, for heaven's sake.*

She furrowed her brows at his unusual expression before transforming her features into a smile. "You might do so, but we have several lovely young women right here in Lincolnshire."

If Mrs. Mercer thought she was being circumspect, she was doing a poor job of it. She had not lowered her voice. Even now she gave a look of significance to Miss Grey on his right and Miss Pasley across from him. The remark had escaped Miss Pasley, who was arguing with Mr. Grey at her side. But Miss Grey appeared to have heard it if the faint flush that stained her cheeks was any indication.

"You do, indeed, ma'am," he replied in a lowered tone. "But you must hold me excused if I do not court any of these worthy ladies. I will need a woman who knows London society and can serve as a hostess when I am there for Parliament."

He brought his gaze around the room, and it confirmed the sentiment he had just expressed out loud. Despite almost all of the guests coming from the gentry, there was no denying that the people here had simple tastes. Perhaps the wife he chose could elevate Horncastle society and aid him even further in his quest to be elected to the larger borough.

Mrs. Mercer looked disappointed but merely said, "I understand perfectly."

She turned to Philip on her left, and Alex knew he must now speak to Miss Grey if he was to behave the gentleman. He flicked a glance her way, then put a bite of steak in his mouth and chewed. She fiddled with a piece of bread on the side of her plate before sending a glance his way.

"Have you received an invitation to the Stuff Ball in Lincoln?" she asked. Her voice was as indifferent as her manner. "It is in two weeks' time."

The question surprised him. It seemed leading, as though to seek out his company, and if he thought she had the slightest interest in him, he would have privately accused her of flirting.

"I received one, but did not know what to make of it." This

was his chance to be more cordial, even if he was not sure she deserved it. "What is the Stuff Ball?"

"It is an annual ball that supports the wool merchants." She sipped the wine and set down her glass, everything performed with a grace he could not reconcile with the first two encounters he'd had with her—and not even with her cold assessment of his mother's portrait. "The Lady Patroness chooses a color each year that everyone must wear, and you must attend in clothing made only of Lincolnshire wool. This year's chosen color is purple."

He had never heard of such a thing, but it sounded like an event of interest. "What types of people attend the ball?"

He supposed it did not matter whether it was mostly gentry or merchants, for both types would give him a chance to speak with his constituents. But the fact would be nice to know so he might weigh how important the event was.

If possible, Miss Grey's voice was even frostier than usual when she answered. "The guests are landowners or merchants who are at ease enough to be able to afford a new coat or gown every year. You often see the same faces there." She let her eyes rest across the table from her on Mr. Grey and Miss Pasley who were still in animated discussion. "It is where many acquaintances are formed and strengthened."

What had caused her to respond so stiffly? He could only confirm his suspicion: that Miss Grey was a cold one. However, despite the reluctance of her response, he had his answer. It seemed prudent that he attend, and he wondered if he could have a coat made up in time—perhaps from the draper in town? Or maybe there was a better one he should visit. He wished to ask Miss Grey for advice but feared she would only find another way to snub him. A different question slipped out instead—one he'd had no intention of asking.

"Do you recommend I accept the invitation, then?"

She slanted her eyes at him, then shrugged. "You must answer that question for yourself, Sir Alexander."

She had indeed found another way to repulse him. He supposed her reply had not been unkindly worded, but it effectively shut the conversation down and made him feel foolish for asking it. In his experience, women were usually more conciliatory than Miss Grey, even ones who had ties to the nobility. He pitied the man who took her to wife.

With Miss Grey now silent, he could not help but turn his attention to Miss Pasley across from him, who did appear to have much to say on the subject of hunting. And much to say in general. As he was a man of few words—unless he was addressing Parliament with a planned speech—he normally enjoyed a woman who could carry her end of the conversation. That was, when it was an actual conversation, and not an expository on the proper way to drive the hunt. As he listened, she raised nothing like admiration in his breast. Mr. Grey, on the other hand, seemed to devote the entirety of the meal to her and ignore Mrs. Townsend on his left—this despite claiming Miss Pasley was beneath him in status.

Even with these small annoyances, the dinner was overall a pleasant affair. There were enough courses and removes for a more-than-respectable repast, but it was not so long that he was forced to converse much more with Miss Grey on his right. Soon afterwards, the women left the room and the men were seated over port. He found himself next to Mr. Grey.

"Did I not warn you? About Miss Pasley?" he asked, leaning back in his chair.

"She is certainly knowledgeable about hunting," Alex answered diplomatically, thankful the man had not asked about his own conversation with Miss Grey.

"Before Mrs. Mercer left the room, she said we should inquire about your engineering project," Mr. Townsend said. "I, for one, would like to hear more."

Alex told them what he had told Mrs. Mercer and was given the chance to elaborate when they asked questions. He described the buckets they had begun to make for other mills whose owners were reproducing the steam pumps. As the conversation unfolded, he felt the warmth of something close to friendship for the first time since he'd settled in Horncastle. These men were more interested in his project than the men he had shared it with in London. There, they had not asked him any questions about the process itself, but were rather interested in its investment potential. Here, the men were curious about the mechanics of it, even Mr. Grey.

After some time with the focus on him, he directed the topic to what he wished to know. "Mr. Townsend, I would like to learn more about your mineral spa."

"Oh, please, I wish you will call me Philip. And call him Gus," he said, with a grin at Mr. Grey. "None of us stand on ceremony. Well, that is...we all still call our host Mr. Mercer."

"I am from a different generation," the older man said with a chuckle.

"Very well," Alex said, touched by Philip's invitation, although he was not sure he was ready to call Mr. Grey Gus.

They had invited him into their circle straight away. It was what he'd had to fight for at Oxford until Roger stepped in and befriended him. And even then, he had noticed that when Roger was not present, his classmates were less welcoming. Here, there seemed to be no barriers to an unguarded friendship.

Upon Alex's inquiry, Philip launched into the story of how his father's abandoned mine had become an important source of revenue for Boden Estate when, after a lengthy period of avoiding the place, he'd discovered it filled with bromine and iodine waters, healthful for the body. He was quick to give credit for the discovery to his wife and went on to say that they had spent longer than intended—a full year—converting it into a space that could welcome visitors who would pay to receive its benefits. The spa was at last open, despite a recent crack they were trying to fix, and they were looking into how they might safely expand and modernize it. All the while, Alex's mind was working, wondering if a steam shovel could be used to accomplish the task, despite the cramped space. He would have to ask to see it.

From there, the conversation turned to the Stuff Ball, and with the gentlemen's urging, he made up his mind to attend.

Finally, Mr. Mercer suggested they join the ladies, and Alex trailed the others into the drawing room, where Mrs. Mercer was setting out tea on a small table and Miss Grey was then distributing to the ladies. Alex had been well satisfied with the gentlemen's conversation, and had even secured the desired invitation from Philip to visit the spa the day after next on his way out of the dining room.

Miss Grey stood at Mrs. Mercer's right and began bringing the tea to each of the gentlemen. "How do you take your tea, Sir Alexander?" she asked him, once he'd sat next to Philip.

Her voice was barely cordial, and he didn't know what he had done to deserve such coldness. Should it not be he who treated her with reserve after the way she had insulted him?

"One sugar, thank you," he replied, then turned back to Philip. He would not give her any more of his attention when she gave him so little of hers. Besides, amid his irritation at her haughty bearing, there was a bothersome attraction he felt toward her that he could not explain and certainly did not welcome.

Miss Grey moved forward to take the tea from Mrs. Mercer, adding a lump of sugar and setting a spoon on the saucer. She turned and began to cross the room toward him, but the Mercers' dog had settled on her path and chose that moment to scuttle backwards. This resulted in her stepping on the dog's tail, and he emitted a pained bark before leaping up and backing into her. The action propelled her forward, sending the cup of tea flying across Alex.

The sting of hot liquid bit into his face and through his waistcoat and breeches, as he leapt to his feet. Philip had received a small portion of it as well but Alex bore the brunt of it.

After shooting him a horrified glance, Miss Grey mumbled an apology, then turned her gaze to the dog who had slinked off into the corner. She went over to him and knelt beside him. "I am so sorry, Rufus," she crooned as she petted him.

Mrs. Mercer hurried over with napkins, and Honoria

Townsend had come to Alex and was peering up into his face. She reached up to touch it, and he instinctively warded off her hands. *What was she doing?*

She instantly stepped back with a look of chagrin. "Forgive me. I should explain that I have skills in healing. I wanted to see if you had been burned."

"No, no," he said, attempting to regain his composure. "I am perfectly fine."

He darted a glance at Miss Grey, who continued to pet the dog, focusing only on the canine. What kind of woman did not even apologize when she threw hot tea over a man? Well, technically she did apologize, but not with any sincerity he could be impressed with. Even the barely audible apology for her insult to his mother had been more properly delivered.

"Let me pour you another cup of tea," Mrs. Mercer said as Miss Grey finally stood and went to sit beside Mrs. Townsend.

Alex wiped his face with the napkin. His waistcoat had prevented most of the tea from reaching his skin, but his breeches were wet and uncomfortable. He knew it was not her fault. But really—how could a woman miss an entire dog?

CHAPTER SEVEN

C hristine sat, leaning against her headboard, her knees drawn up and the blankets wrapped around her. The candle burned low on the side table, and its flickering light sent shadows on the wall. Ichabod was asleep at her side, the only animal allowed to sleep in her room because he was the least likely to playfully nip at her toes in the middle of the night. The cat's soft snores vibrated next to her.

Once again, Christine's mind flashed to the teacup as it flew forward—as Sir Alexander drew to his feet, his eyes wide with surprise. It was hard to breathe from the embarrassment each time she thought of it, this misfortune coming so hard on the heels of her ill-placed comment regarding his mother's portrait. She had known he would be present at the dinner and hoped he would not be seated next to her. When he was, it had taken everything in her to overcome her embarrassment and attempt to make conversation.

Now this. After it happened, she could not meet anyone's gaze and spent the rest of the evening choosing the seats that would allow her to face away from Sir Alexander. Everyone had laughed it off, but it did not soften the mortification. Christine was always careful of her speech and movements so as not to call undue attention to herself. She never spoke unless absolutely necessary, or unless she was at ease in the company. And she never put herself forward voluntarily, precisely to avoid this form of awkwardness. To have volunteered to help Mrs. Mercer with the tea, only to have made a spectacle of herself...well, next time she would stay seated.

Christine dropped her face in her hands. The dinner itself was a disaster of a milder sort. Not only did she fail to redeem herself after their last encounter by conversing in a warm and natural manner, she had failed at polite conversation in general. It wasn't that she was unaccustomed to dining with eligible bachelors—although it was rare enough to do so with ones she had not grown up with—it was just that they had never held any attraction for her. Therefore, she conversed and ate with ease. Not so with Sir Alexander. His appeal added to the burden of needing to raise herself in his image, and it left her tongue-tied around him. The awkwardness had shown as surely as if she'd blurted out that she liked him. Not once had he seen her in the image she strove to present to the world. Each encounter with him showed her only at her worst.

She shouldn't care as much as she did. Her attempts at striking up a conversation at the table had only confirmed what he had already stated to Mrs. Mercer. He wished to know what sort of guests would attend the ball, proving he was a man who cared about what class of people he mingled with—the type who would only take a lady of London society to wife. Good! Christine was sure he would find someone equally shallow and that they would be perfectly happy together. They could live in that big empty house of his, just the two of them, whenever they deigned to make a short stay in Lincolnshire.

With a huff of impatience, she jerked at the cover that had tangled around her legs and slid down into bed, leaning over to blow out her candle. She would have to get some sleep if she was to get anything done tomorrow. There were still the finishing touches to put on Honoria's gown for the Stuff Ball, which they had managed to extend by adding discreet panels on the sides. After that, she would seek out a project she excelled at and restore her lost equilibrium. In no time at all, this would all be a forgotten incident.

She wrapped the blankets around her and turned on her side, at which point Ichabod promptly shifted and placed his tail end in Christine's face.

"Not you, too," she said, pushing the sleeping cat to the far end of the bed. One irritating male per night was enough to contend with.

ALEX'S PLANS TO visit Philip's thermal bath had to be temporarily set aside when he received a letter from his brother announcing that Leonard would arrive the very next day and stay for one night. He threw his brother's letter down in impatience and went to ring for the butler to come.

"We will need to have a room readied, for my brother is to arrive tomorrow. Send Mrs. Mulhouse to see me as soon as she has a menu to propose, and also send the maid. I hope there are spare sheets that do not have holes in them."

"Yes, sir." The butler went off to do his bidding, his face blank as usual, and Alex was suddenly conscious that he had never taken time to learn anything about the man other than his name—Davies. Perhaps he ought to do so, but he feared that the servants would treat him with too much familiarity if he breached the master-servant divide by asking personal questions.

The day was swallowed up by orders to clean the only decent room in which he might put his brother. Some of the larger bedrooms facing west would have been a better choice if only the missing tiles in the roof had not caused damp, mold, and bubbled plaster on the walls there. However, Mrs. Mulhouse produced a menu he thought his brother would be pleased with, and the maid had found clean, ironed sheets that had not even needed to be darned.

The next day, Alex heard the sounds of a carriage pulling up and went out to greet Leonard himself. His brother resembled him in likeness except for an excess of flesh about his middle and the whiskers that covered a chin which had started to sag. He stepped down from the carriage and reached over to shake Alex's hand before looking up at the façade of Gracefield House.

"It has a fine structure. Larger than I expected. A Tudor house?" he asked uncertainly.

"Late Elizabethan," Alex answered, ushering him indoors. Davies was coordinating with the servants to bring in his brother's trunk and to have the carriage sent to the stables. "You didn't mention in your letter what persuaded you to come so far out of your way. I won't flatter myself that it was owing to brotherly affection."

"No, not that," Leonard answered without a trace of irony. "We signed a large client in Lincoln, and I wanted to meet him myself. Once I'd come that far, the visit to see your estate made sense."

"I suppose you're right, although it does add several hours to your journey if it's only for one night."

Alex had accepted an invitation to the Dawsons' for cards the following day and was secretly glad of the short stay. He would not need to bring his brother, who had never seen the need to dampen his bluster, even in refined company.

"In the end," his brother went on, "I've decided to stay for a second night since Martha wrote to inform me she'd accepted an invitation to a party I have no wish to attend." Leonard climbed the steps at Alex's side. "So you will have the pleasure of my company for longer."

"Wonderful," Alex replied with his own carefully hidden irony. He would have to write to Mrs. Dawson to see if an additional guest wouldn't be too much trouble.

They had stepped into the entryway which gleamed white after its fresh coat of paint. Alex was glad Smithson had seen to its renovation before the move, having correctly stated that it was a visitor's first impression of the house and was therefore an important, if small, project before the workers began to repair the roof. Leonard examined the tall ceilings and the majestic staircase that would one day hold the engravings—Alex still thought Miss Grey's idea had been a good one and intended to implement it.

Leonard narrowed his eyes as he stared at the ceiling critically. "They did not paint to the top of it."

"They did not have time." Alex steered him away from the unfinished entry to the drawing room. This proved to be a mistake, for once inside, Leonard emitted a gasp of horror.

"This room is nothing short of a wreck. It's painful to look upon. Are you certain you would not have done better to have razed the bricks and started afresh?"

"You must be joking. Tear down a magnificent house like this simply because it needs a coat of paint?" Alex frowned at him, and when his brother didn't look convinced, he added, "Imagine this room with...with light green walls and a cream base. Then, picture it with gold cushions on the sofas and chairs."

Leonard threw him a glance. "Why not simply buy the furniture new? 'Twill be faster. And these days, chairs and sofas come ready-made in the most fashionable colors."

"Because it's a Sheraton. *Those* are Sheratons," he corrected himself, casting a sweeping gesture over the furniture, unsure of which ones to refer to. "And Chippendales. They are too valuable to toss."

"Well." Leonard folded his arms and took in the entire depressing room. "Although I saw the sense in keeping the mill as Father had it, I could not imagine giving Martha anything less than a brand-new house upon our marriage so she might decorate it as she saw fit. She was mighty pleased to have such clean and bare rooms to work with and told me so."

When Alex did not respond to this he added, "You will have to sign the wedding contract without your future wife coming to visit the house, I suppose. Once it's signed, she will just have to make the best of it."

Alex inhaled quietly through his nose and continued to lead his brother on the tour, his mood growing more despondent as they went through the house, and the quality of the rooms deteriorated. When he'd purchased Gracefield, he knew what a massive project the house represented, as everything needed to be renovated. In many cases, the room would have to be stripped down to the bones to remove damp plaster and rotten floorboards. But he had viewed it as an investment—an inheritance that would one day be passed down to his children, besides being a step into the world of the landed gentry. It had been the largest estate in the area within his price range.

The afternoon was spent riding out on the grounds, which provoked Leonard's admiration more than the house had done. Following dinner, which Leonard was able to compliment with sincerity, they passed the hours by playing cards. Alex did not bother telling Leonard about the Dawsons' invitation until the next day when he had received a positive response from Arabella Dawson.

That night, they were cordially greeted by their hosts, then Theo Dawson led them into the parlor, where the Greys and Townsends were already in place. This did not surprise Alex, as he was beginning to see that the group of friends spent a great deal of time together. They were also introduced to a Miss Reinhart, a woman of an indeterminate age whom, he was told, had recently settled in Thimbleby.

Miss Grey was dressed in another fashionable gown that showed her wealth and knowledge about the latest trends. He wished he could ignore her presence rather than cast furtive glances her way, but it seemed he was powerless to resist whenever he was in the room with her. Despite all the reasons he should feel antipathy toward her, the combination of her enigmatic personality, her beauty, and the fact that she did not seem to want him produced an allure difficult to resist.

He noticed, in one of his furtive glances, that she held herself stiffly and that the bodice of tonight's gown revealed a delicate set of collarbones underneath her graceful neck. She did not deign to notice him after the greetings had been performed. He consoled himself with the fact that his glances in her direction were subtle enough that no one could possibly have remarked upon it.

After a simple repast made up entirely of amuse-bouches and sweetmeats, Mrs. Dawson steered the guests over to two tables set up for whist.

"Miss Reinhart, allow me to pair you first as our guest of honor."

The spinster looked flustered at all the eyes turned suddenly upon her and shook her head.

"Please allow me to watch. I am not a skilled player and would not like to burden my partner. But I should very much like to watch the game being played."

Everyone tried to protest, with Alex the most earnest, certain that it was the sudden addition of his brother to the party that had upset their even numbers. But Miss Reinhart remained unmoved.

"Very well, if you insist." Mrs. Dawson set her hand on Philip's arm and sent him a teasing smile. "Since we have two extra gentlemen among us, I have sacrificed you and Gus to play together."

"I shall surely lose," Philip groaned. "Why not sacrifice your husband?"

"What are you saying? I am skilled at whist," Gus retorted. He plopped himself down on a chair, and with an exaggerated show of reluctance Philip took the chair across from him.

"Mr. Thorne, would you be my partner?" Mrs. Dawson asked Leonard, smiling in a way that would be difficult to refuse.

"With the greatest of pleasure," he replied gallantly.

She then turned to the others, revealing a slim frame that seemed too delicate to carry a child. "That makes up one table. For the other, Honoria, I have put you with Theo." She then added in an off-hand manner, "And that leaves you, Sir Alexander, to be paired with Christine."

Alex should have seen it coming since they were the only two guests who were not related or married. The idea of being paired with Miss Grey flustered him, and he darted a look at her sitting

70

across from him; she did not return it. She was named dealer, and after dealing the cards with a skilled hand, the trump card was revealed to be a heart.

Although the beginning of the game was formal, it was not difficult to fall into the enthusiasm and competition of its players, especially with ones like Mrs. Townsend and Theo Dawson. Both shouted in victory when they won a trick and argued about who had made the unwise move when they lost it. The table next to them was also loud, and he could tell that Leonard was entertained, which pleased him.

But what he enjoyed most about the evening was watching Miss Grey come to life in the enthusiasm of the game. Slowly their dialogue grew more natural, until the game was well advanced and he was given a glimpse beneath her façade when she berated him for not catching on to her play quickly enough.

"Why, sir," she exclaimed in mock indignation, eyes brilliant and her cheeks rosy from excitement. "In that last trick, I most clearly communicated to you *with my eyes* that you should cast one of your honors, so the points would go to us, for I held the trump. Yet, you only put out a seven."

"I did not read your look correctly," he protested, unable to stop himself from laughing. "I thought you were telling me not to waste a good card."

"*Hmph.*" Her lips pinched together to try to conceal the smile, but it only caused her dimples to appear.

He stared at those dimples, then lifted his eyes to meet her gaze, which he held for a moment longer than must be wise if he were to keep her at a distance. He wondered if she was speaking to him with her eyes then, for his heart had certainly started to beat in a peculiar way. Or, perhaps his own eyes were saying something he must deem as ill-advised in a more rational moment. He could not help but be drawn to this side of Miss Grey—this smiling, laughing, bright-eyed version of her that he suspected she did not show liberally.

Leonard broke these pleasant reflections by calling out across the table to him. "You are fortunate in your neighbors, Alex.

When you bring a bride here from London, she will find it to be very agreeable company, indeed." At these words, a sudden silence fell over the company.

It was gauche. And mortifying, and it almost seemed as though the former light atmosphere could not be recovered. Then Honoria slapped down a card, calling out, "My trick!" and the fugue was broken.

Alex did not easily recover from his embarrassment, but there would be no point in taking Leonard to task. After all, his brother was right. It was his intention to bring home a society wife. It little mattered how much Miss Grey attracted him or intrigued him; she did not fit into his plans.

At the end of the night as they headed home, Leonard echoed this sober reminder. "Miss Grey is an attractive woman. No man could say otherwise. But she won't help you reach your ambitions, Alex. You will want to tread carefully where she is concerned."

"I have no intentions toward Miss Grey," he replied, his face carefully concealing any thoughts to the contrary.

"No? You certainly stared at her enough. I am only saying to be careful."

Leonard warmed his hands in his coat, then fished into his pocket and pulled out a cigar, which he cut and lit, the puffs of smoke mingling with their breath in the night air.

Alex drove his tilbury in silence. He had not concealed his interest as well as he thought he had. He would have to be more careful—perhaps even remove to London earlier than planned— if she proved to be a greater temptation than he had bargained for.

Although, upon reflection, he was carrying caution too far. Of course he could resist whatever enticement she might inadvertently provide. He had always been master of his own heart, and that was not about to change now.

CHAPTER EIGHT

I n the days following the card party, Christine recalled
various scenes in her mind to examine them, applying first
one interpretation and then another. She could not deny
her pleasure in observing that Sir Alexander stared at her, as she
had applied careful attention to her appearance. Although she
could only see him on her periphery, for she did not turn her
head in his direction, his regard seemed admiring and not
condemning, even though the last time they'd met, she'd show-
ered him with scalding tea. She wouldn't think about the time
before that.

Her reflections took a sweeter turn when she remembered
how they had laughed together, and how well they played
together. Except for the one trick where he'd failed to follow her
lead, their play was fluid—and fun. Well, that was until Mr.
Thorne had reminded the room at large that Sir Alexander
would not deign to settle with a mere Lincolnshire miss. She had
best put him firmly out of her mind, she told herself. And she
mostly managed to do so, except for wondering on more than
one occasion whether he had decided to attend the Stuff Ball.

The morning they were to leave for Lincoln promised rain.
As Christine stepped outdoors, the clouds above were dark, and
the air felt heavy and unseasonably warm for October.

"Gus, are you certain you wish to ride? Look at the sky," she said, as she brought her portmanteau to the carriage. Their groom had just finished securing their trunk and went to stand with the horses.

"You know I can't bear being cooped up in a carriage when the distance is under fifty miles." He placed his hat on his head and swung up into the saddle, his riding crop in one hand. "No Guinea?" he asked her.

She shook her head. "He doesn't like storms and would probably get sick all over me in the carriage. He'll be well enough staying with Hunter and Artemis with Jimmy to look after him."

She put one hand on the door of the carriage and looked back. "Theo and Arabella are expecting us?"

Gus gave a nod. "We'll join them at Thimbleby and continue on together from there."

"I wager Theo will have enough sense to travel with Arabella," she said with a smirk as some drops of rain began to fall.

Christine climbed into the carriage. She knew better than to argue with Gus, though she privately thought he would have a miserable time of it getting drenched through to his skin. Not even his riding cape could keep out all of the wet when the heavens opened their doors. They set out and Christine settled down as the rain began to fall steadily but not with the force the clouds had promised.

It was too dark thanks to the imminent storm to pull out her book, so she stared through the window and thought about how she would arrange her hair without the help of her maid. Beatrice had come down to wait on her this morning as usual, but her cheek was swollen from a toothache and she was clearly in agony. Christine had insisted she stay home so she could get her tooth pulled, assuring her that she would borrow Arabella's maid to dress.

The rain began to fall in force as they reached Penwood Estate, where they pulled up in front of the house. Christine climbed down from the carriage, surprised at the absence of the

Dawsons' coach in the courtyard. She hurried toward the house while Gus remained in the saddle, but before she could reach the front door, Theo opened it.

"Christine," Arabella exclaimed, exiting behind him. She kissed her on the cheek. "We are not setting out just yet."

Theo jogged over to Gus and shook his hand, braving the rain. "I don't want my wife to travel with the skies looking like this," he called up to him. "I think we should wait until the worst of it is over. Why don't you wait it out with us?"

Christine looked at Arabella, then at her brother. It was true they could leave later—even the next day—and it would change very little. They had decided to travel a day early and visit the town, rather than waiting to go until the day of the ball as they often did. Besides, Honoria and Philip would be leaving tomorrow as well.

"No, let's carry on, shall we, Christine?" Gus said. "I have plans to meet some friends tonight for cards and I shouldn't like to let them down."

At this revelation, Christine stared at him in vexation. He hadn't told her he would be out with friends on their first night.

"Even if he goes ahead, why don't you stay and ride with us?" Arabella coaxed. "We have not seen one another enough lately, and it would be nice to have a catch-up."

Christine hesitated still. It was true that she would like to spend time with Arabella, but then she thought about riding with them in their carriage. It would be an intrusion on their intimacy. Or, she could ride in her own carriage alongside them, but if she was going to do that, she may as well go now. She shook her head.

"No, come and find me at the inn." She smiled. "I will leave word with the innkeeper to have him show you to my room when you arrive. I'll go on with Gus."

"We should be there in time for dinner. This time, we won't be stopping for a pleasure picnic." Arabella laughed and as if in response, the rain picked up.

"Christine, let us go," Gus said. He waved to Theo, who helped Christine into the carriage, then hurried Arabella back into the house. She felt sorry for their groom, Olsen, who was facing the elements as Gus was, but not by his own choice.

They had only gone a mile or two when the rain became a torrential downpour. Christine folded her arms under her cloak as the carriage rocked back and forth over the portion of rough road, hoping for Olsen's sake that the storm would quickly wear itself out. However, as they rode on for more than an hour, it still showed no signs of abating.

She peered through the window at the forlorn image of her brother, who showed signs of fatigue by the downpour despite his hearty constitution. He glanced at the carriage and saw her face in the window, then rode over and said a word to the groom. He tapped on the window for her to open it.

"I'm going to ride ahead and see if the road is still good between Short Ferry and Fiskerton. If there are no problems, I will meet you at the inn in Fiskerton." Without waiting for an answer, he touched his heels to his horse's flanks and rode off.

Christine shoved her window back up in place, irritated and feeling oddly alone. It was just like Gus to do such a thing so he could seek shelter more quickly. And although his decision did not surprise her, she thought that for *once* it would be nice if someone took a little care for her comfort rather than thinking nothing of abandoning her on the road.

They continued on, their pace slow from the muddy road. The rain would begin to slacken but then pick up again, and she finally decided that the rest of the day was unlikely to improve. Voices outside alerted her to the fact that they had reached Short Ferry. Olsen stepped down to ask if she needed anything and when she shook her head, said he would inquire if the rain had caused any problems ahead. After a few minutes he tapped on the window, which she lowered.

The rain was dripping from his hat but no bitterness sounded in his voice. "The road is clear, miss. If ye don't need anything, we will continue on to Fiskerton."

"Yes, do that. Thank you, Olsen," she added.

The carriage lurched slightly as he climbed back up on the seat and they moved forward. Once they left the town, the rain only seemed to fall harder, leaving a damp chill in the cabin. Christine began to ache for the inn at Lincoln where a fire could be made up, and she could order tea. She longed for its comfort.

The road brought them along the River Witham and dipped down alongside it, their wheels turning noticeably slower in the muddy lane. As they went down the decline of the road and over stones and tree roots, the carriage tipped slightly in a rhythmic back and forth, the rain still pelting on the roof.

Without any warning, a loud crack sounded, and the carriage lurched to the side. It stayed fixed that way, tilting precariously with Christine flush against the side of the carriage that faced the river. She dropped her head back on the squabs at this unhappy twist of fate—*of course there would be an upset when Gus had ridden ahead*—but she waited until Olsen came down and opened the door. She already knew what he was going to say. The drunken angle of the carriage told its own story.

"Linchpin must have come off, miss, for I don't see it. And now the wheel's cracked." He leaned down to shove the wheel back underneath to prop the carriage up somewhat as the rain battered down on his black cape. "I think I should unhitch the horses and ride back to Short Ferry to get a new wheel and pin— or a carriage to rent, miss."

The eyes he raised to her were filled with concern, and she knew he did not like to leave her alone, nor did he want to suggest she walk back to town in the rain. To own the truth, she had no desire to do so either, but as there was not even a saddle for her to ride, her only choice would be to walk or remain in the covered carriage. She bit back some choice words for Gus, who had abandoned her to this fate and who would only learn that they had not reached Fiskerton when it was too late.

"Yes, that is a good idea. I will be perfectly fine here," Christine assured him.

She watched the groom unharness both horses from the

carriage. It would not do to leave one of them standing for an excessively long amount of time. He climbed on the lead horse bareback and led the second one by tying him to the bridle. He then progressed up the rocky path to higher ground.

Now, how was she going to bide her time? It would take an hour or two for him to retrace his steps and find a blacksmith, then return with all that was necessary. Christine sat in the dark carriage, listening to the rain continue to thunder down. She was glad Beatrice had stayed home, but she could not help but wish she had brought Guinea with her even if he did get sick. He would have kept her warm and content until Olsen returned.

She sat, lost in her thoughts, listening to the steady drum of rain on the earth outside and on the carriage roof overhead. It was not difficult for her to be content with her own company, but it was more taxing to have nothing to occupy her hands. To have no animals to pet, no cakes to bake, no gowns to sew or little tasks to occupy her. Being idle was something she did not excel at.

She removed her bonnet and massaged her scalp, then wrapped the curls next to her face around her finger to tame them. Thus occupied, it was some time before the shift in the sounds of rain falling outdoors reached her consciousness. It had gone from an echoing, dull sound on the roof and a splattering on the earth outdoors to the noticeable splash of rain hitting water. Christine drew her brows together and tried to peer through the window but did not have a clear enough view of the ground, so she opened the door and looked out. Her lips parted with a sharp intake of breath.

Water rushed by the carriage, swallowing up the lower half of the wheels. She lifted her gaze to the river, where the current had picked up in speed. The banks were no longer identifiable on either side of the river, nor was there any road or field still uncovered ahead of her or behind. She stepped on the footrest of the carriage to look behind her to where Olsen had gone. Only the upper portion of the path was visible, but the water was creeping toward the top. No one was in sight, and the water was continuing to rise, even in the short time since she had first looked out of the carriage.

It took no more than a second's reflection for her to scoot across the carriage to the side closest to the bank. She opened the door there, but the grassy bank was too far for her to reach, even by jumping.

Without sparing a thought, she plunged into the icy water and cried out at the shock of it. It immediately filled her boots and crept up her gown, moving with such force as to threaten her foothold. She briefly considered her hat and portmanteau left behind in the carriage but dismissed the idea of retrieving them. The water continued to rush by with greater force, and the strength of it alerted her to the danger she was in. It was still possible to wade over to the bank but it took all her strength to do so.

With the steep slope of grass before her, Christine managed to grab a root sticking out of the earth before she lost her foothold in the rushing water. With all her strength, she pulled herself up with one hand, then reached higher to grab another stone sticking out from the grass. Somehow, she got a foothold on a root or ledge underneath the swirling water and climbed higher. Without it, her feet slid helplessly on the grass, and she looked for another spot on the bank to position her other foot.

By now, the water had picked up speed and would soon reach the level of the coach cabin where she had been sitting moments before. Impossible to think of that now. Every ounce of her focus was on getting to as high ground as possible, where the flooding river would not reach her. Christine had never been more determined than in climbing those few feet. If she fell, she would be swept away to her death.

At last, with one final heave, she pulled herself up on top of the steep bank and collapsed there, her breath coming out in puffs in the freezing rain. For several minutes she lay face down to catch her breath before turning to a seated position to look at the destruction below her. The sight of the water engulfing her trunk and pouring into the carriage left her sickened. Had she waited minutes more...

She needed to make her way to Short Ferry and try to find Olsen there, and it was imperative she dry off as soon as she could or she would surely catch her death of cold. Christine stood, refusing to give way to the shivering that overtook her, and began to walk in the direction of town. The wind bit into her drenched clothing, leaving her colder than she had ever known. The road to her right was now fully flooded below her, and she walked with trembling steps in parallel toward the area where the road was on higher ground. It was just out of sight, beyond a small circle of trees and bushes.

At the end of the bank, she came to the higher road, only to suffer another shock. The road here, too, was flooded. Her gaze swept past the line of flooded trees, across the body of water. It had gone from a small, gently flowing river to a raging torrent, and the full truth of her situation now dawned on her. The river had cut off her path on both sides. She would not reach Short Ferry on this end, nor would she reach Fiskerton on the other. The only path left to her was through the woods.

Violent shivering overtook Christine. The skies had lightened but were still letting a steady rain fall. To keep from being overcome with fear, she spoke to herself bracingly.

Find shelter, and quickly. You will have to wait out this storm and get dry somehow. Her only option to walk was behind her in the Long Woods, which would not have been her first choice, for she was far from confident of finding a shelter in it and did not know how long it would take to reach the road on the far side. At the very least, she could find reprieve from the rain and wind under the trees, but it would not be easy to find a house where she could get warm. And with the autumn chill in the air causing her wet clothing to stiffen and freeze...finding shelter was becoming a matter of urgency.

Christine stared at the woods in discouragement before looking once again around her; she had been given no choice. The flooded road had formed a natural barrier behind her, leaving the woods in the center like an island. She made up her mind and walked with determined steps in the direction of the woods. As soon as she entered the canopy of leaves, the stillness and relief from the worst of the rain calmed her, and she moved forward with more resolve. There was no clear path that could lead her to think she would find a house anywhere within, but perhaps there might be a shelter somewhere, nevertheless. Anything to allow her to warm up and dry off until her brother could find her. He might be heartless at times, but he would not rest until he had discovered her whereabouts. Of that, she was sure.

Christine's nose began to run and as she walked on, and she rubbed it on her sleeve. She had grown so numb, the rain and cold seemed to have little effect on her. She refused to think about what would happen if she could find no shelter—refused to ponder the truth that even if she found one, how in the world would she dry herself when she had nothing to light a fire and no dry clothes to change into? As she marched onward, she began to doubt the wisdom of her decision to enter the woods. Perhaps she ought to retrace her steps and follow the edge of the tree line to see if she could circle it without being cut off by the rising water. Or perhaps she ought to just stop and rest. She was so tired, and if she sat down, she could regain her force.

A rational voice inside of her whispered that this was not a good idea, and so she moved on, her teeth chattering helplessly. But soon, her desire to rest became impossible to ignore, and she was about to find a place to sit under a tree when the smell of smoke reached her from someplace ahead. Her thoughts were incoherent, but instinct took over at this beacon of survival, and she pushed forward until she caught sight of the smoke curling upwards.

The promise of shelter spurred her on, and she hurried toward it, her movements clumsy. As soon as she broke through the last thicket of leaves, she discovered a small hut, made mostly of wood with one end built in stone. The shutters were open and a flickering gold light was visible from the window confirming the small blaze in the chimney. She stepped up to the door and tried to knock on it, but her fingers were too cold to make a sound, so she turned her hand and pounded her fist on the door, urging the person inside to hurry—hoping desperately the person inside would be someone good and kind.

The door opened, and a dark figure filled the entry. Her fearful eyes traveled upwards until they met those of a gentleman she was amazed to recognize—the one she had been trying to put out of her mind for the last five days.

Sir Alexander! *How...? How could he always be the one I am running into? And at the worst of times?* And yet, the familiarity of his person made her want to fall into his arms.

"Miss Grey!" he exclaimed. He seemed equally frozen in place.

Christine was rapidly reaching a point where her courage would fail her. If she did not get warm soon, she was not sure she would be able to remain on her feet.

"The road was flooded...and Gus is in Fiskerton." She could barely get the words out as her teeth chattered audibly.

"For heaven's sake, come in," he said, taking her by the arm and pulling her inside, shutting the door behind her. He held her arm firmly as he brought her over to the fire. "You are soaked through."

Christine nodded. She could no longer think properly. She moved toward the chair placed in front of the fire intending to collapse on it, but Sir Alexander stopped her.

"You will have to remove those clothes. I have a dry blanket, and that must do for a cover." He did not wait for her to answer but untied the cloak from around her shoulders and laid it on the wooden table.

"I can't." Her hair dripped water down the side of her face and into her neck. "I have nothing else." Without her cloak, the cold air of the cabin accosted her until she could not stop shaking.

"I am afraid you have no choice but to do so." Sir Alexander's voice sounded angry, much as it had been on the day he had nearly run over her dogs. "You risk becoming violently ill—or worse—if you do not get out of these wet clothes immediately." She felt the blanket cover her shoulders and heard him move away.

The sense of what he said finally sank in, and she attempted to obey. She reached back to undo the buttons of her gown, but her frozen fingers would not obey her. After a minute, she heard his steps return and felt the buttons of her dress being undone. She tried to open her mouth to protest but she was shaking too violently.

Sir Alexander seemed to read her thoughts because he spoke in a hard voice. "You need have no fear from me, madam."

His movements were efficient as he unbuttoned her, and she felt the warmth of his fingers on her skin, which caused her to shiver in a different way. Before she had a chance to examine the novel sensation, or to feel exposed, he brought the blanket back around her shoulders.

"Pull off the rest of your dress underneath the blanket and come sit here."

His voice was commanding, and she obeyed him. Her thoughts were too confused to do anything but what he said. She removed the sleeves of her gown, and without the drenched fabric, she felt the warmth of the dry blanket, which was surprisingly soft. She allowed the dress to slip to the floor underneath the covering, and then he led her to the chair. Before he permitted her to sit, he spread another coarser blanket on the chair, which prickled through her wet stockings, but it was also dry and warm.

He glanced at her boots and raised an eyebrow at her in inquiry, which she understood to mean he thought she should remove her boots. She struggled within herself to give up this last defense against complete vulnerability but knew that these, too, were soaked and she would not warm easily while she wore them. She gave a subtle nod and he bent down to remove them, then wrapped the coarse blanket completely around the bottom half of her, making up a snug package around her feet. He stepped back and walked to the opposite side of the hut before pacing back.

"And now, Miss Grey, will you please tell me what in the *blazes* you are doing here, alone and in this state—and what your brother is doing in Fiskerton?"

CHAPTER NINE

Alex watched Miss Grey burrow into his soft blanket in front of the fire and wished he had another one like it so she would not have to endure the scratchy, dirty one he had found in the hut which was now wrapped around her legs. From the unintentional—or mostly unintentional—touch of her skin as he had unbuttoned the dress, he had learned not only how icy her skin was, but also how soft. Such delicate skin should not have to suffer under a rough blanket.

He had been obliged to abandon his tilbury on the edge of the woods when the flood had forced him onto higher ground. The path he had taken appeared to come to an end in a thicket with no obvious way around it. It was simpler to unhitch his mare and cut through the woods in search of another path. He had only his portmanteau and a blanket in his carriage, so he'd carried them with him. By the time he had stumbled on the cottage, he was heartily sick of the rain and preferred to take his chances inside in hopes of waiting out the rain so he could see his way more clearly. If he had known at the start of his journey that the roads were subject to flooding, he would have given up the idea of setting out in the first place. But then, he did not know Lincolnshire.

"Well?" he prodded when Miss Grey remained silent,

huddled against the cold. He didn't mean for his voice to sound harsh. It was just that he was distressed to find her in such a precarious situation. She could easily have perished from the flood, or the cold, and should never have been left alone. Her presence in his borrowed cabin also lay him open to weakness, considering his attraction to her.

She tightened the blanket around her shoulders. "The wheel on my carriage lost a linchpin on the road from Short Ferry to Fiskerton, and the river flooded and broke its banks while I was stranded there. I needed to seek shelter on higher ground." Her lips had a blue tinge to them, and she kept her eyes trained downward. "That led me to the woods, and after some walking, to this house."

Miss Grey's wet hair shone in the firelight, and some of the ringlets stood out against the pallor of her cheeks. She was trembling violently from the cold, and it would take time for her to recover and reach something of a normal temperature. He shrugged out of his coat and spread it around her shoulders on top of the blanket that enveloped her for additional warmth. She nodded her thanks, and he went over to put more logs on the fire. Without the extra layer of his coat, he shivered in the breeze that crossed the hut, but it was nothing to speak of compared to what she must be enduring. His cloak was already drying by the fire and he brought over the other chair to lay her cloak and dress out to dry. All this he performed in silence to keep from staring at her.

"And how is it that you are unaccompanied?" he asked at last. "Without even a groom or a maid?"

"My maid was ill. And when we encountered the problem with the carriage, our groom went to go and purchase a wheel replacement, or see if he could hire another coach at Short Ferry. That's when the river broke its banks. He could not have known that it would when he left me there, for the surge in the water came at once."

Her teeth chattered as she spoke, and he thought about how

perilous it been for her. The bottoms of her gown and cloak, drenched and mud-filled, told their own story.

"Where is Mr. Grey?" he asked.

There was a pause. "My brother rode ahead to see if everything was clear through to Fiskerton, saying he planned to meet me there. He would have made it to the town well before the river flooded over." Miss Grey took the edge of his blanket and wiped her face with it, before drying some of her hair in the back.

The answer was reasonable enough, but he was unreasonably cross with Grey for having put her, and—although he could not have foreseen it—*him* in this position.

There were no more chairs in the small house other than what she sat on and what held the drying garments, so Alex leaned against the rough wooden table and crossed his arms. How could her brother be so careless about her safety? Did he think a sister was something that could be replaced? He suspected Gus wouldn't even treat a horse that way. Alex needed to distract his mind from uttering words he would regret and looked around at the simple hut as he had done several times since he'd arrived, trying to see what other resources it might have hidden. There was an oil lamp on the shelf, a bucket, and utensils for cooking, but as he had not yet discovered anything to cook, those were of little use.

"I suppose your brother will come looking for you," he observed.

Miss Grey's gaze was on the fire and she still shook, but less violently. "I am sure he would if he could reach us. The woods are on the incline, and I cannot be certain that any road can reach it from where he is. I am afraid he must be prevented from returning by the flood waters as well."

"I see."

What was he going to do with her alone in this cabin? He needed to help her to dress properly once she was warm and the gown was dry, but that would take hours. And even with their obvious explanation and with her fully clothed, it might put him at risk to be caught alone with her. There would be expectations of an offer of marriage.

He rubbed his chin and brought his gaze to the shelves, trying to distract himself from the unwelcome temptation of *that* idea. What mattered now, however, was that he do his best by her. One of those saucepans could be filled with rainwater and brought to a boil in the fire. It was not tea, but it would get something warm inside of Miss Grey, which would help with the shivering. He grabbed the small pot and went outside and set it in the yard to catch water. There was already a bucket outdoors that had collected a substantial amount of rainwater. On impulse, he came back in to collect more pots to fill with rain as it came down. He hadn't seen a pump or well anywhere and didn't know how long they would be here.

"I will return shortly," he told her and went out to the rough outdoor shelter to check on his mare. Upon arriving, he'd had time to rub her down and had already filled some water there for her to drink. There were oats in the simple shelter that had been erected near the hut, at least, showing that someone must come here regularly. Even if they starved, the horse would not. He did everything he could think of to see to his horse's comfort, delaying his return as long as he could. Remaining in the shelter would not solve anything, even if he was at a loss to know what to say to Miss Grey.

Again, he mulled over the problem of having a woman dressed only in her undergarments closeted in the same hut as him. It would not look well for either of them were anyone to chance upon them. His only hope was that either the flooding would recede and he could bring her to Farlow with no one the wiser, or that her brother would find them before they were discovered. Surely, he would be out looking for her, would he not? Alex hoped Mr. Grey would not force him to the altar just because he'd had no choice but to open his door to Miss Grey when she sought shelter. As much as he was attracted to her, he could not wish for a match to be contracted for reasons such as this.

It could be delayed no longer, and he went back inside, taking the smallest saucepan full of rainwater. Miss Grey was in the same position, but she had set his coat to the side and indicated it with a movement under the blanket. "I thank you for the use of your coat. I believe I am warm enough now without it."

He did not think she was, but he suspected she was uncomfortable with the gesture as it added intimacy to their situation. Besides, he had gotten wet again just going to the stables.

"You are welcome."

He donned his coat before going to the chimney. He grabbed the long iron hook leaning against it and used it to latch on to the iron grid that could be pulled down from the brick wall behind the fire. He placed the saucepan on it. "I searched the cupboards, but I was not able to find anything to eat. At least the hot water will warm you up."

"There might be a place outdoors to keep vegetables," she said. "If not a cellar, then perhaps a storage place underground, although that can certainly wait until it stops raining." She looked around. "This must be a forester's house, or something like."

The simple conversation set him at ease, and he realized it was the most ordinary one they'd had since they had met.

"Perhaps so, although the path leading to it does not seem large enough to carry logs through. Could be a gamekeeper's hut. There are the trappings of someone who likes to hunt. My question is, who owns it and when is he likely to return?"

"If it is a gamekeeper's, he might use it as a stop on one of the hunts, like the one Miss Pasley spoke of, although it is rather humble for such a thing. In any event, it meets our immediate needs."

She lifted her eyes from where the flickering flames caused the water in the saucepan to send up tiny bubbles. "What brought you here? Were you also destined for Lincoln?"

Alex nodded. "I was on my way to the Stuff Ball you had talked to me about. Not long after leaving Short Ferry, I discovered that the road there had been flooded, so I turned north but was only able to go so far before being forced to halt."

He folded his arms, watching the flames flicker around the saucepan. "The dirt road along the edge of the woods allowed me to bring my carriage to higher ground, but then the road ended. I didn't find a path in the woods large enough to drive through it, so I abandoned my carriage." He briefly met her gaze. "I rode through the woods in search of a way to reach the public road on the far end but decided to stop when I saw the hut."

"And you were able to make a fire," she said, sending him a fleeting smile. Her lips were now pinker, a promising sign that she was beginning to grow warm, but a distracting reminder of what a kissable set of lips they were.

"Yes, and not long before you arrived," he replied.

"I don't believe I would have been able to manage it myself without any flint—or with shaking fingers."

Alex glanced at Miss Grey again. His appreciation for her had begun to grow, and therefore her good opinion of him was of greater value. At first, he had found her a bit strange and unfriendly, but he was beginning to suspect it was more from reserve than snobbery. And he found her undeniably attractive, even without that glimpse of her friendly, laughing countenance at the card party. He would be in grave danger of losing his heart to her were he not a man who, of necessity, maintained an iron will once he had decided upon something.

"I always have certain tools in my possession in case of emergency, flint rock being one of them," he said, pulling the direction of his thoughts to more practical concerns.

He went to search through the cupboards for mugs and found one, plus a small tankard. He wrapped a cloth he'd found lying nearby around the handle of the saucepan to take it off the fire. "In this case, I was mightily glad of it."

Now that the hot water was ready, he continued his hunt in the cupboards and drawers in case he had missed something. His effort was rewarded as he discovered a small sack with a handful of coffee beans in the back of a drawer. They had little scent left in them, but it was better than nothing. He began to smash them with the bottom of an iron saucepan, alternating between banking the pan to crush the beans, and then attempting to grind them. The way he was going about it, the coffee would taste terrible, but it would be better than simple hot water.

He dumped the grounds into a baked clay jug and poured the hot water on top of it, letting it sit and steep. Silence reigned, and he did not bother to break it as he stirred the coffee, then set the spoon down. Miss Grey had not shown herself to be much of a talker either. And although he was glad not to have useless chatter, he wished he was privy to her thoughts.

"I imagine your trunk and other effects are in the carriage," he observed.

"Which was likely swept away," she said, regret sounding in her voice. "I would have been happy to have anything in it right now. For one thing, I would be properly dressed."

At her admission, he could not help but glance at her, and it was in time to see a flush rise up on her neck. He had hoped she would not be too bothered by the fact she was not sensibly clothed, since it had been out of necessity, but of course she would be. The knowledge of her vulnerable condition was one of the things that had kept him outdoors for as long as he was. It was hard to keep his imagination from wandering to forbidden territory, but it must be done.

He had been careful not to look when he had unbuttoned her dress—or rather, he had only looked as much as was required to see the buttons, but rigidly kept his eyes from straying to her smooth skin above the shift. He had never seen a woman's skin up close like that before and had immediately turned away as soon as he could. Then he walked to the other side of the room so he could breathe.

To turn the direction of his thoughts, Alex went over to touch the bottom of her dress. It was nowhere near dry and was still caked with mud and dirt. Struck by an idea, he glanced at her before quickly averting his gaze when their eyes met.

"Should I try to clean this, even though it might stay wet longer if I do so?"

Some women might protest about the extra trouble, but she was apparently too sensible to do so.

"Yes, that would be kind of you. It is not that I care overmuch about my appearance, for it is a bit late for that, but I think the gown will dry more quickly if there is no mud on it. You need not bother for the cloak."

He nodded and lifted the gown. This meant going back out into the rain, but at least there was a covered area outdoors that he could work under—and he would be granted some distance from her. He slipped off his coat, grabbed the gown without a word and went outside, fetching the nearly full bucket and bringing it under the awning. He rolled up his sleeves and plunged the bottom of the dress into the icy water of the bucket. His hands quickly grew numb, and he alternated between scrubbing and rinsing and warming his hands at his sides when the ache grew unbearable. At last, the dress seemed clean enough and he began to wring it out. The water in the bucket was brown, so he dumped it and set it out to fill again in case they needed it.

Once inside, he laid the gown back over the chair to dry and went to warm his hands by the fire. The dress was of a linen material, simple and good for traveling. From the cloth on the bodice, it must have once been a pretty pale blue.

"Thank you," she said, watching him.

He nodded but kept his gaze averted. The intimacy of their situation did strange things to his peace of mind. He slipped his coat back on and went over to the fire to continue warming his hands. Whatever would they find to talk about in the hours until they were rescued? He busied himself once again, opening the cupboards and searching for things they might eat. Everything was bare.

"I had brought cakes with me on the journey," she said as she watched him. "It is a shame we have none of it now. But I will be glad to have some of the coffee you have prepared."

Alex winced. He had forgotten about the coffee—and was certain the brew could not live up to its name. He went over to the jug that held the grounds and water which was still hot, gave it a stir, and let the grounds settle again before pouring it in equal measure into the mug and tankard.

"Here you are, Miss Grey." He handed the mug to her with a bow. "I am not sure it is drinkable, but it will warm you."

She took a sip and shuddered when she sipped it. "I am grateful."

It must truly be awful. One sip confirmed his belief that the beans had been too old to give any flavor to the coffee. What little flavor they did have was ineffective when they were crushed rather than ground. It tasted little better than hot mud.

"Well, I tried, but I cannot rival what you set before me when I came to call," he said.

She darted a look of surprise at his mention of the visit—and from the ghost of a smile that touched her lips, he thought—pleasure. It had only been the truth; her cakes were superior. However, not even *her* cakes could salvage this muddy swill they were drinking.

"There is nothing here to eat in the cupboards or drawers," he said at last. "I will look outside for a root storage as you suggested, but I have hope that we will not need to be here for long."

Miss Grey sent her gaze around the small room. "I hope not. Has it occurred to you, the odds of us being stuck here together?" She looked conscious suddenly and added, "I mean, we are scarcely acquainted and both live quite a distance away from here…"

Her words trailed away, but he knew what she meant, although he did not offer a reply. If she had been the wife he was searching for, he would have lauded it as divine intervention. But in this case, he could not. Fate had a mordant sense of humor.

She gave a sudden intake of breath. "Has it stopped raining?"

Alex had not noticed the stillness until she spoke, but he went over to open the door. "Indeed it has."

He stood there for a moment, heedless of the cold, staring out at the trees on the edge of the clearing where the water dripped still from the leaves. There was something forlorn about the sight. If he had been alone, he might have taken his horse out again to find an alternative way to get home, then come back for his tilbury another time. But he could hardly include Miss Grey on such a mission, and he could not leave her here alone. He was well and truly stuck.

"I won't be long," he said and stepped outside, pulling the door shut behind him without waiting for an answer.

An inexplicable sense of anxiety squeezed at him like a vise, leaving him prisoner to its unwelcome sensation. The small shelter, the blazing fire, and the pretty woman who sat inside of it weighed on his heart like some distant image of domestic bliss he had imagined as a boy. But it was a distorted picture that brought no comfort, for neither the home nor the woman belonged to him.

To steel his resolve, he sent his thoughts to next season in London where he might find a wife to fit into such a fantasy. It proved to be a futile endeavor, however. In his depressed state, it seemed a certainty that such happiness would never be within his reach.

CHAPTER TEN

Christine kept her gaze on the door long after Sir Alexander had walked out of it. She leaned over to touch her gown on the chair beside her, wondering how long it would be before she could wear it again. It was almost dry at the bodice and sleeves, but from the empress seam downward, the skirt was wet. She would only become chilled through again if she put it back on, and that would defeat everything.

At last, she was beginning to grow warm with only occasional shivers, wrapped as she was in blankets and sitting before a blazing fire. She took a minute to offer up quiet thanks for having been spared a disastrous fate, and for being in surprisingly good hands despite how she had begun the adventure.

Just thinking back to those moments in the carriage as the road began to flood brought the realization home. It had been nothing short of a miracle that she had managed to drag herself up the slippery, steep bank with a wet dress and a drenched and heavy cloak, with only some roots for leverage.

Afterwards, the fact that she had not only found shelter, but also a house occupied by a gentleman she knew—even if she could not claim he was a great favorite of hers—in which a fire already blazed was nothing short of the good workings of Providence.

There was only the matter of being alone with him—and the possible repercussions—to disturb her peace. Such an ill-fated circumstance could ruin her reputation as surely as if she had set out to do so. Then came the lowering thought that, if pushed to it, she would not at all mind being married to him, all things considered. But he clearly did not wish to marry her. She must not put him in a position where he would be forced to propose.

In defiance of her noble resolution, Christine contemplated the possibility of a marriage of necessity before stopping herself. Surely the good people of Lincolnshire would look at the situation with an eye of understanding, would they not? After all, it was evidently not her fault that she had been forced to seek shelter because of an act of nature, and that he had shared the same fate. Despite assuring herself that her reputation was secure, she longed to be fully clothed and not sitting in her shift, wrapped in nothing more than a blanket.

She sipped more of the watery brew and made a face. It was awful, but the fact that it contained some flavor, no matter how bad, helped mitigate her feelings of hunger. And it brought about a sense of sleepy contentment as she grew warm.

The door opened, and Sir Alexander entered, a few potatoes, carrots, and beets cradled in his arm.

"An unexpected find," he said, flashing her a smile as he went and dumped them on the table.

No matter how fleeting, the smile settled something in her. It was reassuring to know he was capable of good humor, even in their extreme circumstances. He brushed the dirt off his coat before removing it and rolling his sleeves back up again. Somehow he looked more handsome and rugged like this than when he was impeccably attired. He looked as though he belonged in Lincolnshire.

My word, Christine—stop! What is wrong with you?

"Indeed." She smiled back, pushing aside these unhelpful

musings. The cold had got to her head. "If there is a knife somewhere, I can assist you in preparing them."

He stared at her, wrapped in the blanket, for a considering moment before shaking his head. "No, I will pare them. You will need to stay warm."

"Really, Sir Alexander, I am much warmer now. I cannot sit here idly while you do everything," she protested.

He returned his gaze to her until she felt quite pierced by it and raised an eyebrow. "Neither can you pull your arms out of your blanket and remain decent."

"Oh." Heat flooded Christine's cheeks. That thought had been far from her mind. She tended to forget about her appearance when there was something needing doing. But as he'd pointed out, she was not properly dressed and would be fully exposed were she to attempt to use her hands. If only she could wear her gown again. Keeping her hand clutched around the top of the blanket, she slipped an arm out and touched the garment, but it was as wet and cold as it had been five minutes before.

Sir Alexander turned his back to her and began peeling the beets with a small knife. His efficient movements surprised her. It was as though he knew how to cook, but how could that be? He must have been raised with servants. For a man like him, it could not have been otherwise. Yet there he was, preparing a supper for them with what he had found. The fire sent a warm glow to the area of the kitchen, where he worked over the table with the wooden shelves behind him, creating a lovely domestic picture.

"I have been wondering," he said, not turning around, "where did you learn to whistle like that?"

"Like what?" she asked, after an unenlightened pause.

"The first time I met you," he said. He turned and glanced at her before turning back around. "When you called your dogs to come, you let out a loud whistle, and they came."

"Oh." A laugh escaped Christine. "When I was a girl, I heard Gus and Philip practicing after they'd learned it from Philip's groom. I practiced in secret until I could do it, too."

"Hmm." It was the only reply he gave, but it sounded like he was smiling.

She swiveled to look around the room again. There was a bed in one corner and a deer hide to serve as a rug beside it. On the mantelpiece sat a pewter holder for a tallow candle, and there were pegs by the door to hang cloaks. The hut had a decidedly rustic air, but it seemed not to be neglected. Perhaps its owner would hear of the flood and think to come looking for anyone who might have sought shelter there in the storm.

Doubt assailed her then, for all she had been confident about the good Lincolnshire sense regarding her position. What if the person who found them was not an amiable sort—one who could comprehend how they had got themselves into the situation—and would only assume the worst? This newer, more dire scenario began to prey on her, and the early optimistic feelings fled. She did not want to be forced to marry a stranger because of some ill fate, no matter how handsome a stranger he was.

She looked down at the blanket she wore and had to admit that if someone found them together, they could only make two assumptions about Sir Alexander and her: either they were already married, or she was not a proper woman. Both possibilities made her ill to think of.

"How did you learn how to cook?" Christine's question popped out of her lips without forethought.

He paused in his preparations, then moved to the other side of the table so he might see her. A lock of his hair fell into his face and he turned his attention to his task again.

"A friend from Oxford always insisted we needed to celebrate the end of each hunt by cooking our own stew. It's a quirk of his. We usually have game to put in it, but in this case the vegetables will have to do."

Sir Alexander had finished peeling and cutting all the vegetables into cubes, and with practiced movements he scooped them up into a larger pot he had brought in from the outdoors. He placed this on the iron rack above the fire, then scraped the peelings off the table and into a bowl. He stepped outdoors, pulling the door shut behind him. He was a man of few words, it seemed. That was fine. She was accustomed to keeping her own company.

It was nonsensical, but Christine reached out again to feel her gown. It didn't seem as though it was drying even a little bit. She sighed at her impotence as she pulled the blanket back around her. What would Gus think when he found her missing? That he had got through to Fiskerton without a problem she did not doubt. He was a skilled rider, and he was on horseback and therefore not confined to the roads. Would he worry about her? Probably a little. He was not a sentimental man, but she was his only family after all, apart from their uncle.

The door opened again, and Sir Alexander entered, squatting down to stir the vegetables in the water that had begun to boil. He stood and turned to face her with a measuring look.

"If I were alone, I would ride out and try to see if the roads are passable in any direction. However, I do not like to leave you here."

His look was a questioning one, tinged with hope, she thought, that she would tell him to attempt what he had in mind. She could not do it, however. She was courageous in many things, but agreeing to remain alone in a house that belonged to she knew not whom and contemplating a solitary, overnight stay in the event he did not return removed any sense of courage she had. What if a newcomer arrived who was not as gentlemanly as this one?

"I beg you will not," she answered, lifting her gaze to his. "We are scarcely acquainted, but at least I am sure you are a gentleman and that you will offer me protection. I should not like for a stranger to find me here in your absence."

"I am of the same mind. I only wished to offer you the choice if it might mean being rescued sooner."

He turned away, his voice almost curt, which wounded though she wished it did not. Her request for him to stay must have irritated him. Of course, he disliked being forced to remain with her, but what could she do? She would not be easy if she were left alone.

It seemed he had dismissed the idea, for he went over to the cupboard and pulled down two bowls. "Oh—salt!" he exclaimed, with the first sound of pleasure she'd heard as he reached behind the bowls to retrieve a small covered porcelain bowl.

Despite Christine's discomfort and unease, his joy at finding salt and the knowledge that the supper would be improved by it cheered her.

There was a stone sink near the shelving unit, and after testing the potatoes and vegetables with a knife, he took the cloth and brought the saucepan over to it. There, he carefully poured out the hot water, sending up a cloud of steam, after which he served two bowls' worth of vegetables, sprinkling the top of each with salt. He handed her one of the bowls, along with a spoon.

She hugged the meal of colorful root vegetables to herself, wrapping her hands around the bowl, and allowing its warmth to seep through her blanket. "Thank you. I had not thought to be given such a feast."

"Nor I." He waited until she fumbled in the blankets for the spoon and took a mouthful.

It was one of the tastiest things she had ever eaten, seasoned with gratitude and salt. Christine savored each bite as much for the sense of satiety as for the unexpected gift of having a gentleman cook for her. She had not eaten anything since that morning.

"It's good," she admitted.

He nodded and continued eating, affording her a discreet view of him. His sleeves were still rolled up from having prepared the stew, and he had loosened his cravat. His brown locks were disordered, and with his posture that had relaxed with the setting, he looked more approachable than he had since they first met. He appeared at his ease, despite the mostly stilted nature of their conversation.

Christine remembered his teasing at the card party and

aligned that image with his comforting presence now. He might have irritated her at first, but it had not lasted long. Never had she felt such familiarity with a gentleman she did not know, and it surprised her. With it came an illogical sensation that she had known him all her life. He looked up when he felt her stare, and she immediately dropped her eyes.

When Christine had finished eating, he took the bowl from her without a word and went outside where she heard some splashing from the bucket there. When he returned, she caught a glimpse of the fading light from the skies through the door. What would they find to talk about while they waited to be rescued? How late into the night must they wait? She stifled a yawn as the food settled. At least she was warm now and satisfied. But the events of the day were catching up to her, and her eyes grew heavy.

When she tried to hide another yawn, he turned his eyes to the bed. "You are tired. Why do you not rest while we wait for rescue? I will stay up."

Christine knew she should protest and offer to remain awake with him, but she was not sure what they would find to discuss if she did. It might be more effort for either of them than it was worth. Besides, she really was tired. Perhaps...perhaps she would just take a short nap, then stay up with him while they waited for their rescuers. She hoped her brother would think of the Long Woods as soon as he could find a way to search for her.

"Very well, I will rest a little." She stood for the first time since she'd arrived, and her muscles contracted so that her knees buckled.

In an instant, he was at her side and grabbed her arm then slipped his arm around her waist. Holding her elbow firmly, he guided her over to the bed tucked on the side of the room under the sloping roof. It was a simple cotton mattress, and she was doubtful of how clean or fresh it was. However, when she sank down onto it, using the blanket to protect her hair from touching the mattress, she was pleasantly surprised to find that it was fresh and comfortable.

Sir Alexander stopped, arrested by the sight of something beyond her that was tucked between the bed and the wall. He reached over and grabbed another animal pelt that had been made into a blanket and covered her with it.

"Come to think of it," he said, as he tucked it around her, "this is more likely the house of a trapper."

"Makes sense," she said in a sleepy murmur. She blinked at Sir Alexander's silhouette as he went over and blocked the view of the fire while he stoked it. She yawned again and drifted off.

CHRISTINE AWOKE when the sunlight streamed through the dancing tree branches outside the window across from her, causing shadows and light to fall on her eyes in succession. She leaned up on one elbow to look at the still-dim room. Sir Alexander was sitting on a chair, his head on the table, fast asleep. Behind him, the fire was still burning, which meant he must have stayed up late into the night, or that he had broken his sleep to attend to it. As for her, she had not woken up once. Her body was sore all over, but she was rested.

With stealthy movements, she swung her legs over the side of the bed and stood, wrapping the blanket more securely around her. Her muscles ached awfully.

She crept over to where he slept and retrieved her gown, which was now fully dry, then brought it back over to the end of the room by the bed. There was nowhere she could change in privacy, but she could take advantage of his being asleep to slip her gown on underneath the blanket. Being properly dressed would make it easier, not only to help in whatever chores were needed, but also to allow her to feel less like a victim and more like the capable woman she knew herself to be.

The blanket slipped from her shoulders as she stepped into the bottom of the dress, but her back was turned to Sir Alexander. She was careful to make no sound as she pulled the gown all the way up and slipped her arms through the sleeves. At this juncture the blanket fell to the floor.

Christine gasped and spun around, clasping the bodice of her gown to her chest; the back of it was open wide. Any hope that Sir Alexander was still asleep evaporated when she saw him on his feet. He rubbed his hands over his flushed cheeks and avoided her gaze when he gestured to her dress.

"Forgive me. I did not mean to stare, but I thought the buttons might be difficult to reach in the back. I will assist if you like."

Christine was of a practical nature, and it was true that the buttons in the middle would be difficult for her to reach alone, especially with such stiff, aching arms. It was his flush of discomfort that decided it for her. "Allow me to close what I can, and then yes, kindly button the few I cannot reach."

Sir Alexander faced away from her, and for that she was grateful. He waited as she buttoned the lower buttons and the ones on top, leaving the middle exposed.

"I am ready." She felt her own cheeks heat as he turned around, and she dipped her head to avoid looking at him.

It was awkward—and intimate. But it was somehow not... horrible. To avoid showing her undergarments in the back, she waited until he drew near before turning, then held her shoulders stiff and clutched her dress against her body on each side as he made quick work of the task. Before releasing her, he reached up and closed an overlooked button on the top of her gown. This appeared to be more difficult to manage, for he could not complete the task without fumbling. The touch of his fingers was warm against her skin.

At last this was done, and he stepped away, retreating to the other side of the table. Her gown was now properly closed—her fortress secured.

"Thank you."

Avoiding his gaze, she went over to the chair by the fire that held her cloak and sat to pull on her boots and button and lace those. The leather was stiff and uncomfortable, but at least it was dry. Then, unable either to sit still or to look at Sir Alexander, she went to the cupboards to search in all the places he had looked last night. As she had suspected, there was nothing in them that could be magically whipped into a breakfast. When she felt that she might face him without showing her embarrassment, Christine turned. His chin had a shadow of whiskers which did nothing to diminish his attractiveness. Rather, it made her want to reach for her cloak and put that on, too, for an additional layer of protection.

He had been watching her, but he broke away now and rubbed his chin. "I will see to Millie." At her look of confusion, he explained, "My mare. Perhaps we might try walking back to my tilbury, now that the rain has stopped. It might be possible to find a way around the floods in daylight."

"If we can find a path leading to the north, we ought to reach a road near Stainfield. At least, we will if there is a road that connects it to the path by the woods," Christine said.

When Sir Alexander looked at her in surprise, she crinkled her nose and smiled. "I have lived here almost my whole life. Of course, I know something of how to get home. It will be easier without the rain and now that it's light enough to see."

He gave her a nod and a look she could not quite read. "Very well, let us attempt it."

He opened the door, filling the small room with rays of sunshine, before he shut it again and everything grew dim.

CHAPTER ELEVEN

Alex could not escape the house fast enough and used the need to check on Millie as an excuse. He and Miss Grey had not carried on an extensive conversation in the time they had been stuck together in their rudimentary shelter. It should have been uncomfortable to be thrown together that way, but somehow it was not. He found her quiet presence calming.

However, getting a second glimpse of her delicate shift and the porcelain skin above the cloth made him heated around the collar. He had blurted out his offer to help without thinking, wishing for her to be decently clothed as soon as possible. This would save her from embarrassment and him from something akin to torture. That had been a mistake—as had been the idea to close the top button which had not truly been a necessary service. The minute he drew near her in the soft light of day, now when she wasn't trembling with cold and with pieces of her hair falling from her coiffure to her back, he questioned his sanity.

The chilly air outside steadied him, and he crossed the muddy ground over to the shelter, where Millie greeted him affectionately. He saw that her watering trough was empty, so he left the shelter and went to where he had put out the bucket and pots to catch water. That was when he noticed the pump on the inside of the clearing, almost hidden from sight amid the trees. He hadn't needed to collect water.

He brought the bucket over to his mare, then went out to drink some himself from one of the pans he had set out. As he was about to go in, he stopped and grabbed the last pot to bring inside. Miss Grey must have been thirsty too.

"This is for you," he said when he opened the door and stepped inside. She turned from the window and smiled at him

The sight made him freeze—the image of her petite, graceful form in front of the window with the backdrop of the scenic green landscape beyond it. There was a rightness about the scene, as though they had known each other in a different lifetime. Then, she moved forward, and the spell was broken.

"Thank you." She lifted the pan with two hands and drank her fill.

The sound of a rider approaching on horseback made them both freeze and eye each other warily. Words were not necessary for each to understand the possible danger of the new arrival, and they waited to learn of their fate in silence. Outside, the rider spoke a few words to his horse. Then, a minute later, the door opened, and a man dressed in a simple cloak and patched boots stopped short in surprise at the sight of them.

"Well then, what's this?"

The reserved Miss Grey surprised Alex by speaking first. "Good day. We were each flooded when the river overflowed its banks, and we sought shelter here. Thank you for your hospitality, though we could not request it of you before availing ourselves of it."

The man looked around his small house, bringing his eyes back to bear on them. "You said *each* of you? Were you not acquainted before coming here?"

Miss Grey laughed nervously. "I assure you we are well acquainted, but we were separated on the road."

Alex could see the man was not convinced and feared he would have no choice but to explain that they were married. Once they left the man, it was unlikely word would reach anyone

106

in Horncastle that they had been thrown together in such a way. And they need not say their true names.

"What are your names?" the man asked as though reading his mind.

Before Alex could catch her eye, Miss Grey answered. "I am Miss Christine Grey. And this...this is my brother, Mr. Augustus Grey."

The solution of claiming kinship hadn't occurred to Alex, but he supposed it was cleverer than husband and wife. It allowed even a fictional distance to remain.

"Ah. Brother and sister." The man nodded to himself. "Of course." He peered at them more closely. "You do not look alike."

"I take after my mother," Alex offered, which was nothing short of the truth. But he didn't like the continued questioning. Was there something about them that *looked* guilty?

They needed to leave before they both ended up entangling themselves with their words. It would be pure folly to give this man reason to spread rumors about them, when it should be a simple matter to see their way out of something that happened purely by chance. If they could just make it to Farlow Manor with none the wiser, they would be saved any inconvenience. It occurred to Alex that a show of coin might not be amiss.

"Please allow me to offer you some money to thank you for your hospitality. We ate some of your vegetables and used your coffee beans." He reached into his coat pocket and pulled out a few coins.

The man's grizzly face lightened when he saw this, and he took the coins and pocketed them. "Ye are welcome then. Name's Timothy Duncan, but everyone calls me Duncan. I earn my bread as a trapper." He brought the chairs back to the table and gestured to it. "I've brought back game to roast. Stay and eat with me if ye'd like."

"That is excessively kind of you," Miss Grey said, stepping forward to reach for her cloak from the back of the chair. "But I am afraid it is not possible. There are friends who must be worried about us. Tell me, are the roads passable to Wragby from here through Stainfield?"

The man threw down his sack of game on the table, exposing the legs of a pheasant. "Believe so, though I haven't gone up that far. Ye might try the track along the edge of the Long Wood going north."

He turned to Alex. "That your tilbury I saw near the edge of the woods?" When Alex nodded, he added, "Shoulda known I might have some visitors since mine is the only house anywhere close to the road."

"I could not go farther with my carriage, so I had to abandon it there. Perhaps the roads are passable now, once we take the track to meet them?"

Duncan considered it. "The path along the woods'll take you there, though there's scarce enough room for your carriage. But ye should be able to manage it. That oughta get you to Apely, and from there to Wragby."

"Good." Alex caught Miss Grey's eye. "Excellent. Shall we go...Christine?" Inwardly, he cringed to make free use of her name, but it could not be helped.

She finished tying her cloak in front. "Yes. Do let us, Gus." Unlike him, the name flowed easily from her lips. At least she truly did have a brother named Gus, though it was not he.

"Where are ye from?" Duncan asked them as they made their way to the door.

"From Horncastle," Miss Grey said. "We were on our way to the Stuff Ball in Lincoln, but that will of course not be possible now."

"Never heard of it," Duncan said. "Ye won't reach Lincoln any time soon. The flood'll take weeks to fix." He followed them outside and went over to his horse that was tied to a post near the house. "Well, if ever I'm in Horncastle, p'raps I'll stop by."

Miss Grey did not even flinch at what must be a threat to both of their peace of mind and only smiled at him. "We would be glad to return the hospitality, Mr. Duncan. Good day."

She waited for Alex to go and retrieve Millie, which he did as quickly as he was able. She must not be left alone with Duncan for longer than necessary.

Leading Millie forward, he collected Miss Grey and waved at the trapper as they set out on the small track through the trees. With any luck, they would be able to navigate the path Duncan had mentioned and make it to a main road on higher ground. And if their luck continued, they would not meet anyone who would recognize Miss Grey while she rode next to him in the tilbury. It was a shame he did not have a closed carriage—but then such a thing would likely not have been able to go over the track at all.

They marched through the trees with him leading his mare on his left and Miss Grey walking on his right. He was careful not to let the low branches snap back and hit her. "Why did you tell that man your real name and where you live?"

She picked her way over the uneven ground with graceful steps as though she was accustomed to the woods. She must have been. After all, their first encounter had taken place in it.

"I cannot say. I am not in the habit of speaking falsehoods, although it would probably have been a wiser thing to do in our situation. However, even if he does visit the town, which I find unlikely given the disparity in our social status, I cannot think anyone will pay him heed. I trust the people of Horncastle to look at the situation with an indulgent eye. They know me." She sounded convinced.

"They do not know me, however," he said grimly. "For all they know, I took advantage of you when you were helpless."

She turned her face to him with a look of surprise. "But you did not."

The trust in her dark brown eyes and direct stare melted something inside of him, though it was precisely the thing he wished to keep firmly in place until he found the woman he would marry in London. Briefly, he wondered if his future wife would have shown as much gratitude for their temporary shelter and meal as Miss Grey had.

He thought about her words, which indicated that she had

acknowledged his honorable treatment of her. It was the kind of faith he had always hoped the wife he chose would put in him. However, he must not be naive. His own standing in society, particularly as an MP, was not secure enough, and he could not afford to make any mistakes in his choice of a wife. Although one of Miss Grey's principal attractions lay in her industry—something he admired as much and more than her beauty—this trait was not the most important thing he needed in a wife. What he needed was a lady who could move about in society.

Despite having reached this firm conclusion, Alex knew a sudden, illogical desire to have a bath, a shave, and clean clothes so he might present a better traveling companion for Miss Grey. Someone who looked like he intended her good, not harm. He gave himself a firm, internal scolding when he realized where his thoughts were headed. These ruminations were futile. He would return Miss Grey to her home, after which they would likely cross paths only occasionally. He would finish his renovations in the months before traveling to London. And then he would find the most suitable candidate for his wife. Surely there existed a woman he would find as attractive as Miss Grey, and about whom he would find many other things to value.

He was lost in these thoughts as they walked in silence. Their steps sank into the mud in places, although the leaves had kept the worst of the rain from the ground underneath the trees. His eyes were now peeled ahead for a sight of the tilbury.

"Do you think we will manage to take you safely home without causing tongues to wag?" he asked to break the silence. "I should not like to compromise you."

"Nor I, you," she said, giving him another slight smile.

There was a store of humor underneath her serious demeanor, he was beginning to perceive. An added attraction if he were looking for more reasons to admire her.

"I have some fears over being subject to censure," she admitted, "but it is only from people like Mrs. Pickering, the vicar's housekeeper. She is a known gossip. She, or possibly one of the matrons in town who have nothing better to do than to chatter, might cause me some harm. However, most of the people in Horncastle are good, and they will not rush to assume the worst."

"And is your brother like to?" he asked, realizing how much the answer weighed with him. He would face the greatest pressure from her brother, since Grey was the one who would have the most to say about Alex's responsibilities in the event he thought his sister compromised. Alex would have to propose out of gentlemanly consideration.

"I don't think so," she said, after appearing to give it some thought. "My brother is not likely to raise a fuss if I tell him not to place too much meaning on the event. After all, nothing did happen, and both you and I are innocent. If it is only up to him, this whole affair will go no further. We must simply avoid being seen by one of the few who are bound to cause trouble."

Her words lifted a weight from Alex just as he caught sight of the top of his carriage. "My tilbury is there ahead, around the small bend. It seems a farther distance than when I left it in the pouring rain, but then I was on horseback."

They reached the carriage in silence, and he unstrapped the saddle that he had only loosely tied onto Millie, hooking it to the back of the tilbury, then harnessed Millie to bring the carriage upright. He helped Miss Grey to sit.

"I do not have a bonnet," she said, after settling in. "I feel exposed without it."

He took the reins and nudged his horse forward. "Did you leave it at the hut?" He hadn't remembered her having one when she arrived. No, he was quite certain she did not.

"I had taken it off in the carriage, and it has likely floated away along with my other worldly possessions." Her dry tone seemed an attempt to pretend it did not matter.

"I am sorry about that. Is there anything you cannot replace?" he asked.

Not everyone would have reacted to the loss of possessions so prosaically as Miss Grey did. He was as yet unsure if this showed an unaffected nature or an unfeeling one, but if he had to choose, he would say she was unaffected. Then again, she had had some decisive things to say about his mother's portrait.

"I suppose I regret most the loss of my gown for the Stuff Ball. It was a lovely violet color, and I sewed beads on it with a very pretty result. I spent many hours on the dress, especially the beading, and hate to think of my handiwork at the bottom of the river."

She sent him a look, which he could not see as he navigated the path. "But I am sure you do not care to hear more about my gown."

"I understand what it is like to pour your labor into something and have it be lost," he replied, thinking of the earlier prototypes he had made for his steam engine, before he had found one that worked well enough and was robust enough to do the work he envisioned.

The thicket in front of them that he had thought to be an impasse was merely overgrown branches that could be cleared without too much difficulty. He made quick work of it, then drove his carriage on.

The track was tricky to navigate, as Duncan had suggested it might be. Very narrow with bushes on either side and uneven ground, but it was passable for now. They went as far as they could with the woods to his left before reaching what appeared to be yet another impasse.

He looked around. "This is the end. I wonder where the track is supposed to lead from here."

"Along the hedge there." She pointed. "You can just see the grass flattened from a set of wheels. It is a tight fit, but if we go that way, I think it will lead to Apely, and then to the main road toward Wragby."

He nodded and turned his carriage to where she'd indicated, following the track along the hedge that separated two fields. Now that his carriage was traveling away from the woods, he felt a sense of liberation for the first time since their enforced confinement. He could not wait to get home; he wanted a bath and needed time to reflect on all that had transpired.

It took them almost an hour of attempting to move forward, and he used every bit of his remaining energy to navigate the track. At one point, he got down to lead Millie, and at another, he pushed the tilbury from behind to help it over a clump of mud and straw. They did not speak many words as he did this, but Miss Grey took the reins without asking when he leapt down to maneuver the carriage.

After an arduous mile or two, they pulled up from the track to a packed-dirt road. This was also muddy, but firm enough once they were on it that he was able to resume his usual pace when driving the tilbury. This lifted his spirits.

"I am not familiar with where we are," he admitted. "But if we continue east, we should eventually reach an area we will recognize."

"That way is Apely," she said, pointing. "We may have no option but to go through Wragby—in fact I am sure of it, since I do not trust the smaller roads—but I wish we did not have to be on such a public road. I am not presentable like this."

"Sit back and put the hood of your cloak up," he recommended. "I am sure no one will notice you. There is only one thing that worries me. Are you able to continue on the journey without stopping to eat or have some tea? You've had nothing but water."

She nodded emphatically. "I long for nothing more than to be home. I can very well wait as long as you can." She eyed him uncertainly.

Alex wished for a tankard of ale even more than a bath. It would be filling and quench his thirst, but Miss Grey must be safely deposited at home and their names not connected in any way. He would not take any risks in stopping.

"I do not need anything."

There were few carriages on the road as they went on past the outskirts of Apely, but as they headed toward Wragby, the junction of roads coming from several towns brought more people. He felt Miss Grey tense beside him and sent subtle glances at each person. They could be discovered at any moment, but there was no point in attempting to reassure Miss Grey about something that was out of his control. His best bet was to continue on and hope they made it home without incident.

There were carriages passing by, but no one called out to them as they drove, and Miss Grey gave no signs of recognizing anyone. He kept his eyes trained ahead, and neither he nor Miss Grey spoke until they had cleared Wragby and were on their way to Langton.

"We may be in luck." Alex exhaled in relief, but she did not join him in his confidence.

"I would like to be as optimistic, but we will have to drive near to town before reaching Farlow, and that will be our greatest risk. If we must see someone we know, I only hope we will meet someone sensible."

The road brought them past a modest beer house that he took no pains to look at. However, a woman sitting in a carriage outside of it gasped and began waving frantically, causing him to glance over.

"*Yoohoo! Yoohoo!* Miss Grey, is that indeed you?"

Alex's heart chugged slowly as a coil of dread sprang up in him. He felt the blood drain from his face, even while refusing to believe they would have such poor luck after having cleared Wragby.

Next to him, Miss Grey said quietly, "Sir Alexander, you had better stop since she has seen me."

He obeyed, pulling the tilbury over to where a smiling, energetic woman with bright eyes feasted upon the pair of them. She brought her eager gaze to Miss Grey.

"It *is* you. Mr. Grey has been worried sick, and everyone in Horncastle has been sent to scour the countryside for you. I will go in and tell the men to call off the search since you have been found. You are in luck. The ones on horseback will reach town with the good news even before you do."

"Yes. Be so kind as to do that." Miss Grey's smile lacked warmth. "As you can see, I have been rescued."

114

The woman brought her inquisitive stare to Alex before turning back to Miss Grey. "I believe your escort must be Sir Alexander. But how did this...gentleman find you? Where have you been all this time?"

Alex wanted to help stave off the questions by answering, but he could not read Miss Grey's relationship with the woman correctly and feared to make things worse. Miss Grey hesitated only slightly before offering a reply.

"There was a trapper's hut in the woods that served as a shelter for me when my carriage was washed away in the flood. It was not until this morning that it was safe to venture out."

"And you, sir?"

Now Alex could not avoid answering. "I assisted Miss Grey by bringing her home."

"Oh." The woman's eyes lit with a delight he would have preferred not to read too much meaning into, if only he were not quite sure that he had her measure already.

When neither he nor Miss Grey offered any more, the woman glanced back at the beer house. "Well, as I said, I will tell *everyone* that you have been discovered."

"Thank you," Miss Grey said, giving another tight smile. Her hands were clutched on her lap. "We must continue on now. As you said, my brother is worried about me."

"Good day, Sir Alexander. Good day, Miss Grey," the woman called out, giving a wave.

Alex rode on and did not speak for some distance. He waited for Miss Grey to say something about the encounter they had just had, but she was silent. Too silent. He could take it no longer.

"And that was?"

"And that was Mrs. Pickering," she replied, and without turning her gaze from the road ahead, let out a long sigh.

CHAPTER TWELVE

Sir Alexander brought the tilbury in motion again on the road from Langton, and Christine could not shake the apprehension that had seized her ever since she realized the person hailing her was none other than the dreaded Mrs. Pickering. What luck she had! Of all the people who lived from here to Horncastle, it had to be her. The Mercers and the Reids would have instantly believed in her innocence once she'd reassured them that Sir Alexander had behaved the perfect gentleman. And her own friends would not allow her innocence to be called into question, even if she had been forced into an overnight stay with Sir Alexander. Gus could have been brought around to the idea of ill fate but no harm done if the public at large did not get wind of it. It was not that all hope was now lost, but it would not be as easy to stem the tide of gossip.

"We have been extremely unfortunate," Sir Alexander said in a resigned voice.

She glanced at him, having almost forgotten that he was just as concerned in the affair as she was. *What he must be feeling!*

"We have been. But I would still like to see if we can brave it out. People know Mrs. Pickering for a gossip. Those close to me won't believe what she has to say for an instant."

"But the wider circle can make things uncomfortable," he said grimly.

"I beg you will not worry overmuch until we see what can be done. I must talk to Gus," Christine said. She was hopeful that for all of her brother's faults, he would not believe the gossip and would not take useless measures to protect her reputation once he was convinced nothing had been done to harm it. *As long as I continue to keep house for him*, she thought cynically.

As for her, she supposed a few gossips would not matter a great deal as long as she had her true friends who would circle about her. She did not make enough excursions into town for a few wagging tongues to disturb her peace. And it had not escaped her that Sir Alexander must be dreading that he would be called to account for something he'd had no control over. She would not impose that on him.

They continued the ride, each consumed by his own thoughts, saying next to nothing, though the remaining journey took them nearly two hours. As they entered the road leading into Horncastle, Christine spotted a figure on horseback far ahead. Gus!

He paused in his walk, peered at their carriage in the distance, then must have recognized her because he urged his horse ahead at a mad gallop until he reached them.

"Christine!" He swung down from his horse and reached her in two strides, his arms open.

The unexpected nature of his welcome caused tears to surge in her eyes, and she climbed down in haste and fell into his embrace. He hugged her tight and said nothing for a minute. Then he released her just as suddenly and swiped at his eyes.

"I have been sick with worry." He brought his gaze to Sir Alexander and stepped on the foothold of the tilbury to reach over and shake his hand. "Sir Alexander! How did you find her?"

"It was in the Long Woods."

Sir Alexander must have sensed his explanation was inadequate because Gus kept waiting for more. Christine could not bear for him to be put on the spot that way.

"I can tell you more about it when we get home, Gus. The important thing is that I am well. Shall we continue on to Farlow? I have a great need to wash and change, and I imagine Sir Alexander is keen to go home and do the same."

"By all means." Gus went back to where his horse stood patiently and climbed back up as Christine stepped into the tilbury. He wheeled his horse around to ride alongside them at a walk. This gesture touched Christine. Gus was not someone who would ride at a sedate pace if he could instead ride hell for leather.

"Did you find Olsen?" she asked him as they moved forward. It occurred to her that they would be fortunate if they made it home without seeing anyone who had heard the news from the group in Langton. Her only wish now was for this.

"He rode back to Farlow when he saw that the path had been flooded. He said the entire road was under water and there was no carriage visible." Gus's voice was tight. "I could barely get anything out of the man. He was stumbling over his words, almost bawling like a baby. I felt like doing the same."

She reached over to touch his arm. "You must have known I would have enough sense to leave the carriage when it began to flood. You didn't think to come looking for me in the woods?"

"To own the truth, I wasn't thinking straight. I hadn't connected that portion of the road with the woods by the time I learned of it. I didn't know anything of your whereabouts until late in the night. I waited for you in Fiskerton, expecting you'd had some small delay. But I didn't know about the flood until some new guests came into the inn talking of their near escape."

"So you went to Farlow," Christine said, unsure of how she felt about the fact that her brother had gone home instead of spending all night looking for her. But then, perhaps he couldn't have done so.

"Yes, that's when I took the higher roads to get home in the expectation that Olsen would have had the sense to turn around and bring you there. But he waited in the area, hoping you would walk to Short Ferry."

"I couldn't reach it," she said, reassured by Gus's reasoning.

He did care about her. That led her to think of Olsen's emotional reaction, which also touched her. There were times she felt that no one would notice if she disappeared forever, except for the fact that there would be no one to run the household.

"Where did you spend the night?" he asked suddenly, pulling her out of her reverie. *Ah!* The question she had hoped he would not ask, at least not until they were home.

"I found a trapper's hut in the woods and was able to take shelter there," she said briefly. "Did you see Arabella and Theo this morning? I hope they did not end up setting out after all. They were right to wait. And did you warn the Townsends? They were supposed to leave this morning."

Gus ignored her questions. "Was no one in the hut when you arrived?" He turned his gaze from her to Sir Alexander. "And you, sir. How did you manage to find my sister?"

She felt Sir Alexander tense beside her, and although she could not explain it to herself, she knew a longing to protect him. He had been a perfect gentleman, and only she had the power to bring them both out of this predicament. For if she made it seem as though she were compromised in any way, no matter how small, then people would believe it. He would be forced to offer for her hand. On the contrary, if she did the opposite, her word must carry power.

"Now, that was a piece of luck," she said, with a nervous laugh. "Sir Alexander had taken shelter in the same hut I stumbled upon, and what was most fortunate was that he had started a fire in it, which was blazing by the time I arrived. I was wet through, let me tell you."

Her brother was now looking at Sir Alexander from his superior position on horseback, waiting for him to say something. Sir Alexander brought his eyes up from the road and looked at Gus.

"I had been flooded out as well. I left my tilbury on the edge of the Long Woods, near the track that leads to Apely, although I did not know where it led until the trapper gave us directions this morning. When your sister arrived, I made sure she was dried off and warmed."

"And he cooked me dinner," Christine explained, thinking to impress upon her brother how remarkable such a thing was. After all, when had Gus ever cooked anyone dinner? It was only belatedly that she realized mentioning the dinner made it sound like an assignation.

"Sir Alexander, I trust you know how this looks," Gus said in an austere voice—more serious than she had ever heard from him. It was ridiculous. He sounded like their father.

"I understand perfectly," Sir Alexander replied, his face and voice bleak.

"Wait, both of you." Christine stopped their speech with her hands up. "Gus, you and I will talk more about this when we get home, but I do not wish for Sir Alexander to be under any oblig- ation. He may very well have saved my life, for I cannot tell you how cold I was. He helped to remove...to warm me."

She stopped short in horror. *What* had come over her? When had she ever permitted herself to speak without thinking? She had come within a hairsbreadth of admitting that he had undressed her! It was as if she had wished to sabotage Sir Alexander's freedom. What must he think? She darted a glance at him, and his face was still set in the same firm lines. She could read nothing except grim resignation in his look.

"Christine, there is no need to say any more. I perfectly understand the situation." He glared at Sir Alexander. "Believe me, I do."

She couldn't stay silent as guilt piled on to the dread, and it made her speak tartly. "Gus, for heaven's sake, will you stop being ridiculous?"

Both her brother and Sir Alexander met this reproach with silence. They turned down the road that followed the Waring and led to their house. Another carriage rode by them with the baker and his wife in it. They both stared hard at Christine before continuing to ride on and leaning in to speak to each other. Not even a greeting!

"Do you see what I mean?" Gus said between clenched teeth. "Somehow word has already got out and they are all thinking what I am thinking."

"Why do we not wait until we are in the privacy of your home?" Sir Alexander said. Tension was radiating from him, and his voice sounded strangled.

They all fell silent now, and although Christine wanted to continue to protest, she could not do so. It seemed awful that Sir Alexander should have to suffer from what was his likely belief that she was attempting to entrap him. After her thoughtless prattle, he would surely think so.

Well! It would be some time until they could discuss this rationally, and there was nothing she could do until then. In her wish to clear herself, there was one thing she held on to to keep from getting distracted. Once she released Sir Alexander from all obligation, he would know she had never meant to trap him in the first place. He would then exonerate her of that at least. It was this future hope that kept her lips sealed.

They finally entered the gates of Farlow, and as soon as the carriage stopped, Christine turned to alight without assistance. Unable to meet Sir Alexander's gaze, she curtsied.

"I owe you a debt of gratitude for rescuing me, sir. I am certain any repercussions from our misfortune can be discussed in a sensible way."

She turned to walk into the house but heard Sir Alexander address her brother. "I will return home and make myself presentable, then call upon you this afternoon if that is acceptable to you?"

"It is," she heard Gus answer curtly. She was tempted to slam the door behind her at her brother's stupid, obstinate stance. Instead of thanking the man, he had plans to...*oh*, she knew he expected that Sir Alexander would offer for her, but he would see how wrong he was when she refused him.

Although she wanted nothing more than to slip into a bath and eat a hearty breakfast in complete silence, she waited for Gus in the drawing room, knowing he would expect a conversation. Beatrice walked by the entrance to the room and upon seeing Christine, gave a cry, then ran over and hugged her. Guinea trotted into the room at the sound and began yelping and leaping around her feet. The maid was sobbing incoherent words, and Christine patted her back, soothing her.

She had not had time to think about Beatrice other than to briefly wonder if she'd had her tooth extracted and was relieved of her suffering. It had been providential that the toothache kept Beatrice from accompanying her to Lincoln—even if her presence would have kept Christine from being alone with Sir Alexander. But what if her maid had not been able to climb out of the flooding carriage and up the bank to safety? So it had all been for the best.

"I am well, as you see, Beatrice." She was touched again at these signs of welcome and affection. She reached down to pick up Guinea, who wiggled around in her arms, attempting to lick her face everywhere. "Would you have a hot bath poured for me? And do tell Olsen I am safe. He will want to know. And ask Cook and Mary to prepare something to eat. Gus will want something as well."

"Yes, miss." The maid wiped her tears with her apron and hurried to the kitchen to do Christine's bidding.

Gus came into the room as Christine set Guinea down. Petunia had begun to wind her way around Christine's skirts, and she picked the cat up in turn and nestled her face into her fur.

"We need to talk. I want to know exactly what happened," Gus said.

"And we will. But first I am going to take a much-needed bath and change my clothes. Beatrice is seeing that both of us have something to eat. Let us postpone this conversation until we have done so." She added silently, *or you will be intolerable, my dear brother.*

He grunted, which she took for a yes. She knew she couldn't avoid their talk and didn't wish to. But she also knew him well enough to know he would be more indulgent when he was well fed. And in this instance, she would have a better rein on her temper when she was, too.

The bath was heavenly, although it took time for Beatrice and Jimmy to bring up enough hot water to fill the tub as full as she liked. For once, she did not help them or try to rush and do something else while she waited. She sat in her dirty gown and shoes until Jimmy left her alone, then allowed Beatrice to assist her to remove her clothing.

"Put out my yellow cambric gown. And please take that pile to be washed. I hope I will be able to wear it again, but it will take some effort to remove all the stains."

"Yes, miss." Beatrice came over and held out her hand for Christine to grasp and helped her into the bath.

As soon as the maid had left and Christine was alone, tears slipped out of her eyes from exhaustion, and from the heavenly sensation of sitting in clean, hot water. She grabbed the soap on the stand next to her and began removing the dirt, along with the cold and the memories of her near escape.

As she dipped her head under water, then lathered her hair with the soap, she couldn't help but think that it could all have been much worse. She might have missed the hut entirely and would very likely have frozen half to death in the woods. She could have found it but have had no one there to receive and help her. Or it might have been someone else—a man with no morals. Christine supposed she should be appalled after reflection on all that might have happened, but she could only focus on what had. She had been kindly treated by the hand of Providence.

The water had grown dirty and was now swiftly cooling. She stood, letting the water slough off her and reached for the towel to dry herself. Beatrice had evidently been hovering nearby because she knocked and entered, hurrying to assist Christine with a clean shift and her gown, then to towel dry her hair. She separated the strands to dry them as much as possible, but Christine told her to just pin it up wet. It would hardly be noticeable as long as the curls on the side of her face were dry.

"Your breakfast is ready, miss. Mr. Grey is waiting for you in the dining room." Beatrice stepped back and picked up the wet towel that had fallen to the floor.

"Your toothache is better?" Christine asked.

"Oh, don't ye worry about me, miss. I am right as a trivet. Ye must be right starving." Beatrice offered her a smile, and Christine went over to the door. She was famished.

Gus waited for her in the dining room, and as soon as Christine took a seat, he served her a cup of tea. He then filled her plate with kippers, and toast with cheese, and set it in front of her. He pushed the basket of fruit closer to her as well.

"Thank you." On the heels of his embrace, this additional gesture let her know how much he had worried. She had no recollection of him ever serving her food before. She sipped at the sweetened tea, and her eyes brightened. This, she followed with a bite of toast.

Gus tucked into his food, taking her suggestion to eat first seriously. Good! She needed it as much as he. Hers was a considerable appetite to satiate, and every mouthful was as delicious as the last. She ate more slowly than he did but had staved off the worst of her hunger by the time he put his fork down. He pushed his plate forward and folded his hands on the table.

"Now," he said, pinning her with his gaze. "Let's have it. The whole story. Do not leave anything out, if you please."

Christine gave up on eating and set down her fork. She began with the broken wheel and the rapidly flooding road, describing how quickly she had to abandon the carriage. He sat back and folded his arms when he heard about her climbing up the hill that bordered the road and using the roots as a foothold. When she paused, he rubbed his face in his hands.

"I am sorry. I should never have left you." He exhaled, blinking rapidly. "That was foolish of me. I'd never have forgiven myself if something had happened to you."

"Gus." Christine's voice softened, and she was filled with a rush of affection. "Do not think anything more of it. I am well.

We cannot prevent every ill from happening in life. And you must remember, I am no longer a girl."

"You're not an old spinster, either," he retorted, in his normal tone. "Go on."

Christine was torn between the lingering affection of all these signs on his part that he did care for her and her usual frustration at his fractious ways. She resumed her recounting of walking in the woods and how cold it was—how grateful she was to spot the hut.

"I saw the smoke from the chimney and knew someone was there. It no longer mattered who it was and that I was unaccompanied, for I was too cold to stay outdoors any longer. It had been some time since I had been able to feel my fingers and toes. I knocked, and Sir Alexander opened."

When Gus waited for her to continue, Christine told him that he asked why she was alone, watching as a flash of some emotion crossed Gus's face. Then she told him about how he got her warm by assisting her in taking off her dress.

"The devil he did," Gus snapped, and Christine grew irritated.

"Have *you* ever been drenched through in the cold of autumn?" He thought for a minute and shook his head, so she continued. "Well, let me assure you that it is impossible to get warm when you are. Sir Alexander must have known it because he wrapped me in a blanket and merely offered to unbutton my dress when I couldn't—"

She paused as he opened his mouth in outrage, then cut him off before he could say anything. "Let me remind you that women cannot easily dress or undress without assistance. And immediately upon helping me, he turned away while I removed my gown under the blanket for him to lay out to dry. He sat me beside the fire and removed my wet boots, then covered me in another blanket *and* his coat."

Christine spoke heatedly, and the realization caught her short. She was so practiced with speaking in measured tones when dealing with difficult people that she had forgotten there was any passion within her. Even her argument with Sir Alexander over her dogs had been out of character for her and brought about by extreme fright. Otherwise, ever since her mother had fallen ill, she never allowed herself to display anything beyond her usual placid demeanor. But Gus's insistence on reading something into Sir Alexander's benign help sent her over the edge.

The memory of Sir Alexander's fingertips grazing over her skin came upon her like a flash, making it difficult to breathe. *He didn't mean anything by it. It is clear he has another type of woman in mind to marry.*

Gus listened to her defense with more attention than he usually did. It gave her hope that he was truly listening for once. But then he sighed, grabbed the napkin on the table, wiped his mouth with it, and threw it down.

"Christine, you must know you are compromised. If I had been there...if I had come that morning, even if you had been there overnight with him, we could have pretended that I had been with you all along."

"Well, you were not there, because you left me. Do not lay the consequence of your lapse of judgment at Sir Alexander's feet."

He blew out harshly, stood, and paced away from her. "You said the trapper came home. Who else saw you?"

Christine's lips twitched in a grimace, and she directed her eyes past him to the opposite wall. "Mrs. Pickering."

"Mrs. P—" Gus threw up his hands. "No wonder the baker and his wife gave you the cut. They must have known about it before you even reached home, although how that could be..." He puzzled over this, and Christine gave him his answer.

"Some of the men on the search were on horseback, so they would have reached town before us. They were able to use a more direct track."

Gus looked at her pityingly. "You see what this means, do you not? If Sir Alexander is a gentleman, he will have to make you an offer. I expect it of him and will have something to say if he does not." He raised his brows and sent her a meaningful look. "And *you* will have to accept it."

Gus turned away before he could see the obstinate lift of her chin that told its own story to anyone who knew her.

CHAPTER THIRTEEN

Alex was partially restored after having eaten and bathed, but he couldn't shake the heavy feeling regarding what would be required of him next. He would have to go to Farlow Manor and make an offer of marriage to Miss Grey. In the past, when he thought about marriage at all, he had, of course, hoped for a woman he found attractive. Someone adventurous and kind, who would be a companion to him. She must have a high station in society—he had always known this element was essential—but her other attributes were important. And above all, he must have a choice. Miss Grey had many excellent qualities, but besides her lacking the necessary one of helping him with his political career, his proposing to her was not of his own choosing.

To marry sensibly but without love he could accept for the good of the family name. Or to marry for love, though the decision lacked sense, he might countenance. But in this case, the union lacked both love and sense.

What wretched luck! If only he had not taken shelter there—or Miss Grey had not stumbled upon that same hut. But then, she might have wandered on in the cold woods and died alone. This brought about an immediate image of her collapsed on the forest floor on a bed of decaying leaves, her face deathly white, impossible to rejuvenate. It caused a sensation of horror to well up in him. No, he could not wish for that.

He wandered through his study, one of the rooms he had not shown to Miss Grey and Mrs. Townsend. It had been stripped of the wall hangings and new ones had yet to be hung. He stopped and stared at the room in which he spent most of his time, whose bare walls had never bothered him before.

Gracefield House is a thoroughly depressing stack of bricks. It was the first time since he'd acquired the estate that he felt no joy in contemplating its ownership. To be sure, he did not regret his acquisition, but at the moment, it was difficult to find anything hopeful to dwell on.

He went over to the desk and picked up the letter he had received from his brother, skimming its lines. If he had received one so soon on the heels of Leonard's visit, it was because his brother wished to deliver a subtle reminder of how necessary a strategic marriage was. He went on to remind Alex of his two nieces' presentations one day and how much training was geared toward preparing them for it. Leonard suggested Alex waste no time in finding a wife—especially one of good birth and standing in society so the Thorne plans would succeed. Impeccable timing, this reminder.

He dropped the letter on the desk and walked over to the window, his hands clasped behind his back. At what time should he go to Farlow Manor and meet his doom? He almost laughed at himself for such a dramatic turn of thought, except that it was little short of the truth. His brother would not understand— would be incensed at his not fulfilling his part of the promise— considering he'd gained his portion of the mill for which he did not have to work, a large part of which allowed him to buy the estate. Yet what choice did he have? Should he go now and get it over with? Have Mr. Grey think there was a grain of truth to his suspicions because he had presented himself at the earliest opportunity? Should he delay it until the last possible minute?

No, he could not do that. Because then Miss Grey might think he would not come, and he would not have her suffer another moment's anxiety. Alex walked over to the small side table near the door—one of the pieces of furniture that he happened to like—and picked up his hat and gloves. It may as well be now.

He reached the Greys' residence, where a footman answered the door and admitted him with a bow and all that was proper for a guest to the manor. This time, there was no disheveled Miss Grey to receive him. Recalling the image would almost make him smile were it not for the dire predicament they were now in.

Mr. Grey entered the room and shook his hand, gesturing to the seat. "I will call for some claret in a bit. But first I thought we might come straight to the point of your visit today. My sister has been compromised, although I will do you the honor of believing it was not your intention."

"Good of you," Alex responded in a dry tone.

"Nevertheless, the facts remain. And so?" Mr. Grey opened his hands and waited. The gesture only fueled Alex's irritation, but he had been educated a gentleman, even if he had not been born one. He would go through with this.

"I have come prepared to make your sister an offer. You may have no fears on that head." A vein in his temple began to throb. "Before we begin to speak of financials, however, I believe I should be certain this is what Miss Grey wishes for. After all, we do not know each other."

Mr. Grey's eyes popped open, and he stuttered on his first word. "That cannot matter. You must know how precarious her standing is. Of course she will accept you."

Alex was not handling this well. His prepared speech was coming out stiff and ungenerous. He would have to do better when he spoke to Miss Grey.

"And she will have my offer, I give you my word. But I think we should begin with that, if I may be granted a private audience with her."

After a brief pause, Mr. Grey nodded and stood. "I will go and fetch her, and then we may discuss the particulars."

He quit the room, and Alex was left with the heaviest spirit he'd had since the day, in his childhood innocence, he was made to understand that his mother had died and wasn't coming back. What he was experiencing was akin to grief, he realized. Putting aside a future one had always hoped for meant those hopes were dead. One must naturally grieve its end. If he could just get through this meeting, he would worry later about what he might say to his brother.

Alex let his gaze roam around the drawing room, noticing for the first time how pleasant the arrangement was. The last time he was here, he had been so caught up with the strange household, the lively conversation brought by Miss Pasley, and the delicious cakes, he had not observed his surroundings.

The wall hangings were bright, as though they were brand new, and the furniture had been polished to a gleam. There were intricate *papier-mâché* framed decorations covered with gold leaf, and the articles placed around the room on tables and shelves were a mix of comfortably rustic and elegant porcelain. It was evident Miss Grey was capable of running a well-ordered house, even if he had been convinced of the contrary on his first visit. Gracefield would benefit from this talent, but it was not for such a reason a man liked to propose!

The door opened, and he turned to see Miss Grey standing just inside the room. He scrambled to his feet, her appearance sending his thoughts into incoherence. He was conscious of the strange familiarity they shared that came from having spent extended time together. He was also cognizant of her beauty whether she was dressed in elegant clothing with styled hair or covered in mud and wrapped in a blanket.

She was somehow more beautiful than she'd been at the card party, because he knew something of her now. Miss Grey measured her words, had a hidden sense of humor, and her infrequent displays of vulnerability raised some protective instinct in him. The fact that he would have to propose marriage to her when they were not even intimate enough for him to take her hand—and the wild jumble of emotions on just *how* he would do this—chased all logic from his head.

Miss Grey curtsied. "Sir Alexander, I hope you have had time to recover from your adventure." She smiled and moved toward him as though firmly in control of the situation.

Right. He was here to make an offer. He bowed. "I must hope the same for you. It was undoubtedly a more difficult ordeal for you, Miss Grey, and I hope you are on your way to being restored."

She nodded, then gestured for him to resume his chair, which he did. Sitting across from him, she sucked her lips in and pressed them together as though to repress words that threatened to leak out. This brought him to the object of his visit, and he hurried to begin his speech. This must not be made any more awkward than it had to be for either of them.

"I believe you know why I am here, Miss Grey." He cleared his throat. "And I want to reassure you that I have come without any hesitation on my part."

This little falsehood slipped out, surprising him. He was not given to polishing his words, except for what speeches he prepared for Parliament. However, it would not do either of them any good to dwell on how circumstances had forced him to do the honorable thing.

He brought his gaze down to his hands and placed his fingers together before lifting his eyes to hers. Although her posture and features were relaxed, her face was impossible to read. There were neither signs of apprehension, nor relief. Yet she could not like this necessity any more than he did.

"I am hoping you will do me the honor of accepting my hand in marriage."

There! He had got it out. Since he could not wax about tender sentiments, nor could he speak of mutual affection when they'd not had time to get to know one another, this was the best he could do.

Miss Grey shifted in her seat, then placed her elbows on the arm rests. Only her tangled fingers revealed any signs of tension.

"I thank you for your offer. I understand why you made it, and I honor you for it. I..." She swallowed quickly, revealing more of her unease. "I will have to turn down your gracious proposal. Unlike my brother, I do not believe the misfortune of our circumstances need lead us to this. My friends will rally around me, and the whisperings will die down."

It took a minute for her words to register. Once the initial shock of being released of his obligation had penetrated his senses, Sir Alexander felt nothing but the most extraordinary respite. It manifested in a shaky laugh, which he curtailed quickly. She must not know how relieved he was, for it would only insult her. Now, how best to answer her? He couldn't very well thank her, although it was what he wished to do. He decided on caution.

"I honor your decision, but I feel duty-bound to make you aware that the gossip may be more destructive than you imagine. Perhaps you might take a day or two to think it over with a sober mind before giving me a definitive answer? You have been through much in the last twenty-four hours."

She was shaking her head before he had finished offering this piece of gallantry. "No. Truly, there is no need. You have been most kind and gentlemanly. But I am certain I can see this through."

Miss Grey stood and gave him another smile. "I will call Gus to come and speak to you, but don't let him bully you. You can send him back to me, and I will repeat my answer. He will have to accept it, for I am of age."

She curtsied and began to leave him, but turned back before she had reached the doorway.

"Please remember that you have done the right thing. It is my decision not to accept your kind offer, and if I suffer as a result, then it is my own fault." She left without giving him a chance to respond.

Alex would not have known what to say, even if he had been given the time. He let out a long, quiet breath, his mind suddenly whirring with thoughts.

Why did she refuse? Was it for my benefit or hers? Does she not think me a fit candidate for husband? Another thought struck him. *Is there someone else she loves?* The latter brought a pang of disappointment, although why it should he could not explain to himself.

When Miss Grey had stood to leave, he rose as well and stayed like that awkwardly, waiting for her brother to return. That she would refuse him was one outcome he had not expected. He was relieved—yes—but the aftermath was a sort of emptiness he could not put his finger on. Perhaps...was it because he had secretly hoped to have the business of finding a wife done with? That the process of finding the right one was not a quest he looked forward to?

But no, it could not have been that. He wanted to have the freedom of choice when selecting a wife, and he had that now.

Gus opened the door, and his pleasant demeanor and the bottle of claret in his hands gave Alex a clue that he had not been apprised of his sister's decision.

"Well? All right and tight now? I imagine Christine was relieved. To be honest, I wasn't sure she would ever marry. She hardly has a chance to meet any eligible men here in Horncastle, and the ones she has met she has never taken to. But becoming a wife, and mother to a brood of children, is just what she will like best." Mr. Grey set the bottle and two glasses on the table in front of the sofa.

Alex's uncomfortable expression had not seemed to register to Mr. Grey, and he was forced to speak.

"I think you are under a misapprehension. I did propose to Miss Grey, but she refused me." This intelligence was met with a long pause. And then—

"Refused?" Mr. Grey's eyebrows stretched toward his hairline. His face grew a dull red as though an explosion was imminent.

"And so," Alex continued, "I am sure you will understand me if I do not trespass upon your hospitality any longer." Suddenly, he needed to leave the premises and as quickly as possible. Flight was cowardly, but he didn't care. He picked up his hat and gloves.

"You know where to find me if you need. I don't plan to leave Lincolnshire any time soon."

"What's this? No—stay. I must make her see reason." Mr. Grey started after him, but Alex was already near the door. He reached it and bowed.

"This is something you will need to discuss privately with your sister. I can't imagine my presence will be either useful or welcome to her." Alex stood to the side, waiting for Mr. Grey to open the door. It was the man's own house, after all.

"I have to disagree with you there. She *will* see reason. You should not leave until everything is finalized between the two of you." Mr. Grey started toward the opposite end of the room where an archway led to the interior of the house.

"Miss Grey was quite determined," Alex called out after him. When his host did not turn back, he added, "You will understand if I must be off. Perhaps we will have the pleasure of meeting soon."

The footman was nowhere in sight, and he opened the door and let himself out, breathing deeply of the fresh, chilled air. He strode toward the stables, where he hoped to have his horse saddled before Mr. Grey could run out after him and try to urge him again to stay. As he crossed the courtyard, he lifted his head to the second floor. Miss Grey was seated near a window looking out, her face unsmiling. When she spotted him, she turned away and let the curtain close, hiding her from view.

This brief glimpse of her face stopped Alex in his tracks. What was he doing? He was running from his duty, that's what. What if she was putting on a brave face and wished only for some coaxing on his part for her to agree to matrimony?

But that was absurd! It would be like professing a love he had never had time to develop. Still, he stopped for a moment longer, hesitant, his gaze still on the window. Something did not sit well with the situation, and the relief he had initially felt at being free evaporated. In its place was a dull weight that felt like guilt.

He turned to walk again more slowly, now reluctant to go. Even so, the fact remained. She had said no. And nothing would serve to bear witness to a family squabble while her brother tried to push her toward a yes. The woman must decide for herself. After all, when it came to matrimony, only the bride and groom had any right to decide their own future. Not everyone might see it the same way, but it was something he firmly believed.

Still, although he did not wish to marry Miss Grey, he wished he knew what had caused her to refuse him. It would be nice to know her better so he could guess what was on her mind. Some enigmas were worth figuring out.

CHAPTER FOURTEEN

Gus stormed into Christine's bedroom without knocking. "What in the devil are you about, Christine? So help me...turning the man down? Haven't you any notion of self-preservation?"

Christine stood and moved quietly toward the dressing table, hiding her inner turmoil. Sir Alexander had caught her looking down on the courtyard, and he had stopped in his tracks. It had seemed to her that he hesitated. Of course he must not sacrifice himself, but the thought that he might insist was more tempting than she feared she might be able to resist. It was not lost upon her that she was giving up the chance to be mistress of her own home, married to the most attractive man she had ever met, whose initial irritating qualities had lately been overshadowed by his more compelling ones. However, it was better to be alone than paired with someone who would only grow to resent her.

Without quite knowing what she was doing, Christine began to arrange the bottles on the silver tray there. "I am firm in my resolve, Gus. I've had the morning to think about it, and I believe you were too hasty in forcing Sir Alexander to the point. You have too little hope in the goodness of the people who live here and who know me. I have faith that they are better than that."

She turned and folded her hands in front of her. "I am certain Mrs. Mercer will come as soon as she hears, and she would never be so unkind as to cut me. She will use her influence to good effect, you will see. My friends will gather around me, and together we will find a way through this situation. I will simply plan a trip into town in their company and let everyone see us going about our usual business. That should still the wagging tongues."

"You honestly believe that? That you alone of all the innocent maidens in England can escape criticism?" Gus leaned against the door jamb and crossed his arms. "That is a mighty foolish hope you have there—a naïve one. It only shows how little you know of the world."

Christine lifted her chin. "I do not claim to know the world. I only claim to believe the best of the people who live in Lincolnshire. We are not of London society, which feeds off gossip. We belong to a more intimate circle who strive to see the good in our neighbors."

She thought of Mrs. Pickering, then the baker and his wife, and amended her words. "At least, the ones who truly matter."

Gus shook his head. "You are going to change your mind once you get a taste of their censure. Or if you have any sense, you will."

"I won't. So you may as well let it go. And you might find something else to do before we get into a row and stop speaking for a week."

At his obstinate expression, she grew still and added softly, "Please just let me be." He let out a harsh sigh, spun around, and slammed the door behind him.

Christine sat on the bed and tucked her hands between her knees. There, she remained frozen in thought. The situation she was in was more perilous than she would allow herself to contemplate or own to Gus. But marriage was so final. Was it not better to see if they could not calm the situation some other way? There was something abhorrent about forcing a man to the altar, which was clearly what it would be in Sir Alexander's case. The way he had practically bolted after she had sent Gus to him told its own story. It was hardly his fault that fate had led him to the same hut she had been forced to seek shelter in.

The silence of her room usually calmed Christine, but now it grew oppressive. The afternoon shadows darkened it, and she made no move to light a candle, or even to seek out the more comfortable armchair near the fire. Her thoughts wandered back to recent events and to Sir Alexander's considerate treatment of her.

He had wrapped her in a blanket, his fingers efficient as he unfastened enough of her buttons so she could remove the wet gown herself, then turned away so she might have privacy while being exposed. He covered her more thoroughly, knelt before her as he unlaced her boots and slid those off. Then he wrapped her feet in the folds of the blanket to warm them. He had built up the fire, brewed a hot drink, and prepared a stew with the little he found. Finally, he gave her the bed while he fell asleep with his head on the table.

Then today, without a second's hesitation—not one that he had shown at any rate—he came and offered the protection of his name to a woman he scarcely knew. Not to mention a woman who had first berated him, then greeted him covered head to toe in filth, who had insulted his mother, and finally who'd thrown a full cup of hot tea all over him in a clumsy moment. A man like that hardly deserved to be forced into anything.

Christine knew she should go downstairs and give instructions to the servants for dinner, but she could not be motivated to do it. They would likely prepare something without her help, and if they did not, Gus could request a meal on his own. After all, that's what he would have to do if he married her off.

She kicked off her shoes and pulled the stitched counterpane back, climbing underneath it with a deep sense of relief. If she were going to stay in bed, she should ring for a maid and change into a nightdress. But then, it would likely only be for an hour or two since she never could bear to be inactive.

There. I will just close my eyes and forget about everything for a little while.

EARLY THE NEXT AFTERNOON, a knock sounded on the door that Christine heard even from the garden, where she was petting Hunter and Artemis. Her heart skipped a beat from an irrational hope that the visitor was Sir Alexander coming to insist she change her mind. She dusted off her hands and walked indoors, where Jimmy was already opening the door to Sarah Pasley.

"Sarah." Christine greeted her, forcing a smile. She was not ready to see anyone and should have given instructions not to be disturbed. She turned to the footman. "Please have Mary bring us a tea tray, and maybe some of the currant cakes."

She gestured Sarah to a chair, then sat across from her. After sleeping right through dinner the night before, Christine had woken up with the crow of the rooster that morning and had kept herself busy through noon. That way she would not be required to think.

"How have you been?" she asked Sarah politely, wondering how long she would have to endure the visit. "I assume you and your brother did not make it to Lincoln for the ball either?"

"We started out, but it was hours after you did. By the time we had reached Short Ferry, we knew of the flooded road and abandoned our journey." Sarah turned at a movement in the doorway, and Gus entered the room and came to sit in one of the chairs.

"Ah, Sarah. I thought it was you." Christine stared at his use of Sarah's Christian name, and he seemed to realize what he had done. He frowned at her. "Did you send for refreshments?"

"Yes." Christine had mostly managed to avoid Gus that morning. She'd had breakfast before him and spent most of her time in the kitchen or garden—or in reassuring Olsen that the incident was due to poor luck and not through any fault of his own, and that of course he was forgiven. At some point during that time, Gus had gone out riding and had been gone for a long time.

"Good, good." Gus fidgeted, glancing up at Sarah once or twice, then pushed off the chair to his feet. "I suppose I will leave you two to talk."

He turned to walk out of the door, and Christine brought her eyes to Sarah, whose face held an amused look.

"Well that was strange. He asked about refreshments, then left before they arrived. What can it all mean?" She laughed and dropped her gaze.

Christine thought she saw a blush stealing up toward Sarah's blonde curls, and her suspicion grew, but it was too early to question her. She was also too depressed to attempt it.

Sarah cleared her throat and sat forward. "I only think it fair to tell you that Gus came to visit Martin and me twice yesterday, and again this morning." She brought a clear-eyed gaze to Christine. "He told me what happened with Sir Alexander."

"Oh." Christine sucked in her breath quietly. She didn't know what to make of that. Of course she trusted Sarah, but it felt like a betrayal that her brother would talk about her personal life with someone outside of their family. "He told you about it yesterday?"

"Yes. He came because he was worried that he did not know what had become of you and asked my brother to join in the search." She smiled and tilted her head. "Then, he returned to tell us of his good fortune in having found you. But Martin had already learned of your...rescue in Langton. He knew that you had been forced to seek shelter, and that you were not alone."

"Sir Alexander had already sought refuge there when I arrived," Christine said faintly.

"I see. When Gus came again this morning, it was to speak to me." Sarah lowered her voice with a glance at the open door leading to the corridor. "He thought I might prevail upon you to reconsider Sir Alexander's offer of marriage, and he asked me to try."

Christine felt tension creep into her shoulders. That her brother's betrayal had gone to such a degree! He was asking a near perfect stranger to interfere in her life! Oh, perhaps not a perfect stranger, for she truly did like Sarah, but they were not on such intimate terms as she and Honoria were. Even Arabella was closer to her than Sarah, although she was a later addition to Christine's circle. She found it difficult to meet Sarah's gaze directly as she wrestled with feelings of indignation.

"I told him I could do no such thing," Sarah said. She waited for the words to sink in and for Christine to look up again, this time in surprise. "And said I wouldn't be so impertinent as to try."

Now her dimples were in full evidence, and a laugh escaped Christine, feeling some of her tension leave her. Perhaps Sarah was a better friend than she had considered.

"He did not take it well, I imagine," Christine said.

Sarah lifted a shoulder. "Oh, he knows what to expect from me. So, if you are wondering why I have come, it is only to take tea with you, and to listen to anything you might wish to confide after your ordeal. Or talk on any harmless subject, like how many jars of tomatoes you managed to store up for the winter."

Christine took a moment to reflect on how much she did want to reveal. In general it was very little, and if she confided in Honoria, it was because the friendship was a lifetime in the making. Her closeness with Arabella was brought about by the dramatic event that threw them together. It had been forged when they traveled to London to save Arabella's son, David, from the clutches of his uncle. And they were the only two friends she had allowed into her confidence. Until now, Christine had been content to keep her talk with Sarah to lighter issues. Was she ready for that to change?

The maid entered, carrying in the tea tray, and Christine went to the cupboard to fetch the tea leaves. "Thank you, Mary. That will be all."

She used the time it took to stir tea leaves into the hot water to gather her thoughts. When she had served Sarah some cake and poured them both tea, she sat back again.

"I value your friendship," Christine said, now more composed. She had come to the decision to explain something of her reasoning in refusing Sir Alexander.

On this, she was not allowed to elaborate, for another knock on the door cut her short. Honoria was peering through the side-light across the room, and she caught Christine's regard. Jimmy entered the room to answer the door, but Christine waved him off and went to open it herself. Outside stood not only Honoria, but also Arabella, whose folds of her cloak were extended by her swollen form. Her confinement was to be sometime in December.

"Come in, come in." Christine greeted them both with a kiss. "Sarah Pasley is here."

Arabella and Honoria greeted Sarah as they took off their cloaks and bonnets. Mary was efficient, for she was already returning with another two plates and cups, and the two latest arrivals took one of the free chairs to form a cozy circle. They did not know Sarah as well as Christine did, but they all shared something in common. Her brother, Martin, had helped to solve a mystery that tied Arabella's former brother-in-law to his criminal acts and freed her from his stronghold. It had given them a degree of familiarity they might not otherwise have had.

Christine poured the tea, content to listen as they exchanged commonplaces. When these had been exhausted, a silence stretched as though everyone was waiting for someone else to begin speaking on the subject that mattered. Christine fingered the fringe on the bottom of her reticule at her side, unwilling to break the silence.

Honoria looked around the room with an exaggerated movement. "Gus is not here? There is cake." Sarah choked on her tea, and everyone laughed, breaking the tension.

Christine smiled at her. "It is inexplicable."

When another small silence fell, Honoria carefully set down

her cup. "I suppose he is leaving us in hopes that we will speak to you. He came to visit me and Arabella, you know."

"You too?" Christine was ready to march off and tell Gus how unwelcome she found his interference, but she waited to hear what Honoria would say. It was unlikely her friend would come at her brother's bidding any more than Sarah had.

Honoria glanced at her, then at Sarah. "I am only introducing the subject in front of Miss Pasley because he told me he had already spoken with you."

Sarah nodded, adding, "I wish you will call me Sarah, if it is not too forward."

"Sarah, then," Honoria said with a smile, turning back to Christine. "It means all of us are aware of the delicate situation you find yourself in, and there is no point in avoiding it, even if you would rather we did so."

Christine now looked at Arabella, who was even shyer than she was. Well, not that Christine was shy. Hers was more of a reserved nature. But she wondered what Arabella made of it all. It was probably best to come to the point and find out what everyone truly thought.

"What are they saying about me? In town, the servants—tell me everything." Christine steeled herself for their responses.

"I have little news to share with you," Arabella said, "for I have not been out. But Theo heard some servants bandying your name about, and he threatened to relieve them of their posts immediately if he heard any such nonsense coming from our house again. *And* he said if he learned that someone else had heard the news from a member of our household, he would send that servant off without a character. I've never seen him so angry."

Her soft mouth grew determined as she added, "I told our servants I fully supported him in this."

"Thank you, Arabella," Christine said softly, thankful for their loyalty. However, a tendril of concern seized her in learning that the Dawsons' servants were speaking of it when they knew their master and mistress were close friends with her.

144

Either the gossip was too choice a morsel to resist, or they thought her reputation deserved to be discussed in the servants' quarters.

She looked at Honoria, who met her gaze and reached over to squeeze her hand on the arm rest. She gave her a fortifying smile before sitting back. When she did not add anything, Christine was forced to prompt her.

"Well, Honoria?"

Her friend sipped her tea and set the cup down carefully, returning her gaze to Christine.

"I have not overheard my servants speaking about you. They respect you so well I cannot think they would dare try."

This news strengthened her until Honoria continued. "However, Samuel and Barbara stopped by because they had to find out *if it was true*." The last words were uttered with heavy irony.

Christine's jaw dropped. She was not particularly close to Honoria's brother, but she had thought there had grown a small degree of affection between her and his wife. She had invited Barbara over for tea several times to help her feel more included in the neighborhood circle.

Honoria made a face. "I know. I was thoroughly disgusted with the purpose of their visit, and I had no hesitation in letting them know it. I expect they will come around and realize that no good comes from anticipating a person's downfall." She gave a small huff. "At least they will learn they'll have nothing from me."

Christine glanced at Sarah, who had kept quiet. "And you? You live in town."

Sarah looked away and pressed her lips together. After a moment, she brought her eyes back to Christine's.

"There is talk. Unfortunately my sister-in-law, Helen, has said things, and she seems to be turning my brother's mind against your family with her stricture. He was cold to Gus this morning when he came to ask me to come and visit you."

"Oh no," Christine said, softly, thinking of Gus. He could handle himself, but would this affect a courtship it seemed he was attempting to carry on?

145

Sarah then sat up straight as though fortifying herself to say the rest.

"And...Mrs. Reid stopped by to ask me what I had heard. When I played dumb, she shrugged and said something about being careful with whom I spent my time considering I was yet unmarried."

"Mrs. Reid?" Honoria said, shock sounding in her voice. "We have known her our whole lives. I cannot imagine she would take such a view when she *knows* Christine. She must know she's innocent."

Mrs. Reid suspects me? Christine was reeling from the news. It was hard to hear that anyone gossiped about her and was willing to think the worst of her, but it was especially hard to learn it about someone she had trusted and looked up to. Mrs. Reid was a respectable farmer's wife, and she had thought both her and Mr. Reid to be family friends. She blinked rapidly, and both Honoria and Sarah reached for her on each side. Arabella clasped her hands and sat forward.

"I will be here for you," Sarah said quietly. "If you must suffer a downfall in the eyes of the gossips through no fault of your own, then I will go down with you. What do I care for the opinion of others?"

"And I," Honoria said stoutly. "But you knew that."

"And I," Arabella added. "After all, you have been there for me in my worst moments. I will never forget—" She pressed her fingers to her mouth as tears welled up in her eyes.

"Thank you." Christine's words came out strangled. She was overwhelmed by the kindness of her friends, and her emotion came as much from their support as it did from the disappointment over people she thought she knew. "Perhaps with your support we might turn the tide of their opinion?"

Christine looked at each one in turn, but not one of her friends seemed overly optimistic. She must attempt to brave it out, but she couldn't help but think of Sarah's words: *If you must suffer a downfall in the eyes of the gossips through no fault of your own, then I will go down with you.*

She had no doubt that not only Sarah, but also Arabella and Honoria would support her. But was it fair? What might be acceptable for her to endure, she was not entirely sure she ought to force on any friend—and most particularly one who had yet to find a husband, as Mrs. Reid had not hesitated to intimate. People were ruined by association, and if she was truly bent on refusing Sir Alexander, then she ought to distance herself from everyone she held dear.

If only the thought of keeping Honoria and Arabella at arm's length was not so difficult to bear. Even her association with Sarah, who was a newer friend, needed a period of reflection. What if there were indeed something between Sarah and Gus? What if Martin Pasley forbade the marriage on the grounds of his sister's association with Gus's family? That was something else entirely to consider.

Did she have a choice in the matter? She would have to make one, but it seemed someone was to suffer either way. Her brother might lose the woman who was his perfect match because of her. Or Sir Alexander would be shackled to a woman he did not love for the rest of his life. Neither option was satisfactory. Neither brought her anything but dismay.

CHAPTER FIFTEEN

T he sound of a rider approaching Gracefield reached the study where Alex sat and brought him out of his reverie. It had been two days since he acted out of honor, offering his hand in marriage to Miss Grey, which had been denied. It was not exactly how he had pictured his very first proposal of marriage to go.

Surprisingly, he was no closer to enjoying the unexpected freedom of having escaped a match he did not wish for. Gus had not come pounding at his door ordering him back. No letter had arrived penned in Miss Grey's hand, expressing her change of mind. It appeared he was well out of the affair, and he should be rejoicing over it. Instead, he felt...unsatisfied.

For one thing, he couldn't help but think that Miss Grey had been hasty, and perhaps...ungrateful? After all, he had not hesitated before rushing to protect her name. His one trip to town after the flood had been unsettling. Flurries of whispers and stares—some furtive, some open—followed in his wake as he walked down High Street, like the ripples off a rowboat.

A tradeswoman in Mrs. Reid's creamery had even had the audacity to ask him if he planned to offer for Miss Grey, or if he was bent on ruining all of the ladies from Lincolnshire before running off to London to escape the consequences. As he left the shop without purchasing anything, he heard her say in a loud undertone that it was not the way a man should act if he hoped to be elected to Parliament.

The tradeswoman's impertinence burned every time he thought of it. Not even at Eton, when he was forced to prove himself, coming from a trade background as he did, had he met with such audacity. In his school days, he had quickly learned how to portray the correct image in order to be accepted, and he'd finally achieved what he desired. But if the tradeswoman was to be believed, he could lose everything in an instant, including the election he'd hoped to win.

At last, a knock came on the front door, and Alex stood in expectation of the visitor to be announced. He had little desire to see anyone and would likely send the person away just as quickly. The aftermath of this unfortunate affair was beginning to dawn on him, and it covered him like a cloak of failure, for it could damage his social standing in Lincolnshire beyond repair.

And for what? For doing the right thing? The gentlemanly thing? It was preposterous and undeserved. And it was not as though he and Miss Grey could meet in company now—it would be intolerable to both of them—and that meant shunning all those who had presented him with offers of friendship. Local genteel company was not extensive enough to form a separate set of friendships, so he would likely have to sell his new home. Having only just acquired Gracefield Park, he would be forced to give up the estate which represented the pinnacle of his dreams.

"Alex!" a cheerful voice sounded from the entryway that he recognized instantly but had trouble crediting through his gloomy thoughts.

A man with disordered blond curls, wearing a broad smile, entered the study without ceremony, leaving Alex's butler to hurry behind with a troubled, guilty expression on his face. Alex's astonishment turned to delight.

"Roger!" He strode forward and shook his hand, then turned to the butler. "You need not mind him. Mr. Garrick is a friend of mine come to visit."

Alex came to a halt and turned to Roger with some doubt. "You are staying, are you not? I had no letter from you, so I've prepared nothing for your visit."

The butler was holding Roger's hat, and he now collected his gloves as Roger looked around the room.

"Didn't write. But even had you time to prepare, I hardly think you could have done much to improve this place in time. The decorations must be a century old! If this were my house, I would have started with this room."

Alex gestured for him to take a seat and sat on the chair with a lumpy cushion across from him. "Davies, bring us some burgundy, would you?"

He crossed one leg over the other, his spirits lifted by the surprise visit. "I *am* starting with this room. Can you not see that the wall hangings are in the process of being replaced?"

Roger laughed and lifted his brows. "I dare not imagine the state of the rest of the house, then. But from my view of the outside, I must say it is a fine house—unless, of course, the roof is about to fall in, which I hope it will have the courtesy not to do while I am under it. My congratulations."

Roger Garrick was Alex's closest friend from Oxford, and they had met in the first week there. He had not looked down upon him despite the fact that he was the son of a gentleman with ties to nobility and Alex had no such claims. He had a ready sense of fun, which lightened Alex's own sober, hard-working nature. For some reason, Roger had taken to him, although Alex suspected the initial reason was to see if he could corrupt him in some way—to see if he could get him to leave off his studies and join him in his pranks.

In the end, though, it was Roger who had discovered a knack for academics that included an interest in engineering, although he would not need to earn his livelihood from it. This strengthened a friendship that had already the benefit of sharing the same humor and pastimes.

"Well, what have you been up to since I last saw you in

London?" Roger asked, as Davies returned with the burgundy and two glasses.

Alex poured some for each of them, his eyes fixed on what he was doing. It occurred to him that a truthful answer might be a bit difficult to explain. That would have to wait.

"Why, nothing really. I have been trying to put the house in order, but it is proving more difficult than I thought it would, as you have so kindly mentioned."

Perhaps Roger would learn nothing of his encounter with Miss Grey if he was careful not to mention it.

Roger drank, then looked at the contents of his glass. "*Ah*, this is good. You'll have to show me your cellar—I'm surprised you have anything in it. Do you have a cook?"

Alex nodded. "I do, and can at least promise you some good dinners, which is more than you deserve showing up without notice."

"And how is local society? Will we entertain?" Roger flashed him a grin, entirely ignoring his previous comment. "I've even brought my breeches in case we are to dine with stiff, old-fashioned gentlemen, who will not consider pantaloons acceptable dinner attire. I hear there are still some like that tucked away in the country."

The thought of entertaining brought an uncomfortable smile to Alex's face. How could he explain there was no one he dared to invite? He was beginning to see that he would not likely escape Roger's questions if his stay were to be an extended one.

"Well, as soon as we are finished here, I can show you around the house. Better not change out of your traveling clothes, since there are rooms that are not fit to walk through. Tomorrow we can ride around the estate."

"And we must visit the town, too, of course," Roger said again. "Following that, I hope, you will have some entertainment to propose. I am only here for a fortnight, you know."

"I didn't know it," Alex answered wryly. "Again, you never wrote."

Roger gave an impish smile and tossed back his wine.

THAT NIGHT, the dinner Alex shared with Roger was, of necessity, a simple one, but their laughter echoed through the house as they recalled Oxford days, which cheered Alex immensely. For one thing, he momentarily forgot his trouble. Besides, it was how he had always hoped the house would sound. There was nothing advantageous about buying a large house if it was only to keep it empty. One day, if all went according to his wishes, it would be filled with the sounds of children.

Oddly enough, when he thought of children, he now pictured Miss Grey sleeping and wrapped in a blanket. And of course *now*, his entire dream of all he wished to make of Gracefield Park was in peril, for he might be forced to sell it and start over elsewhere.

The next morning after breakfast—which they ate as Roger poked fun at him for the damp sheets and mold creeping up the walls in Gracefield's finest guest bedroom—they saddled up and took a turn around the grounds together. It reminded Alex of how much he had grown to love his estate in the short time he owned it. Roger's appreciative comments cheered Alex further. It was nice to have his closest friend—and a gentleman, besides—think well of it.

Later, after they had finished a cold collation, Roger pushed his chair back and slapped his legs on his knees. "A visit to town, then?"

"Why not?" Alex said, his heart sinking. He did not know what they would find there, but it was not likely to be anything good. He had his pair of roan carriage horses hitched to his phaeton and waited while Roger climbed up beside him. He touched the reins to his lead, and the carriage moved forward.

"Did you know that my estate is only a three-day journey from here?" Roger said.

"Only that?" He had not thought to calculate the distance and could not raise any interest in the fact with the town as their destination.

"Well, it is not as far as London, at the very least. So"—Roger eyed his sleeve and brushed off some imaginary lint—"when I am married, you will have no excuse for not coming to visit us."

Such a declaration coming from Roger caused Alex to turn to him in surprise. "Married! Have you found a lady to fill the role of wife, then?"

"I have." Roger's grin was smug, but Alex read through it a sort of vulnerability his friend did not often show to others. "We are corresponding."

Alex smiled at the road ahead. It took his mind off the visit into town. "Well, if you have found the woman you wish to make your wife, you had better tell me her name and something about her."

"You shall have it. She is Miss Mary Corning. Her father and brother sit in Parliament." Roger gave him a knowing look, and he had not erred. Alex did indeed know them.

"William and Frank Corning. Whigs, both of them and with rather prominent noses. Of course, I know them. I hope she takes after her mother." He hid a quiver of laughter that sprang up when he saw Roger's flash of ire.

"Her mother is dead, but she must indeed, for she is the fairest woman I've ever seen." Roger said in a quelling voice.

"I am sure she is. Please accept my best wishes for your happiness." Alex was truly glad for his friend and left off the teasing. "Shall I meet her, then?"

Roger folded his arms and lifted his chin a notch. "Not until I've secured her hand. You are far too handsome for your own good."

Alex laughed. His friend was being ridiculous, but it was nice for once to see Roger discomposed. He had never imagined love could do such a thing to him.

They were approaching Horncastle, and at the sight of the short row of buildings on the other side of the river, Alex began to grow uncomfortable. He had not found a good reason to deny Roger his wish to see the town, and he feared it meant an end to his anonymity. Traveling through the town was sure to raise a stir, but such a thing would have to be faced eventually, he supposed.

"Are there any centuries-old inns we must try?" Roger asked, studying what signs of town life were visible as they crossed over the River Waring.

"None that I know of. Perhaps in Lincoln," Alex replied, his eyes roaming in front of him for an unwelcome glimpse of someone who might recognize him.

They drove to the stables on the edge of town, where Alex left his carriage and the sense of protection. Being on foot was more exposed and would make for a less hasty retreat. He pushed his hat far down onto his head.

Leaving the mews, they turned onto High Street and began to stroll along it, passing first a millinery shop with tiny glass windowpanes and bonnets on display. Next to it was the apothecary, and across the road, a tavern. Farther down was Mrs. Reid's creamery, which they would be avoiding. Alex's thoughts circled around the unpleasant memory of the rude tradeswoman as Roger took in everything.

"How quaint." He tipped his hat to a pretty young woman of the merchant class who sent him a saucy wink in return.

"'Tis." Alex walked on, every movement controlled, but he continued to send discreet glances to both sides of the street. It was just as he'd feared. The whispering had not stopped, and Alex's heart began to sink. It could not be long before his friend noticed it, and it was too recent and raw an event to endure any teasing over, even from a good friend.

"Stay." Roger grabbed his arm, bringing him to a halt, and Alex waited for the inevitable. Roger had finally noticed the whispering. Instead, he pointed across the street. "Is that a sweet shop?"

It took Alex a moment to realize he was not on the brink of being forced into a confidence he was not ready for, and he relaxed his shoulders. "It is. Shall we go and buy some? I know you've always had a weakness for confections."

"We most certainly must," Roger said, leading the way forward.

The street was full of activity, with the fine weather and late hour when much of the day's work was done. Alex noticed a few faces in the crowd that had grown familiar to him in his month in Horncastle. More glances were sent his way, but he decided he was going to be resilient and ignore them. In this way, he would ride the gossip out.

This decision made, he brought his gaze forward again, and his steps came to an abrupt halt. Walking toward them was Miss Grey, her arm linked with Mrs. Townsend's, leaning in to listen to something she was saying.

Roger paused his own steps and glanced from Miss Grey to Alex as a look of curiosity grew. "What's this?" he asked quietly, drawing the question out, a smirk on his lips.

"Nothing," Alex muttered. There was no sense in attempting to flee the situation. It must be faced sooner or later. He came up to the two ladies and bowed deeply.

"Good afternoon, Mrs. Townsend." Then, after the briefest pauses, "Good afternoon, Miss Grey."

He made every effort to look the latter in the eye but such was not easily done, especially when she appeared painfully conscious of their surroundings. The crowds around them began to slow in both directions with the irresistible chance of witnessing the meeting and trying to catch a word. He had no doubt it would be discussed over supper tables that night across this part of the shire.

"Sir Alexander, will you not introduce us to your friend?" Mrs. Townsend asked in a cheerful voice.

Her question pulled Alex's whirling thoughts into focus. "Yes, this is my friend from school, Mr. Garrick. Roger, please allow me to introduce you to Mrs. Townsend and Miss Grey."

"Your obedient servant," Roger said with a broad smile, bowing before both of them. The two ladies returned a curtsy.

"Are you in town for long?" Mrs. Townsend persisted. Her voice carried, and Alex began to understand she was attempting to foster an air of normalcy in their conversation to show the onlookers that all was well.

"Only a fortnight. But I hope we shall have an opportunity to meet again," Roger replied. His inquisitive gaze turned to Miss Grey and rested there.

"How delightful. Mr. Townsend and I will be sure to send a dinner invitation before you must leave us." She turned to Alex. "I will have one delivered to your house and hope to have the satisfaction of seeing you both there."

"Yes, of course—delighted," Alex murmured.

He hardly knew what he said. Miss Grey was looking anywhere but at him, and her face was flushed, her eyes dull. This alone told him how much of a strain it was for her to be in public like this. On impulse, he bowed again, and this time to her.

"Miss Grey, I hope we will meet at the dinner."

She darted a glance at him and mumbled something incoherent. With a hurried farewell, Mrs. Townsend moved forward with Christine on her arm. She must have seen that too much of this performance would only distress her friend beyond what she could bear.

As though released from a spell, Alex, began walking again, although he had been troubled by Miss Grey's joylessness. "The sweet shop?"

"Hold on, my boy." Roger placed his hand on Alex's arm, although he allowed their pace to continue. "Why is everyone staring at you? What's between you and Miss Grey? And don't tell me it's nothing, for I shall not believe you."

Alex's eyes were trained ahead, and he caught the unfortunate sight of Mrs. Pickering, who renewed her whispers as soon as she spotted him. She peered over someone's shoulder to where Miss Grey had gone, which meant she had seen her, too.

This was intolerable. His entire life, he had always acted above reproach. Always. He had shown the Baron Winton that he would have no cause to regret his patronage. Alex had worked hard to imitate the gentlemen at school, so he would do nothing shocking to hinder his reputation there. He blended into the background, so people would forget where he had come from. But now, *one* unlucky event had caused all that to change. And he could not even ride out the scorn with his head held high, for there was something of truth in the rumors. He *had* been alone with her, and now he was being viewed as the man who ruined young ladies and left them to bear the disgrace.

Why had Miss Grey said no? Surely, she could not abide being the object of such scrutiny and idle talk? As hard as this was for him, it was not as though she could move about in public as easily as he. Men never endured as much censure as women did. Could she not see that she really had no choice but to accept his offer? There would still be gossip, but she would not be shunned like this. And what was more besides, if she'd said yes, no one would dare to look at him as though he were a man to trifle with a gently bred woman and not make her an honest proposal.

"There has been a complication," he answered at last before opening the glass-paned door to the sweet shop. "But we will not talk of it here. I will tell you all when we return to Gracefield."

Roger accepted this wordlessly, and their stay in Horncastle did not last long after that. Although Roger kept up a steady stream of conversation and prattled about which sweets to buy, he seemed to sense Alex's discomfort and did not poke at him as usual. It was only when they were riding over the bridge from town that he requested an explanation—which Alex gave in succinct terms.

"So after all that, you proposed and she refused?" Roger knit his brows.

"She did."

His friend dropped his gaze to his folded arms. "It was a most unfortunate situation to be caught in, and you did the right thing. Perhaps she will see that she must accept your offer in the end. And I must say that if she does, you appear to have been lucky in your partner in misfortune. Miss Grey is a comely girl and seems to be a modest one, as well. It could have been much worse." He glanced at Alex to see how he took the statement.

"I agree. One could do worse than Miss Grey."

A rapid series of images flashed through his mind: the little fury in the woods, the disheveled mistress of the house, the clumsy hostess, the poor iced creature about to collapse on the doorstep. Then his thoughts went to the sweet smile as she thanked him, the dignified refusal, the image of her looking down from her bedroom... It seemed remarkable that he should share so many memories with a woman he had only just met, each one equally as vivid as the last.

"However," Alex went on, "For now, she has refused. And as I am sure I have already told you, my aim is to marry a woman who is capable of navigating London society. That is certainly not Miss Grey."

"Yes, for the nieces you must launch," Roger mused. "But a lifetime seems a lot to pay for the benefit of two seasons."

It did indeed, although it had not seemed so before he had been forced into the dramatic situation with Miss Grey. It was not as though he had changed his mind about wanting to marry her. He still needed to be practical about his future. But something in his situation had changed. He could not contemplate with any degree of equanimity the idea of Miss Grey being left in Horncastle to fend for herself, while he was free to go to London. And, odder still, he could not immediately imagine pursuing any other woman.

"Ah, I suppose it does not matter. After all, she said no."

CHAPTER SIXTEEN

"That was not easy," Honoria admitted, as soon as they had left Horncastle. They were walking back to Farlow Manor via the tree-lined road along the river.

"It was not," Christine agreed, finding it difficult to lift her eyes from the path in front of her. She had not experienced such despondency since her mother died. "And I thank you for not attempting to make me feel better. It should not have worked."

"I know it." Honoria reached across and squeezed her arm. "Oh, my friend. I would not have believed it of some of our acquaintances. How could Mrs. Reid allow such gossip? Or spread it! My mother will have something to say about that, and she is not without influence."

Mrs. Bassett and her husband had recently moved into the smaller house near the mill, giving the larger house to Samuel and his wife. The change made it easier for Mrs. Bassett to come into town, even in her rheumatic state, and to engage in local society.

"I am grateful to your mother," Christine said quietly. At least not everyone had turned away from her.

Honoria switched her basket to her other hand and slipped her free arm into Christine's. "I own to some hesitation about how quickly this will die down. I had thought it would have to some degree by now, but people are bent on thinking the worst of the situation. I don't understand it."

She stopped suddenly and looked at Christine. "Oh, but *ha!*—do you know what Arabella Dawson did? She marched right into Mrs. Reid's establishment and told her what she thought of her tradespeople spreading rumors about one of our own." Honoria laughed and shook her head. "She is something to behold when she sees injustice."

"Did she?" Christine smiled despite herself. Meek Arabella coming to her rescue. It was touching to think of it.

What had been less pleasant was to see Martin Pasley and his wife's reaction when she entered the apothecary with Honoria. Sarah had immediately welcomed them, of course, but Martin behaved in exactly the way Sarah had warned her he might. Since he had married Helen the year before, he had become stiff and concerned with what was correct, in keeping with his wife's Methodist standards.

Martin nodded stiffly to Christine, then excused himself to go into the back room where she could hear a low discussion being carried on. Before she and Sarah could converse for more than a minute, he had called his sister to come to the back, saying he had need of her. Sarah's expression revealed a flash of anger, then regret. She excused herself, and Christine did not want to stay any longer.

"I think Gus and Sarah Pasley might have feelings for each other," she said, unable to keep this new revelation from her best friend.

Honoria nodded, looking unsurprised. "I had thought they might. I think they are made for each other. Sarah does not idol-worship him, nor is she put off by his rough edges. He needs a woman like that."

"She does keep him on his toes." Christine allowed a smile to touch her lips. "But Martin's reaction today worries me. Did you notice how unfriendly he was? He could not escape my presence fast enough." She glanced at Honoria who answered with a reluctant nod.

160

"His behavior is as ill-natured as it is unfair. You even gave him some of your herbs when his herb bed was flooded out."

Honoria went silent for a time as their footsteps crunched on the autumn leaves. "It is all his wife's influence. But Sarah is not the kind of person to listen to what her brother says. She will not heed him, even if he disapproves of the match, don't you think?"

"I agree with you, but Sarah and I share something in common. Martin is the only family she has, and as much as Gus can drive me to distraction, I would be unhappy to be estranged from him. I would not like a permanent rift to come between us, and that might happen to Sarah if she marries against her brother's wishes."

"I suppose you are right." The sky above them darkened as a cloud passed in front of the sun. "What are you thinking?" Honoria asked as they veered off on the fork in the road that led to Farlow.

Christine sighed. She seemed to be doing that a lot lately. "I am thinking that my refusal to consider Sir Alexander's offer is hurting more people than just myself."

Honoria clucked in sympathy. "Perhaps, but those people of whom you speak are grown, and they can all take care of themselves. We all can. It is you I am worried about."

The air was still, and there was silence before she went on. "Sir Alexander seems a kindly man. He is certainly a handsome one. Are you quite sure you can develop no feelings for him, should they be given time to grow?"

"My feelings do not matter. The idea of forcing a man to the altar is insupportable." She had thought this through many times recently, and the idea grew even more distasteful the longer she pondered it.

Christine pinched her lips and shook her head. "I know Sir Alexander to be a good man, and I would not suffer from the match. After all, I would gain a large home and an independence I could never have as a single woman. I would have children." Christine broke off suddenly, unable to continue.

Honoria lifted her head to the tall iron gates of Farlow Manor

161

where the gray clouds were visible through it. She pulled Christine to a stop. "You would gain all these things. And so...?" She let the question hang.

"I could not bear for my husband to despise me every time he looked at me, simply because he had not had the opportunity to choose me." She did not meet Honoria's gaze. "I could not bear knowing I had forced him to the altar. It is worse than anything. Even worse than the pitying looks, or whispers and smirks—worse than the cut direct. Those I will bear outside of the home. But his scorn I would bear every minute inside of it for the rest of my life."

She covered her eyes with her hand, and Honoria hastened her into the courtyard, out of sight of the prying eyes of anyone who might chance by on the road.

Inside the courtyard, Christine wiped her eyes, striving to restrain her emotions. Jimmy rounded the house, but upon seeing her tears, he turned his face away from the private scene. Christine was grateful for the faithfulness and goodness of her servants. Not one of them would stand for any gossip being said about her.

"Come inside," Honoria said, bringing her to the front of the house. "The excursion has been distressing, and you need rest. And probably something to eat to restore you."

Voices reached them from inside even before they had opened the door. It was Philip talking to Gus while he watched Matthew's progress along the furniture.

"Where is Nurse?" Honoria asked as soon as they were inside.

"In the kitchen. She's within earshot should I need her."

Philip glanced at Christine, then at his wife with a questioning look. She gave a little shake of her head, but Gus had caught the movement.

He stood and bowed to Honoria, waiting for her to take a seat. "Of course her first trip into town did not go well, even with you there to bear her company, Honoria." He sent Christine a dark look. "She is an innocent in every way and had to experience it for herself to believe it."

"If I am innocent, then I should not be forced to endure criticism or expectations as though I were not," Christine replied tartly.

She had had about enough of her brother. But then, she thought back to Sarah in the apothecary and a twinge of guilt pinched at her. She might be the unwitting cause of his unhappiness.

"We saw Sarah and Martin," Christine said. She was not sure why she brought it up, except perhaps to provoke him to a reaction. She had never spoken openly to him about any hopes he had in regard to Sarah.

Honoria went over to her boy and held him by the back of his dress as he toddled forward, adding, "Martin was aloof with us, and I was not pleased with him."

"Was he?" Philip asked, resuming his seat now that Matthew had his mother nearby.

"Yes, well..." Gus frowned. It was a minute before he continued. "If he was, he is acting above his station. He should not think he can cut my sister who is, after all, a gentleman's daughter. And what is he?"

"It is fine, Gus," Christine said wearily.

"We also saw Sir Alexander," Honoria continued, which was not a piece of information Christine had planned on revealing. "He was visiting town with a friend of his from school. Philip, I promised Sir Alexander I would send a dinner invitation to them both. Perhaps we might all dine together. All of us," she added with a significant look at Christine.

"No." Christine looked away.

"You cannot avoid the man forever," Gus said.

"But I can until he leaves for London. What will happen in a year's time will be an entirely different matter. The talk will have died down by then."

In truth, Christine could not imagine the torture of dining with Sir Alexander as though nothing had happened and was surprised that Honoria had even suggested it. She thought her friend knew her better than that.

"Who else would you invite to a dinner party?" Gus asked. He was seriously considering it! He probably thought to use the dinner to push her into an engagement, but he would see how wrong he was.

"Well, you both and the Dawsons, of course—and Sarah. Sir Alexander and his friend, Mr. Garrick, although we will need another woman to even the numbers. I think it is a good idea to have Martin and his wife attend so they can see that he's making a big fuss over nothing and that no one of consideration agrees with him. Speaking of which, perhaps we ought to invite Sam and Barbara for the same reason."

Each mention of an additional guest to the party caused a pain in Christine's head. "You realize I cannot attend such a dinner, do you not?" She stood and went to Honoria's side, where Matthew waved at her from his spot next to the sofa. She returned it, though it was a somber little gesture.

"I cannot thank you enough for your support, and I know your intention is to bring me nothing but good. But I will never survive such a large crowd, knowing that there are some who have not always believed in me."

"That is precisely what you need to think about," Gus said staunchly. "Where is Mary when we need some tea?"

"Yes, you're getting tetchy. We could set the clock by your stomach," Christine replied with begrudging affection. Any irritation she might ordinarily feel toward him paled at the knowledge that her obstinacy might bring Gus and Sarah's budding courtship to a standstill and steal their future hopes as well.

Mary had already prepared a tea tray, and she brought it in. It was as copious as if Christine had overseen it herself. A flicker of satisfaction filled her at this evidence of her orderly home, small comfort though it was.

As they ate, Christine feeding Matthew little bits of cake, the conversation turned to lighter subjects. Just having her friends present and talking about ordinary events helped Christine to swallow more than she had been able to eat in the last couple of days. The nourishment then gave her more energy to ruminate on her situation, although she was not any closer to a solution.

When the Townsends left, promising to send over the dinner invitation, Christine resumed her seat and took up her embroidery. She half hoped she would have a chance to talk to Gus about his feelings—a daunting concept, since most of the time they both pretended he had none. Not even when their mother died had they been open and vulnerable with each other. But it was becoming something of a necessity to discover if Sarah was as dear to him as she suspected.

Gus appeared to have nothing of importance to do and walked over to the fire, where he poked at it restlessly, then sat and helped himself to the remaining piece of cake.

"Gus, I would like to ask you something," Christine began, taking the plunge. She set her embroidery down and met his gaze.

"You have lost weight," he said at the same time, "and you've dark circles under your eyes. You need to eat more and sleep." Those critical words were about the kindest thing he had ever said to her. He had *noticed* her. A warm sensation nestled into her heart. "What is it?" he added, a little less graciously.

She kept her eyes steady on him. "Why did you go and see Sarah Pasley when I was missing?"

His eyes started out of his sockets, and he froze for a minute before answering. "I went to see Martin. I needed him for the search."

"Then why did you go again afterwards to tell her that I had been found?" she persisted.

He folded his arms, and although he still seemed defensive, it took him less time to give an answer. "Why, of course Martin needed to know that you had been found and that there was no reason to search any longer."

"But by that point, Martin had already gone, had he not? And he would learn it, just as everyone else had, through the means of Mrs. Pickering's unfiltered tongue."

165

She pinned him with her gaze, wondering if he would admit it—if he would have the courage. He had liked Arabella and been open about that, but he had never shared any sort of connection with her. He had encouraged Honoria's childhood admiration for him, but he had never been tempted to pursue her.

There was something different with Sarah. They bickered, yes. But they had much in common, and above all—given the way they were always drawn to each other—it seemed they were interested in each other in equal measure. Any woman would be fortunate to have a husband who returned her regard and did not waver in it.

"Why all the questions?" he asked at last.

Christine decided to state it outright. "I think perhaps you went to see Sarah because you have feelings for her."

"Of all the things you go on about." Gus snapped his brows together and stood, walking back over to the fire. "Next you will imagine that I plan to offer for her."

"There might be worse things," Christine persisted, swiveling to look at him as he turned suddenly to leave the room. She stood and went after him. "I think if you have feelings for Sarah, you should stop dallying and ask her."

Gus came to a halt and turned around. "She is not a gentleman's daughter." He was still frowning.

"She is close enough to one with their uncle's fortune left to them. And she was trained by a governess and is not without a portion. That should not matter anyway," Christine said. "You share common interests. And she is not awed by you."

Gus turned and rested his hand on the archway that led to the corridor. He paused for a brief moment, then started to leave the room without answering, but Christine stalled him.

"Gus, I have rarely asked you for anything. But I would like to know something now. Do you have feelings for Sarah Pasley? Do you see yourself with her? Will you please, just this once, share a confidence with me?"

He turned back, and she was caught by the look in his eyes. There was vulnerability there—and, she thought—fear.

"I admire her, but I am not sure if she is the right wife for me. As you said, we often fight, and I've always thought I would be better off with someone of a more docile nature." He stopped short, his gaze on the floorboards, before saying, "But...as much as I try to reason my way out of it, I cannot get her out of my mind."

He sent her a grim smile. "There's your confidence. Now leave me be."

CHAPTER SEVENTEEN

The blanket of fog that shrouded the woods in Gracefield Park did not hinder Alex and Roger from going out to shoot that morning, and they even managed to bag two birds due to a fortuitous break in the clouds that permitted a ray of sunshine to give visibility. This sporting success was followed by a hearty breakfast and a period of a few hours for each to read the newspaper and catch up on correspondence. Roger's efforts consisted only of a letter to Miss Corning, which he wrote with a deliberation that was as astonishing as the fact that he had written to anyone at all.

As long as Alex looked over his accounts or answered letters, he was spared from having to think about his recent entanglement with Miss Grey. *Entanglement* was not quite the right word to use for their situation, but he could think of none other. He would certainly not call it a disappointment, although the way his heart chugged along in a heavy and dull manner, it surely resembled that.

In the afternoon, they sat over a game of cards in the library when a knock sounded. Since he had not received a single call since the flood and its aftermath, Alex puzzled his brows at a loss to guess who it might be.

Within minutes, the butler announced that Mr. Mercer had

come to call. He told Davies to show him into the library, explaining to Roger, "He's a neighbor of mine. A decent fellow."

Mr. Mercer was shown in, and they stood, Alex bowing in greeting and gesturing to Roger. "Mr. Mercer, please meet a friend of mine who is visiting, Mr. Roger Garrick." He signaled to the butler. "Bring us a bottle of scotch and some glasses."

Roger and Mr. Mercer exchanged a few pleasantries, and Mr. Mercer spotted the forgotten game of cards on the table. "I fear I have interrupted your game."

"Think nothing of it. We are honored by your visit." Alex's practiced civilities came easily, but it was no less than the truth. There was something about his older neighbor that he liked and respected. And he had felt a friendship with him ever since the Mercers' dinner party. He appreciated his visit now in light of everything that had happened.

"Mr. Garrick, where do you come from?" Mr. Mercer asked as Alex indicated for them all to be seated.

"From Wolverhampton. In Staffordshire." The door opened, and Davies brought in three glasses and the scotch, which Alex poured for everyone.

"I can't say I know the area." Mr. Mercer took a sip and leaned back. "Are you enjoying your stay in Lincolnshire?"

"It is a beautiful shire, and the people have all been very pleasant. Have you lived here for long?"

Alex allowed his mind to wander as Roger and Mr. Mercer discussed the light personal details he already knew. Part of him wondered what had brought Mr. Mercer to visit, and Alex was not entirely sure what he hoped for. It was clear the gentleman had friendly intentions, and he was glad to find he had not got caught up with the town gossip. He could not help but wonder, however, if Mr. Mercer would allude to the topic that was on everyone's lips. He and his wife knew Miss Grey well. Perhaps he would find a way to raise the topic, and Alex would learn what he thought. However, their visitor could hardly do so with Roger here.

"Mr. Garrick, I hope you will excuse me if I request a private word with Sir Alexander?"

Mr. Mercer's face held the same kindly expression, and Alex could glean nothing from it. It must be serious if he requested a private audience. Roger took the cue and stood, dipping his head.

"Of course. Alex, you will find me in the billiard room. I believe I'll practice my shots."

"Ask the footman to show you where the balls have been placed. The cupboard is warped and not easy to open," Alex replied. He then turned to his guest.

Mr. Mercer took another sip of the scotch and set it on the table, his fingers still wrapped around the glass. "My visit is more delayed than I would have liked, but I wished to come and thank you in person for rescuing Miss Grey. She is something like a daughter to us."

His ensuing silence prompted Alex to respond. "I was only glad to be in the position to render her such a service."

Mr. Mercer absorbed this as he fingered his glass idly. He seemed to be considering his words.

"I understand the aftermath has not been easy for you. Your rescue has had consequences for Miss Grey, certainly, but it has also had consequences for you." His smile was understanding. "Philip Townsend came to see me and apprised me of the situation. I know you will not take it unkindly that he did this, as his intention was not to meddle. Nor is it mine," Mr. Mercer was quick to reassure.

He let a silence fall again, and this time Alex did not break it. He waited for Mr. Mercer to come to the point.

"Philip knows that Miss Grey is just as dear to us as Honoria. We have known both ladies since they were born. But, you see, Miss Grey has no father or mother to look out for her, and Philip thought we might be wishing for news, since they'd had none from us. My wife had taken ill, you see, so we were not making visits." He brought his regard to Alex. "When Philip

170

came, he informed me that you'd offered for her after the local gossips began causing mischief, and that she refused."

Despite his respect for Mr. Mercer, Alex was not accustomed to having his personal matters spoken of so openly, nor did he like it. And he could hardly say which was worse—to allow people to think he was unwilling to offer for Miss Grey, or for people to know he had done but that his suit had not been deemed worthy of acceptance.

However, Mr. Mercer's reminder that Miss Grey's own father was no longer alive and in a position to assist her led him to look upon this breach of his privacy with leniency.

"You are correct, sir," he said.

"Although I consider Miss Grey's affairs to be something of my business, I am well aware that your own affairs are not. I will therefore spare you the impertinence of questioning you on how you took her refusal. However, I must tell you that had she accepted you, she would have made you a very fine wife." He raised a bushy eyebrow as he peered at Alex. "In case you were inclined to view her refusal as a lucky escape."

The comment caused Alex to shift uncomfortably, and he cleared his throat. It was irrational, but he suddenly disliked Mr. Mercer. He was not sure where the displeasure came from. His neighbor was only stating a truth Alex had scarcely allowed himself to admit. There was also a tinge of accusation threaded in the man's statement, whether or not it was intended. But Alex had not viewed it as a lucky escape—well, at least if he had, the sensation had been brief—and after all, he *had* offered. He had done all he could. Formulating the series of justifications prevented him from giving an answer.

After a moment, Mr. Mercer added, "Well, as I said, I shall not press a confidence, and I do thank you for sparing our Miss Grey from freezing to death."

This softened Alex, and he asked the question that had been foremost on his mind since they began the private audience. "While I am sensible of your gratitude, I am wondering if there is another reason you wished to speak with me."

"Ah." Mr. Mercer sipped his drink and set it down carefully before answering. "I'll confess 'twas Mrs. Mercer who asked me to pay you a visit. She is worried about Christine, you see. She has not spoken with her directly due to her convalescence, but Honoria told my wife that Christine has been on the receiving end of several direct cuts from local members of society. She hardly goes out anymore."

Mr. Mercer paused, but Alex had an idea of where this was headed. His neighbor had come to plead Miss Grey's case and ask him to step up again with another offer. He should have been indignant at the interference, or panicky of its implications, but his main sensation was one of relief. Perhaps the issue might finally be resolved.

Still, it would be wise to be cautious and make sure he fully understood what was yet unspoken.

"What is it you are saying? What are you asking of me?" When it was Mr. Mercer's turn to look uncomfortable, Alex could not hold back the argument that had blocked him each time he thought to bring about a change to the situation.

"I have been refused. I can hardly offer for her again when she finds the idea of marriage to me not to her liking."

Mr. Mercer made a soothing motion with his hands. "I know it. I told Mrs. Mercer it was highly irregular for me to interfere in such a way. It is just that it pains my wife, and me as well, to see Christine suffer under the hands of mischief makers such as Mrs. Pickering."

"If Mrs. Mercer has not spoken with Miss Grey, I can only assume she has no idea if another offer would be palatable to her." Alex left the rest unsaid. After all, this was not a love match. He was not going to beg.

"I'll not presume to know Christine's mind," Mr. Mercer admitted. He tapped his fingers on the edge of the arm rest. "Will you do me the honor of confiding your willingness to offer for Miss Grey again in the event that she has come to regret her hasty refusal? Perhaps time has given her a different perspective."

More than once, Alex had thought the same but had always

drawn the unsatisfactory conclusion that he could do nothing more. He could hardly approach her again when her refusal had been so definitive, and he didn't even know her well enough to pay a social call. But the supposition left him frozen and unable to move forward. If she had changed her mind, he might settle this once and for all. He thought about how to answer.

"I think it only fair that Miss Grey be given a second chance to save her name should she so wish it." Alex's words came out emotionless, hiding his inner turmoil. "I will propose to her again, but only if I have her assurance that the answer will be an affirmative one." This brought about a sudden shift in his visitor's countenance.

"I am pleased to hear it, and I honor you for your noble intentions." Mr. Mercer beamed at him. "Are you to attend the Townsends' dinner tomorrow night?" When Alex said that they would, Mr. Mercer added, "Then perhaps it might serve as a betrothal announcement if all goes as we hope."

Alex looked at him in surprise. "It is rather sudden when I know nothing of the lady's mind."

"Mrs. Mercer is waiting to hear the result of my visit with you, and if it is favorable, she will go and see Christine today. I might send over word tonight as soon as I learn of her decision."

Alex put his hand over his eyes. It was all too much. He had gone from an unenthusiastic but determined resolution to offer for Miss Grey on the day of their return to Horncastle; to relief then disappointment over her refusal; to the surprising sensation of having lost his way when she had said no. Now that he had expressed a willingness to offer for her again, he was expected to do so immediately and announce it at a party the next day? That was a bit much to ask of him.

"Miss Grey has been suffering much from her ordeal." Mr. Mercer's steady gaze did not spare Alex. "It need not be a grand announcement, but if you made this gesture, it might go a long way to setting her back up in society. Perhaps rushing into such an announcement is something of a sacrifice, but it would certainly be a kindness."

Alex could not keep the sigh out of his exhale. "Send me word as soon as you learn of Miss Grey's decision. I will visit her tomorrow if she returns a favorable answer."

"Excellent. I promise to come tonight if it is."

Mr. Mercer stood and held out his hand, which Alex shook. He could not decide if Mr. Mercer's sudden end to the visit was because he was relieved that Miss Grey might be spared from criticism she did not deserve, or simply that he had fulfilled his mission and had no more reason to stay.

Mr. Mercer walked only a few steps before turning back. "You are most truly a gentleman, Sir Alexander."

Alex bowed. This was not something he could return an answer to, but Mr. Mercer's words touched him. He supposed by now he did qualify as a gentleman since he had been educated as one and held a title and an estate—even if he did still need to work to maintain his living.

But Mr. Mercer had called him a gentleman based on his behavior. This left him with a warm feeling that remained as he saw Mr. Mercer to the door and went to join Roger in his game of billiards. To his friend, Alex spoke of his neighbor's gratitude for having rescued Miss Grey but not of the prospect of a renewed proposal. After all, nothing might come of it.

But as the day wore on, he allowed himself to reflect more seriously on the likelihood of marriage with her. Despite all of the reasons not to align himself with Miss Grey—none of which he had forgotten—he found himself dwelling on all the reasons why the match might prove beneficial.

She was the daughter of a gentleman, though Leonard would balk at the fact that she could not further his daughters' careers in London. She was industrious, which was something Alex could admire. And she had the prettiest features, though they would be brought to advantage if she smiled more. And she had skin like alabaster, which was something Alex would not think about at all.

After all, most women would jump at the chance to snag a wealthy, titled man—at least the ones in possession of even a small degree of worldly sense. But Miss Grey did not appear to be one of them. Until she showed herself willing to consider his proposal, he would be smart to regard her as little more than a stranger—one whose skin was therefore firmly off limits. Besides that, she had not yet returned a positive answer, and there was no surety that she would.

CHRISTINE SAT in the dim housekeeper's room in perfect stillness, listening to the sounds of activity in the kitchen nearby as Mrs. Bunting prepared that evening's meal. They had not had a housekeeper since before leaving for Bath years ago in the hopes of finding a cure for their ailing mother. Upon their return, Christine had leapt into the role of housekeeper and mistress of the house as a way of keeping her mind off their recent loss. This had worked as she was naturally industrious and found pleasure in her domestic duties.

For once, however, she could think of no activity to pour her heart into. It had been well over a week since she had rejected Sir Alexander's offer of marriage, and her life had turned upside down. No visitors had come to call, other than her closest of friends, and she had lost the heart to attempt to go into town a third time, even when accompanied. The whispers and stares were simply too much, as was the cold treatment by the shop-keepers who had always been as respectful as they had been friendly.

It had become clear to her that although she had had a fortu-nate escape from a cold, icy death in the river, the life she'd always known had not survived. It had been carried off by the current along with the carriage, and had met its own death.

The carriage itself had been found, broken and muddied, washed up on the shoreline of the Witham near the town of Fiskerton. Her trunk and her brother's, however, had disap-peared. She would never be able to wear her lovely violet gown that she had spent so many hours decorating with the tiny beads.

It had been the loveliest thing she had ever created or owned. Christine leaned her arms on the simple desk, her hands clasped in front of her, staring into nothing.

Not that I would have anywhere to wear it now, she thought. The Stuff Ball had gone on as planned, even without those who had been prevented from attending. And she would not likely attend a ball ever again, not now with the loss of her good name.

In the distance, a knock sounded on the front door, and she continued to sit without curiosity, letting someone else answer it. There was no point in anticipating who it might be or looking forward to a visit that might bring pleasure. If it *was* for her, it would only be Honoria or Arabella—Sarah had ceased to come—and there was nothing else her friends could say that would promise a brighter future.

Jimmy knocked softly on the door to the housekeeper's room. "Miss, ye have a visitor. Mrs. Mercer."

Christine lifted her gaze in surprise. Mrs. Mercer had not come before now, and the only assumption she had been able to draw from it was that Mrs. Mercer viewed her in the same way Mrs. Reid did—as an object of disgrace. It had been a bitter pill to swallow, and she had cried many tears over it. Despite the promising sign of Mrs. Mercer appearing at her doorstep, she would do well to see what her neighbor wanted first. It might only be to deliver a scathing denouncement of her character and the severing of all ties.

She stood, smoothing the skirt of her gown. "Tell her I will be right with her."

Jimmy nodded and left, and Christine stayed with her fingers on the smooth wooden table, steadying her breathing. When she was ready, she went into the kitchen to tell Cook to prepare a tray of tea and cakes before stopping herself. There might be no need for one if Mrs. Mercer did not intend to stay, and it would be humiliating if the tray was brought to a drawing room already empty of visitors.

Instead, she walked past the kitchen and pantry and followed the corridor to the drawing room, where she stood out of sight.

It would be best to simply get this over with, but somehow her legs refused to move forward. This visit might be the end of everything. She would learn what Mrs. Mercer thought of her and perhaps bid farewell to a connection she had thought would last a lifetime. The idea was more than she could bear in her present state.

Jimmy exited the dining room on his way to the kitchen and stopped short to see her frozen in place. "Mrs. Mercer is...that is, I've told her you'll come, miss," he said. Christine nodded, steeled her resolve, and walked into the drawing room.

When Mrs. Mercer saw her, she stood and held out her arms, walking forward without hesitation. "My dear."

In the past week, Christine had trained herself to hide her emotions and show only a stoic demeanor, but she could not be insensible to such a sign of grace as she crumpled into Mrs. Mercer's arms. Despite herself, her eyes filled with tears, and her shoulders began to shake as their kindly neighbor patted her back and soothed her with murmured words.

"Come, let us sit down," she said, leading Christine to the chair. "Dry your tears, and I will go and speak with Mrs. Bunting. I think I might not stand on ceremony in your home since I was friends with your mother."

Christine could only nod and attempt to stem the flow of tears. She had kept this weakness from her staff and did not wish for anyone to see the traces of it now. Perhaps her face might resume its natural color before the maid brought in the tea tray.

Mrs. Mercer was gone for a short while, and when she returned, she took the chair nearest to Christine, resting her hand on her arm.

"You must forgive my not coming before today. I had a rather bad cold, and it has taken me a week to recover enough to be up and about. Even though Mr. Mercer spared me from worry by not telling you had gone missing, he could not keep from me your dramatic rescue and the ensuing challenges. He would not even allow me paper and pen to write to you until I was recovered, however, saying that the excitement would be injurious to my health. And by that time, I wished to come see you myself."

She examined Christine, who said nothing, then continued. "I know you have not had the easiest time of it. I've heard there are whispers all over the countryside." Her mouth tightened in displeasure.

"Mrs. Pickering saw us," Christine said. "So of course there was gossip...but then Mrs. Reid..."

She could not continue, and Mrs. Mercer merely patted her hand and nodded. Guinea, who had been sleeping in the pantry, trotted into the room and went over to the visitor, who bent down to stroke his neck.

"Troubling times reveal the true nature of people. I will certainly give Mrs. Reid a piece of my mind, but I do not believe those who are bent on gossip can be reasoned with."

Christine shook her head. "I would not have thought it of her, but I believe you are right."

Mary brought in the tea tray, and Christine suspected their kindly cook had begun to prepare it once she heard the visitor's knock. Mrs. Bunting refused to believe that anyone could suspect Christine of behaving in anything but the most ladylike manner—or go so far as to cut ties. Such a thing was unthinkable for her mistress. When Mary had set everything out, Christine went over to the tea cabinet and took out the tiny key to open it. Habits dictated rituals in times of grief, she'd noticed.

In silence, she prepared and poured the tea and gave Mrs. Mercer a plate with lemon cakes. They both sipped the tea, and Mrs. Mercer set her cup down, turning to her.

"I would like to see you eat something. Your gown is fitting you too loosely." She placed some of the cakes on a plate and handed it to Christine, who ate obediently, though she tasted little of it.

"I understand Sir Alexander offered you marriage, and you refused?" Mrs. Mercer asked after a beat. She was not put off by Christine's silence, for she continued. "Honoria came to see me when I was well enough and told me all. She has invited us and her parents to the dinner party she is holding tomorrow night. It is becoming quite a large event."

Mrs. Mercer's laugh was like a soft wisp. "She believes our presence will help establish your position in society, particularly since Mrs. Reid holds Mrs. Bassett in high esteem. And although Mrs. Reid won't be invited, perhaps she will stop her malicious gossip when she sees that her own position might not be so sure."

Christine managed a little smile. Even though she had practically been bullied into attending, all this effort everyone was making for her deserved a show of appreciation. "It is kind of Honoria and her family to take up my cause."

"Sir Alexander has confirmed his presence at the dinner. Mr. Mercer paid him a visit before I came here to see where he stood on the whole situation."

Christine knit her brows at that piece of news. Why would Mr. Mercer take it upon himself to do such a thing? It was not that she could resent it, for Mrs. Mercer was quite right. They had been family friends for many years, and in some areas, they served her and Gus in ways their deceased parents could not.

"To what end did he visit him?" It seemed like the safest question to ask.

Mrs. Mercer adjusted her position as Guinea grew tired of waiting for more caresses and pulled himself up on the sofa beside her.

"No, you may not have any cake. I suspect it is not good for you," she admonished the pug before turning to reply. "He went to discuss you, my dear. His friend Mr. Garrick was at home, but he asked for a private audience with Sir Alexander."

Christine's heart rate sped up at the idea of a discussion occurring that tied her to Sir Alexander, but she could not tell what she wished for. In the week since the flood, she'd had plenty of time alone to think, to ponder, to regret. She did not regret her refusal...precisely. But her treacherous mind *would* dwell on all she admired about him and what she had lost in saying no. He was proud, to be sure, but he was not lazy. He had a home that required a mistress, and in the deepest, most secret place of her heart, he was cast in the role of the masculine ideal.

"What specifically did they speak of?" The words came out in little more than a whisper.

Mrs. Mercer's eyes searched her face. "Mr. Mercer thanked Sir Alexander for rescuing one so dear to us, and he raised the difficult issue of your precarious position in society. He finished by inquiring if Sir Alexander would be willing to propose to you again."

"It is so humiliating." Christine buried her face in her hands. *To have to beg a man to take her!*

"He said that he would indeed propose again," Mrs. Mercer continued as though she had not spoken, "if you gave your assurance that his proposal would be met with a favorable reply this time."

Mrs. Mercer announced this with a triumphant air as if it was the greatest piece of news, but Christine was sunk in the humiliation of anyone having to go and beg a gentleman to propose to her. Unable to give any response, she sat for some minutes simply wringing her hands.

Mrs. Mercer prodded her. "Well? What do you say to it? Mr. Mercer said Sir Alexander was quite willing—earnest, even."

It was simply beyond her ability to give an answer right away. She was not given to impulsivity, and this was *marriage*. It was permanent.

"I must have time to think," Christine said. She had felt an immediate attraction to Sir Alexander, but it was not until she came to know him better that she had been impressed with his character. It troubled her deeply to be forced to entrap such a man as he. Meanwhile, she needed to consider her brother's suit and the prospect that it might fail because of her. He might never find a better match than Sarah.

Her eyes were on her lap, and she raised them to meet the gaze of her kindly neighbor. "I ask that you not speak to Gus about this. I will give you my answer tomorrow."

CHAPTER EIGHTEEN

C hristine knew she would accept Sir Alexander's offer, despite her request for more time. However, she came to the resolution that she would give her acceptance directly to Sir Alexander and not have it passed along through the Mercers. She would have this one independence, at least.

One thing that had spurred her decision to accept was watching Gus grow unhappier as time went by without meeting Sarah. The other that decided it for her was experiencing a week of what her life would be like, shunned and alone, except for the kindness and faithfulness of a few friends. This had shown her the unhappy future that was in store for her if she made no change.

She was grateful that Sir Alexander was willing to offer for her again. And she had one comfort, at least, that her acceptance of his marriage proposal might not be entirely self-serving. Gus had let some comment slip about Sir Alexander's rapid downfall in popularity in town, saying it was sure to cost him the election for Parliament. This was as unfair to him as the censure had been to her, but her acceptance must surely turn the tide and give him a chance to gain his seat. She could offer him this benefit, at least.

The knowledge did not stop her from grieving a life where she could be mistress of her own fate. If Sir Alexander was kind to her—and she had seen evidence of that—he would give her free run of his home. But it was highly unlikely he would give her his heart, since he had been allowed no choice but to bind himself to her. How could he ever feel anything but a lifetime of resentment after such a beginning?

However, if he was indeed earnest in his offer of marriage...if it would not be quite dreadful to him? In that instance, she could accept with something of pleasure, even. Perhaps she would read something in his face when he came.

Though her decision was taken, she dozed off in the wee hours of the morning and was granted only a few, fitful hours before she needed to rise from her bed. For once, she was not ready to receive Mrs. Mercer when she came to have her answer and had to dress in a hurry, slipping on her simple earrings and necklace while Beatrice styled her hair.

"I apologize for keeping you waiting," Christine said as soon as she entered the room.

Mrs. Mercer cocked her head and examined her with a critical eye but said nothing about the haggard look she presented. She waited until Christine sat beside her before taking her hand.

"Well? Have you come to a decision? Mr. Mercer had promised Sir Alexander he would come yesterday if he had news of your acceptance."

This caused Christine's heart to race again. Sir Alexander had been expecting to learn of her answer yesterday? What if this morning he thought himself well out of the situation, only to be plunged once again into disappointment when he learned he must offer for her after all. She could not lift her eyes when she answered.

"I would like to give my decision directly to Sir Alexander."

"Is that so?" Mrs. Mercer pulled back and knit her brows. "But you realize he expressed his determination to come only if he was sure of being received favorably?"

"I am aware of it," Christine replied. "Mr. Mercer may tell him he will suffer no inconvenience by his visit."

It was the closest she would come to giving a promise to the Mercers. It was easy to read her unspoken thoughts, but it was her last salvo at pride. And she was fully aware that her words contained a false promise. In no way could she guarantee that he would suffer no inconvenience in coming to make her an offer. For who was to say he had any desire to make one at all?

Mrs. Mercer must have read Christine's unspoken decision, for her voice went up in pitch and she squeezed Christine's hand. "Why, that is precisely what I had hoped to hear. I will waste no time in telling Mr. Mercer, so he might visit Sir Alexander and apprise him of it right away."

Although this should have come as no surprise, the idea that so many were discussing her intimate dealings brought fresh mortification. Christine could not keep from voicing her fears. "Sir Alexander expected news of my answer yesterday."

"He is a gentleman. If he gives his word, he will not go back on it." Mrs. Mercer gave one final squeeze to Christine's hand and stood.

"I know you will understand if I do not tarry in my eagerness to return and deliver your answer to Mr. Mercer. Perhaps you might have Beatrice add some color to your cheeks, my dear. Not much, mind you. I know it is not in your style, but you will not want to receive your suitor looking pale."

Christine accompanied Mrs. Mercer to the door, which she opened herself, rather than calling for a servant.

"Thank you for your kindness on my behalf." It was all she could manage, although she did not precisely know what she was thanking her for.

"Never mind that. I could do no less for a girl I've known since the cradle. Your mother would have expected it of me and rightly so." Mrs. Mercer gave a bracing smile and slipped outdoors into a biting autumn wind.

Christine remained at the sidelight, watching as Mrs.

Mercer's groom opened the door to the carriage. She must not have expected to stay long since the carriage was still waiting by the door.

So, it was done. She had given her acceptance which would be carried to Sir Alexander, who would presumably arrive at some point to offer for her a second time. Gus would be glad of it, she thought dully. She had not seen much of her brother since his latest disclosure about his feelings for Sarah. Perhaps the admission had been too much for him, especially since Sarah had not come to visit in several days and she didn't think he had gone to see her. It did not bode well for his suit.

After a long moment of staring through the window without looking at anything in particular, she turned back to seek the privacy of her room. Despite Mrs. Mercer's advice, she would not be adding any color to her cheeks. He would get her as she was, not as some painted puppet. None of it mattered anyway. There was nothing she could possibly do to her appearance that would likely stir any romantic feelings in Sir Alexander's breast.

ALEX WAS SITTING with Roger in the library, each with a book in front of them, a routine that suited them both. They had taken to riding or shooting in the morning before breakfast and spending hours of leisure after that. They had not returned to town since that first uncomfortable episode.

Roger lifted his eyes from the morning paper that had been sent from London. "Tonight is the dinner at the Townsends', is it not?"

Alex nodded. He was now glad he had not spoken of the true purpose of yesterday's visit. Mr. Mercer had not returned last night with a favorable answer, which meant that Miss Grey had not changed her mind about refusing him. He should be glad of it, but he could not help but wonder what was wrong with him that she should remain so opposed to the match when her reputation suffered as a result. And there was something else that rankled about her obstinacy that he could not quite put his finger on, and it was that which had kept him up at night. He tried to discern why he was so bothered by her constant refusal when it only liberated him, but a rational response eluded him.

"Good," Roger said cheerfully. "At last, I will be provided with some lively conversation. I am beginning to feel as though I've joined a funeral procession rather than a pleasure party."

Alex looked up, startled. "Am I that bad? I do apologize. My mind is elsewhere."

Roger was grinning at him. "You are, but do not worry. I am accustomed to your dour face when you are preoccupied with something. I can only hazard a guess at what is preoccupying you now."

"You would be wrong," Alex retorted, but he smiled begrudgingly. "I am sorry. What shall we do this afternoon before we have to dress for dinner?"

"We might go into town," Roger proposed. "We've not been back."

Alex was spared from having to make up an excuse for why that was a terrible idea by a knock announcing a visitor. Despite himself, his heart ticked a faster rhythm. It might still be Mr. Mercer announcing a different fate than the one he had planned for himself, although he was not sure what he truly wished for. He was incapable of continuing the conversation until the butler opened the door.

"It is Mr. Mercer, sir."

"I'll see myself out," Roger said with a wink and put his words into action as Alex told Davies to show the visitor in. Mr. Mercer and Roger greeted each other civilly as they crossed paths, and Alex met his neighbor in the middle of the room as they shook hands.

"As you are now aware, I was unable to come to you last night," Mr. Mercer said, as soon as they were seated and in private. "It occurred to me that you might have wondered what to make of it. I believe I did suggest I would come yesterday if a positive answer had been given."

"You did."

"I had no answer last night, however. Mrs. Mercer returned with the news that Miss Grey needed time to think about it."

So no announcement at the dinner tonight, Alex thought. *But will she be there? What will it be like to meet her again?* His mind rushed to think of all the implications, but it was useless to sort out what he felt on the matter.

"Mrs. Mercer visited her this morning to have her answer, and Miss Grey has expressed her willingness to receive you."

"What?" Alex was powerless to keep that one word silent. "Are you saying she will accept my proposal this time?"

Mr. Mercer inhaled and lifted his eyes to the ceiling, breaking the gaze. "She did not quite say that. She said she would receive you, but it is my belief she would not do so if she was inclined to reject your suit. Despite having the appearance of a meek little thing, Christine is a strong woman, and I think she merely objects to others deciding her future on her behalf."

Alex had never thought of Miss Grey as a meek little thing.

Mr. Mercer regarded him steadily for a moment. "Allow me to remind you of what I said yesterday. Although she might not be the woman you would have chosen, I am convinced she will make you happy if you allow her to."

"Yes, of course." Alex mumbled the words. He wanted to bury his face in his hands. He needed time alone to adjust to this sudden switch in fate—again. His well-ordered life had been in tumult ever since he and Miss Grey had been thrown together. In fact, it had been ever since he'd met her.

"I am sure you have much to do before tonight," Mr. Mercer said. "I will not presume to advise you, although I am twice your senior. But, out of concern for Christine, I will ask that you consider calling upon her without delay so that you may both agree upon your future. Her comfort at this evening's dinner is dependent upon your next step. Will she arrive tonight as a woman betrothed—or a young maiden with a stain upon her reputation through no fault of her own?"

With little else to say after these weighty words, Mr. Mercer soon took leave of Alex. He could not move from his chair and was grateful that Roger stayed away so he might have time to think. He would be proposing again, it seemed. He was to be married. It would mean writing to Leonard about the sudden shift in the plans they had spoken about for years. Well, that Leonard had insisted upon and Alex had not seen anything to object to. Should he pretend it was a love match, or share the details of how it was forced on him to appease his brother? He could not fathom which was best.

At last, he went to seek out Roger, and one of the footmen told him he was outside playing a solitary game of croquet. Alex went over to the stretch of lawn where his friend was playing, grabbing another mallet on his way. He dropped a ball in the middle of the game and began playing where Roger had left off.

"I am to be a married man. Probably before you." Alex whacked the ball and sent it through the hoops driven into the grass.

"That so?" Roger hit his own ball, roqueting Alex's and sending it spinning away. He hit his ball again and missed the hoop. "Have you ridden over to Miss Grey to ask her? I did not think I had been playing long enough for that."

"Not yet, though I must do so." Alex focused on his next hit, unsurprised that his friend knew exactly who he was talking about.

Roger grabbed the mallet from his hand and leveled his gaze at him. "Go and change your coat and do it now. Don't leave the poor girl waiting. We all have a dinner party to attend tonight and I, for one, am desperate for some proper entertainment before I leave you."

"Oh, are you leaving me?"

"Indeed so. All this mooning about has left me depressed." Roger's easy grin was back. "I finally wrote to Mr. Corning to ask permission to pay my addresses to his daughter and received my answer this morning. So we shall see who is to be married first."

"Not everything is a competition," Alex grumbled.

"No, it is not. But if you don't take the lead that has been handed to you, I shall lose all respect for you." Roger got into position again and eyed his wayward ball. Then he glanced up and smiled at Alex, before raising his brows. "Now go."

In under an hour, Alex was standing on the doorstep of Farlow Manor, and he paused to collect himself before knocking. Just the sight of the painted white doorway set in bricks brought out strong emotions in him. Nothing about his visits here had ever been ordinary.

The door opened before he raised his hand to it, and Gus, who was about to step out, stopped short at the sight of him. "Sir Alexander!"

He seemed at a loss, and at once Alex understood that Gus had no idea he had come to propose again to his sister. She had clearly not confided in her brother. It was awkward, but he didn't feel as though he should offer up the information that there had been negotiations behind the scenes regarding Miss Grey without his knowledge.

"I have come to speak to your sister, if I may."

Gus furrowed his brows and stepped back to allow Alex to enter. "You most certainly may, but I must own to some surprise at seeing you here. Christine has led me to believe her decision was final."

"You have my word that I will respect her decision, but I wish to speak to her all the same if she is amenable."

"Certainly." Gus's look of confusion had not changed, but he closed the door behind Alex and moved toward the corridor. "I will send a servant to fetch her. Please have a seat."

Alex did not have long to wait, and the slight fear he held that Gus would come and plant himself by his sister's side while he attempted to propose again did not materialize. She walked into the room alone, wearing a drab gown the color of her surname and a complexion as pale as day-old snow. It was not that she was unattractive. Such a thing could not be said of a woman with such simple beauty. But she looked careworn.

He stood and bowed. "Miss Grey, your servant."

What an idiot. What a thing to say to a woman you are about to propose to! But then he could not begin spouting flowery speeches either. It seemed his first attempt at proposing had not prepared him in making the second one any easier.

"Sir Alexander." She curtsied, equally as somber and formal as he. Then they both stood mutely and stared at each other.

"I will come straight to the point." Alex cleared his throat. He was about to say that he suspected she was ready to accept him now but then thought it not quite the thing. This was miserable business.

He plunged back in. "I have not given up hope that you would reconsider my offer of marriage, and I have come to ask you again if you would do me the honor of becoming my wife."

A wan smile flitted past her lips that didn't reach her eyes. "You honor me with your proposal, and I am grateful that you have offered again. I accept."

The words fell like resounding gongs in the stillness. He could hardly believe what he was hearing. There would be a wedding! *His* wedding. He was indeed to be married to Miss Grey. Belatedly, he realized he must react, and he pushed his sluggish features into something like a smile.

"I am glad to hear it. I believe we will deal very well together."

"I will do my best to make it so," she replied. Her smile was still strained, and it occurred to him that she might fear he made the offer wholly against his will. "You will wish to speak to Gus, I imagine."

Despite having seen Gus before his sister, he had not thought about the fact that they must, of course, discuss terms. Miss Grey and he had shared so much without his involvement that the simple and necessary courtesy had slipped his mind.

He bowed. "Yes, I should speak to your brother."

She turned to leave, but he held out his hand. "Wait, please.

Tonight is the dinner at the Townsends'. It would be a good time to announce our betrothal if you are not opposed to the idea."

When she looked back at him, he saw the doubt in her eyes and was now certain that she was afraid that he had proposed against his will and did not wish for the match. He needed time to think about what that would mean and how he could reassure her that the contrary was true when he was not even sure of it himself.

"I have no objection." Miss Grey waited another instant, as though she wished to say something else but then simply curtsied and left the room.

Alex paced to one end of the room, mulling over that look of doubt. Yes, he had been forced into it, but had not she as well? He was not entirely sure Miss Grey saw him as an equal match, although he certainly hoped she would come to view him that way. She was still an enigma. Was she accepting against her will? No, she could not be, because her brother was unaware of his second proposal. So she was accepting him of her own volition, but she looked unhappy. Was it simply because she could not bear the censure she had received and felt she had no choice but to accept a man she could not admire? It was a lowering thought. But no, there had been doubt as well.

Gus entered the room with a look of puzzlement on his face, and with it a spark of something like optimism. "Christine said you wished to speak to me?"

"Yes, I do. I have made Miss Grey another offer of marriage, and she has accepted it. I thought we might discuss the particulars. We are planning to announce our betrothal tonight at the Townsends' dinner."

Gus blew out in a loud exhale, then laughed. "You astonish me, sir. But I must say how glad I am to hear this news. My sister can be a stubborn one, and I thought all hope was lost for the match. Come, come. Let us go into my study where we can negotiate the details in comfort. I will have my solicitor draw up a contract once we have agreed to it."

When Alex finally left Farlow Manor and climbed back onto

Gypsy, dusk had fallen. He would not have much time to change before the dinner that night. He must make haste, even if he dreaded the evening ahead of him. It would be hard to make his engagement public, but for once he was confident he had done what was right. With that confidence came a determination regarding his newly betrothed, and it was to remove the look of uncertainty in her eyes. He would give Miss Grey not only his hand in marriage, but his heart as well.

CHAPTER NINETEEN

C hristine went upstairs to change for the dinner while her brother and Sir Alexander negotiated the contract. She was now an engaged woman. It was a shocking turn of events after everything, but her heart lightened at the change in her circumstances despite the somber face she had shown him earlier. Why she should feel any better defied reason. It was not as if she knew Sir Alexander any better, or that her life with him promised more than it did before. But the awful sensation of betweenness was over. She was not her former self, settled and respected in town as a young maiden who had no set plans for marriage, nor was she the shadow of herself she had been in the last two weeks, shunned and reclusive.

Beatrice came at the summons, and Christine went over to the wardrobe to examine her gowns, which also served to give her something else to look at rather than at her maid.

"Sir Alexander and I are to announce our betrothal this evening at the Townsends' house, so I will wear my ivory silk with gold embroidery. And...I think I will wear the pearl combs for my hair." Her heart fluttered to say the words out loud, but she had to start somewhere.

"Oh, miss. I am right glad for ye, I am." Beatrice, her round face flushed with pleasure, walked over to Christine's side and pulled out the requested gown, then laid it across the bed.

"Thank you. You may tell the other servants after we have left for the Townsends'." Christine sat to have her hair done, and she smiled up at her maid in the mirror. It would spare her from having to repeat herself to each servant, although she would have to hear their congratulations.

"Yes, miss. They will be as glad as I am to hear it." Beatrice began to unwind her simple hairstyle and comb through the curls, engaging Christine in a series of light observations more in line with her usual manner. Lately her maid had been silent, sensing her depressed mood and giving her the space she needed.

After having dressed and applied a light perfume with notes of amber, Christine went downstairs and found her brother waiting for her in evening attire. He went over and kissed her on the cheek.

"Sir Alexander and I have sorted everything out to both our satisfaction. You did the right thing in accepting him."

Gus's smile was sincere, and gone was his typical offhand manner. It left her feeling unsure of herself. He had been kind to her since the flood and its aftermath. That was unusual enough, but that he continued in this way without gloating when she had done what he thought best was worthy of notice—and completely inexplicable.

"Shall we go?" she asked.

He nodded. "Jimmy had the horses put to. Do you feel up to the announcement? I know you don't like attention centered on you, and tonight there will be plenty of pairs of eyes directed your way."

Christine turned to stare at him in surprise. Despite her nerves, she laughed. "Gus, are you well? I feel I hardly know you. I might die from the shock of your solicitude."

"Oh fine," he said. "I'll stop if it's so disagreeable to you."

"Don't stop, brother. It's nice." Christine slipped her arm through his and walked with him outdoors. It was good to go early. She would rather they arrived before anyone so she did not have to make a grand entrance.

Despite the early hour, the Dawsons had already arrived for the party, as had Honoria's parents, the Bassetts, and her brother Sam and his wife. Christine's breath quickened to see a crowd already assembled. It was beginning. None of them knew of her changed circumstances, and Barbara had not approved of her when she thought her compromised. She feared their first encounter now and had to admit to some relief at being engaged. It gave her a degree of protection that was as welcome as it was novel.

There was a bustle as they entered, and Gus began speaking to Theo, Samuel, and Philip, leaving Christine to stand there uncertainly. Barbara, Honoria's sister-in-law, stayed at Samuel's side and made no move to greet her. Mrs. Bassett called Christine over to where she was sitting next to her husband with a little wave.

"Christine, I beg you will show some kindness to an invalid and sit by me for a moment."

The friendly gesture brought Christine comfort, and she went to sit on the other side of Honoria's mother, just as Honoria and Arabella came from the direction of the kitchen.

"Christine, you've arrived. Excellent!" Honoria glanced at her sister-in-law, now standing forgotten at her husband's side. "Barbara, won't you join us? The men appear to be talking about hunting and won't have a thought to spare for anyone else."

"I can see I am not wanted here," Mr. Bassett said with a wink at his daughter. He placed his hand on his wife's shoulder and went over to join the men.

Eventually, Barbara came and took one of the chairs so that the five of them sat in a circle that included all the women present. Christine could see what Honoria was doing. She was making sure that at least her family and closest friends were behind Christine before the party began.

"We don't have much time before the other guests will arrive. Christine—"

Honoria's words were cut short when a clamor went up from the men that sounded like a cheer. She looked at her husband with raised eyebrows, and he left the men to come over, his eyes now on Christine.

"Allow me to congratulate you on your engagement, Christine. I am to understand we will announce the good news tonight?"

"What?" Arabella turned to Christine with her lips parted. This quickly turned to a smile.

"Is that so?" Honoria exclaimed, her voice exultant. "What *excellent* news! We have enough of Horncastle society here that the rest of town should hear of it even without Mrs. Pickering's kind offices."

Christine blushed at her friends' outpouring of pleasure—she could feel the heat creeping over her cheeks—and blushed even more deeply because she could not hinder the smile that touched her lips. It revealed feelings she preferred to keep hidden, since she was not sure she deserved to be happy over a marriage that had been forced upon them both. It was not often she was the object of congratulations, however, and she could not help but bask in them.

She only hoped that Sir Alexander would not look too miserable at their announcement tonight. He had been stiff and formal when he proposed to her both times, so he could not be experiencing any sort of pleasure over the change in his fortune. For him to show his reluctance publicly would be humiliating.

"I must wait until Sir Alexander arrives, but I believe we will indeed announce our engagement tonight," she replied as soon as she was given the chance.

She glanced over at Gus, and he sent an encouraging smile her way. She remembered his words, that he knew this was hard for her, and was touched by his consideration. Even announcing it early before Sir Alexander arrived showed that he knew her better than she had realized, for she needed to ease into such an announcement.

There was a knock on the door, and her heart beat helplessly inside her chest like a fish flopping about on land. The servant answered it, but it was only the Pasleys who entered. Sarah, her brother Martin, and his wife Helen, who took one look at Christine and frowned, pulling back. Honoria did not allow her time to make a disparaging comment, but rushed over to Helen with a broad smile and a brief curtsy for the new arrivals.

"Welcome to Boden House. As this is your first time here, Helen, please allow me to show you some of the rooms before more of our guests come." She linked her arm through Helen's, who could not remain cold to such distinguishing treatment, and led her away.

Any discomfort Christine might have felt, or any lingering hesitation over her choice, was whisked away when she saw her brother smile bashfully at Sarah and walk over to her, trying unsuccessfully to retain some of his swagger. Sarah met him partway and made some teasing remark that caused him to retort with something like his old manner. This was a happy result of Christine's acceptance, for she would not knowingly destroy her brother's happiness if it could be helped. Even Martin had appeared to relax without his disapproving wife present as he participated in the men's conversation and made no move to protest Christine's presence.

There was another knock, and this time the footman admitted the Mercers, along with Sir Alexander and Mr. Garrick. As soon as Sir Alexander stepped into the room, he sought her gaze with a conscious look in his eyes. The corners of his lips tipped upwards, and she returned the smile, hiding her hands behind her to keep from fidgeting.

Her heart gave a puff of happiness. He did not look displeased. Arabella moved to sit next to Christine, and Mr. Garrick approached them, coming to stand at her side.

"Good evening, Miss Grey." He leaned forward and murmured, "Allow me to offer my congratulations. I understand you have done my friend the honor of accepting his proposal."

Christine forced a tight smile and hoped he would not think her unfriendly. With her nerves so tightly wound, she could not reply to this. "Do you know Mrs. Dawson?" she asked instead, indicating Arabella.

"I have not had that pleasure. Delighted to make your acquaintance, ma'am."

Sir Alexander disengaged himself from his conversation with Theo and came over, bowing to both her and Arabella.

"Good evening, Mrs. Dawson." He paused a minute before adding, "Miss Grey, would you walk with me a bit? Philip said you know the house well and might be willing to show it to me."

"Of course, Sir Alexander." Christine stood quickly, trying to combat her nerves, and hoping that one day she would regain her usual equanimity and not live in such a constant state of upset. She placed her hand on his arm and allowed him to lead her away from the guests into the silence of the corridor. She pointed to the room on their right, which was lit with candles that provided a cozy warmth.

"This is the library." They entered it, and their steps wandered toward the bookcase, where they pretended to examine the books there.

"Are you well tonight?" he asked, turning to her. "Are you quite comfortable?"

Christine had been raised to keep her true thoughts to herself, except for the rare occasion when they slipped past her defenses. But she would be married to this man. And he had been considerate enough to ask. If such a thing were possible, her wish was that they could be true to one another—to know each other. It was this hope that caused her to take a leap of faith and speak with candor.

"I am nearly frozen with nerves," she confessed.

He turned to face her, an interested light in his eyes as the candlelight made shadows on his face. His gaze was unnerving only in its intensity and her experience of having, for the first time, a man study her so openly. She tried to hold it but quickly dropped her eyes.

"It so happens that I am as well," he said at last. "It is my first time announcing a betrothal, you see." It sounded to her ears like humor, so she risked a look and found that the same half smile lit his face again.

Sounds of Honoria and Helen Pasley's conversation neared as they walked through the small corridor that led to the library. They must have started with the dining room and were coming this way. Christine did not want to be here when Martin's wife entered it, for fear it would leave her open to attack.

"Shall I show you the main stairwell and the dining room? Of course, we will soon enough see the latter."

She didn't wait for his reply but led him to the door, where they were forced to give way as Honoria and Helen entered. Helen ceased talking, and her eyes narrowed to see Christine and Sir Alexander so brazenly together, alone in a room, and she felt ready to sink into the floor.

Honoria stepped once again into the breach. "Helen, I know I can trust you to keep this little secret for another hour or so. Sir Alexander and Christine are about to announce their betrothal, and we wished to have a celebratory dinner for them." She stood back with a sweet smile on her face, waiting for Helen's reaction. It came swiftly.

"Why, that is wonderful news!" she said to Honoria.

Under the circumstances, Martin's wife could only express her pleasure without being labeled as entirely uncivil, but it seemed that Helen's surprise held a promising element of approval in it. Christine peeped at her to be sure and found warmth in her regard. Perhaps she simply had a sensitive conscience and was relieved to be able to approve of Christine, now that her reputation was beyond reproach.

"Please accept my congratulations," Helen said, now addressing Sir Alexander and Christine. "Of course, you may trust me to keep this quiet until you have a chance to announce it for yourself."

"You have our thanks," Sir Alexander said.

Christine had thought she'd had enough surprises for one day, but she had been wrong. It was the first time anyone had replied on her behalf, and the novel sensation stole her wits. She brought her eyes to rest on Sir Alexander's face, but he appeared to be unaware that he had done anything out of the ordinary. When she turned back to Helen, her smile came more naturally as she murmured her thanks.

Sir Alexander led her out of the library, saying, "If you will permit it, Mrs. Townsend, we were going to visit the other rooms on this floor that are open to visitors before we are summoned to dinner."

"I will permit it, Sir Alexander, if you will please call me Honoria. After all, you are to marry my best friend." She rested one hand on her hip in playful challenge.

"Honoria, then," he said with a bow and another handsome smile. They moved forward and left the small corridor to a set of stairs that led up to one wing of the house.

"This is the stairwell, as you see." Christine gestured to the broad wooden staircase that had a new runner nailed down in the middle of it.

In giving the tour, she was conscious of a novel desire to please him, to be accommodating and interesting. She wanted him to be...not unhappy to be married to her, especially after all he had done to protect her name. It was her turn to make efforts for him.

"Very nice," he observed. "I hope you will find my stairwell as fine as this one, once I have finished hanging the Merian engravings."

She sent him a timid smile, pleased to learn he had taken her advice, especially when not all of it had been graciously delivered. She thought regretfully back to her comment about his mother's portrait.

Sir Alexander followed her as she led him through the doors of the dining room. She had slipped her hand from his arm earlier when they stood staring at the bookcase, but he had taken it again as they reentered the corridor. Warmth came from his side, along with a scent of something woodsy. It suited him, she realized, especially since her encounters with him had largely been in the woods.

"The dining room is quite the feature of Boden House," she said, attempting an air of normalcy. "You can see how large it is, and how useful for entertaining. The silverware and some of the place settings are from the original owners of the house."

"You know a lot about Boden House." He pivoted to look at her.

A smile came to her lips and vanished just as quickly from nerves. "I helped Honoria to redecorate some of the rooms and choose the fabric to reupholster the older furniture."

"Ah, so that is where your expertise comes from." His smile teased her. "As you well know, Gracefield is in desperate need of repair. It is fortunate you are already in possession of this fact, or I might have despaired at the thought of showing you the house for fear you would change your mind."

She laughed, more as an escape for her nerves than anything. But there was also that promising sign of humor again, which gave her much hope. She warmed to him and answered with playful enthusiasm.

"Why, no project is too daunting for me. Decorating is what I love to do above all things. Except perhaps baking. I can only properly work with a cook who will share her kitchen with me."

"As I have tasted your seed cakes," Sir Alexander said, "I can only confirm that any cook of feeling should step aside so you might bake to your heart's content."

Christine grew warmer yet and ducked to hide her pleased smile as she took another step toward the far end of the dining room. Never in her life had she blushed, and smiled, and stepped out of character with such frequency. But then, never had she met a man who overturned her composure so easily.

"You are too kind."

She came to a sudden decision and stopped to face him before she could think the better of it. "Sir Alexander." She licked her lips before continuing. "I wish to thank you for the sacrifice you are making in offering to marry me. You are a man of honor, or you would not have done such a thing. I will endeavor to make you a good wife so you will have no cause to regret your decision."

Her words hung in the air, almost echoing in the empty dining room. In the ensuing silence, he regarded her for a weighted moment. She feared she had said too much, had been too vulnerable, until the light pressure of his hand on her arm brought her closer, and his face hovered above hers. For several long, heart-thumping seconds, she attempted to hold his gaze while wondering if he intended to kiss her. And then she tried to keep at bay the frantic thoughts of what it would be like to kiss him back. It caused her to blink rapidly and grow flushed.

"I offered for you because I wanted to marry you," he said softly. Releasing her arm, he added, "And I think we might address each other by our Christian names when in private, don't you think? My brother and closest friends call me Alex. I hope you will make free use of it."

"I am Christine," she replied. Stupidly, she thought. The man knew her name. Her mind was in a whirlwind after his disclosure and his manner of giving it. Her heart would not stop racing.

"Well then, Christine. I am glad we have been granted a moment's privacy to be in a more informal setting before we make any public announcement. Although," he murmured, "I would not object to being given more privacy."

Given his casual tone, she could only surmise that their proximity had not affected him at all and realized how inexperienced she was. And why did he wish for more privacy? *Was* it to kiss her?

He studied her for a moment as her thoughts reeled, then asked, "Is there anything you wish for me to say when I announce it?"

She darted a glance at him, trying to follow his conversation despite her discomfiture.

"I suppose you might say anything as long as you...I hope you will not allude to..." Embarrassment prevented the rest of the words from leaving her lips.

After a moment's hesitation, he said, "I think I know what

you are attempting to say, Christine, but I do not wish to presume. I don't know you well enough to read your mind. Will you finish your sentence?"

Of course she would have to be clearer. That was only fair, and it spoke well of him that he did not suppose he knew what she wished for without her stating it. She gathered her courage and faced him.

"I am of a mind to announce the engagement as simply as possible tonight. Naturally, we cannot speak of attachment. But if we could avoid addressing the forced nature of our engagement, I would take it kindly."

"I see." Alex paused before saying, "I will try not to be offended that your opinion of me is so low you believe me capable of announcing our engagement in such a gauche manner."

She glanced fearfully at him but saw he was smiling to take any potential sting out of his words. "I am sorry."

"Forgiven." He steered them back toward the sitting room, where the increase in volume indicated that guests had likely all arrived. "And you need not fear it. I would not dream of insulting my betrothed in such a manner."

Somehow Christine felt chastised, although she did not get the sense that Alex was attempting to belittle her. Surely he must understand where her fears came from. She hardly knew him, so how could she guess what he planned to say? It made her wonder if he was the type of man to be forever correcting or belittling her. But no, that could not be so because he had smiled. And he had asked what she meant without assuming he knew. Such a man could not change personality so radically from one instant to another.

They had reached the entrance to the drawing room, where the guests were grouped together in pockets around the room. He paused and looked down at her.

"Well, Christine? Are you ready?"

Her fears evaporated at his earnest expression and the intimate use of her name. They were about to make an announcement regarding their future to the people she had known her whole life, and she could *almost* believe they had chosen one another of their own free will—not as a love match or even as a match for practical purposes—but as two minds who would suit very well together. She smiled at him.

"I am."

CHAPTER TWENTY

Alex led his betrothed into the drawing room, taking care to release her arm before they were seen so that their arrival did not announce the news precipitously. Samuel Bassett noticed it but turned away when Alex looked in his direction.

Christine's open admission of how nervous she was had settled something inside of him. He had thought that if only, in their marriage, she might always say what she thought and not make him guess, they might rub along well together. And he was beginning to feel they would indeed be comfortable together. They might even be happy.

The memory of her looking up at him under her long lashes while he drew near enough to kiss her flashed before him. In that moment, he had been tempted to kiss her, wild as the idea had been. Who could have thought someone as reserved as she would welcome it? And yet she had not shown any inclination to move away. The pull had been strong, but fortunately wisdom had reasserted itself. Their first kiss would be more enjoyable without the risk of someone intruding upon the moment.

He followed his betrothed with his eyes as she went over to Arabella's side, allowing himself to admire her graceful figure. He knew how fortunate he was to be forced into an engagement to someone he found attractive. When he had praised her seed cakes, he had been given a glimpse of her shy smile and how it transformed her icy beauty into something intimate and approachable. He didn't know if she simply had no reason to smile, or if she was more likely to reserve it for those she was intimate with, but he made it a private goal to make her smile more often.

His thoughts were thus agreeably engaged when the reality of his position struck and a sudden surge of terror went through him. They would be irrevocably bound together—and he had not even told his own brother about it.

Philip Townsend skimmed his gaze around the room, and he caught Honoria's eye before clapping his hands lightly to draw everyone's attention. Slowly, the guests realized their host was attempting to address them, and their voices trailed away as they turned towards him. Mr. and Mrs. Mercer moved to the front of the crowd and stood to Alex's right.

"Thank you, everyone, for coming to our dinner party—our largest since our wedding. In addition to the usual reasons for inviting you," he continued, glancing at his wife again as though for reassurance, "there is an announcement to make that will bring many of you great pleasure."

"Honoria is expecting," Samuel Bassett called out, shooting his sister a provoking grin. His wife sent him a severe look and Mrs. Bassett spoke his name in reproach, but it was clear both his wife and mother were accustomed to his mordant sense of humor.

"Is she?" Philip turned to look at his wife with mock surprise.

Everyone laughed, even Honoria, who turned pink and said, "Samuel, your bawdy sense of humor is hardly fit for polite company."

Philip cleared his throat. "My announcement is of quite another nature. Actually, it is not my announcement to make, so I will give the floor to the ones whom it concerns. That is probably for the best, given that the tone of the conversation has gone downhill."

As Philip spoke, Gus moved to the front of the crowd and took his place beside Alex and the Mercers. Alex glanced behind him in time to see Martin Pasley's eyebrows snap together. With a flash of understanding he guessed that the apothecary feared that Gus was about to announce his own betrothal.

"Sir Alexander?" Philip's eyes were on him.

Alex stepped beside Philip to address the crowd, and his eyes settled on Christine, whose pale face was nearly expressionless. He was beginning to understand that although her natural reserve led her to display a disinterested mien, she was a woman of feeling. He brought his gaze back to the general gathering.

"Good evening, ladies and gentlemen. I believe you all know of me, but for those to whom I have not been introduced, I am Sir Alexander Thorne, and I hail from Derbyshire. Allow me to present my friend who is visiting, Mr. Roger Garrick, who must unfortunately leave us tomorrow."

Roger gave a general bow to everyone in the room, and Alex continued. "As most of you are aware, I purchased Gracefield Park a year ago, though I moved into it only last month. This now gives me the distinction of being your neighbor. And just recently"—he paused, catching Christine's gaze again and holding it—"I have asked for Miss Grey's hand in marriage, and she has done me the honor of accepting."

He paused, as the conversation in the room erupted in exclamations of surprise and pleasure. Honoria smiled and leaned in to say something to the woman he thought was her sister-in-law. He raised his voice over the hub.

"Gracefield Park is to have a mistress, who is one of Lincolnshire's own."

The pitch rose in the room, and the guests congregated around them both. On his side, there was much slapping on the back and voices of congratulations that were as familiar in nature as if he had grown up with these people. He smiled at the well-wishers, filled with an odd sensation that he had truly announced an engagement to a woman he had pursued for love.

He glanced over at Christine, who was still pale, surrounded by so many people seeking her attention. But her eyes were fixed on Samuel Bassett's wife, and she was smiling, so he knew his fiancée was being treated kindly. Somehow, having made a match that brought so much pleasure to everyone around him, and which saved Miss Grey's reputation—no, *Christine*, she would be to him now—made him feel as though he could not have done better for himself. As though he had pursued her from the beginning.

He turned and caught Roger's glance above the crowd. Someone had served him a glass of wine, and he lifted it in a salute. Alex smiled back and raised his own empty hand in a wave. At least he had one friend here for this momentous occasion. He would have to ask Roger to return in a month for their wedding, especially if Leonard could not, or would not, attend it. He hoped Roger could come.

Earlier, when Alex and Gus had discussed terms, Gus thought it wisest to have the ceremony as soon as could be. So they would read the banns for the next three weeks and would have the ceremony in a month. He would worry about who would stand for him at that time. Right now, with such gaiety in the evening's assembly, there was nothing in the announcement that felt like a forced marriage. It felt simply like a celebration.

ALEX AND ROGER met for breakfast the next day, having planned to take the meal on the early side so Roger could have an early start to his journey. Alex had eaten enough the night before that he settled for coffee and a roll, but Roger said between bites that his full day of riding ahead of him required he not break his fast so moderately.

When they had both had their fill, Alex set down his cup and eyed his friend. "Would you come back for my wedding in a month? I'd like to have you there."

"Of course. You may rely upon it. And if I am successful in my mission, you must stand up for me at my own wedding. I have no brother, you see." Roger smiled, but Alex detected an edge of nerves.

"You can count on me." Alex furrowed his brows. "Speaking of which, I might need you to stand up for me as well. There's no guarantee my brother will take the news well or whether he will think it a worthy enough event to leave the mill for the time it takes to come."

Roger lifted his brows in surprise. "Leonard would miss his own brother's wedding?"

"He could very well." Alex shrugged and said wryly, "He was easier to get along with before he married up."

Roger gave a bark of laughter. "It is always the ones clambering up the societal ladder who are the most particular." He stopped short at what he had just said. "My apologies. I had no intention of giving offense."

"None taken. And you are very right. No one is more concerned with what is good *ton* than my brother who grew up with no notion of it."

Alex laughed, but it was weak. He was not looking forward to receiving his brother's response to the letter he had to write that day. He did not wish to have his fears that his brother would feel himself unjustly treated confirmed. It would be much pleasanter if he could simply be happy for him.

Alex saw Roger on his way, then sat down to write the letter to his brother, which he could not put off. It took several drafts before he was even a little satisfied with it, especially since he had decided not to inform Leonard of the forced nature of his engagement but rather to let him think it was for love. If all went as he hoped, it would be.

He then took care of other urgent correspondence, such as giving instructions to his solicitor about the marriage contract and seeing that the banns were read, as well as writing to the project manager in Boston, where they were using his steam pump to drain part of the fens.

He had sadly neglected his project as the events of the past weeks had nearly driven it out of his mind. It could not be helped; he would need to put it off longer and focus on his upcoming nuptials. It was fortunate his manager was competent and even had a natural aptitude for understanding the mechanics of the pump so he could make small alterations when it stopped working.

When this was done and the butler sent the footman off with the letters, Alex wandered through his house, attempting to resist the temptation to visit Christine so he might see her again. They had not spoken of their next meeting when they bid farewell the night before, and he did not want to appear desperate, as though he could not go a full day without a glimpse of her face. He paced back and forth in the drawing room, imagining how it would look after she gave orders for its decoration. His heart lifted as he imagined the house in her capable hands.

After a few hours of solitude, he found the temptation to see her beyond what he could resist. After pacing back and forth a little more, he finally settled on the reasoning that they had much to discuss about matters such as the ceremony and wedding breakfast. It would therefore actually be a sensible thing to visit her. She must surely be expecting it and wondering why he had not yet come.

When he was admitted to the Greys' residence, he discovered Honoria already there. He wasn't sure if this was a good thing or not. On one hand, it would make the visit potentially less awkward; on the other hand, he would not get time alone with Christine, which had been his object in setting out.

After the greetings had been exchanged, Christine hid again behind her reserve—he would have to find an excuse to be alone with her so he could break through it—and they sat down and waited for the tea to be brought. With Honoria present, Alex was at a loss to know how to bring up any of the wedding details he had thought of on the ride over.

After a moment's silence, Honoria turned to him. "I had forgotten to ask about your tenants on our visit to Gracefield House. I've been treating the ailments of some who live on your estate even before you purchased it. Have you been able to meet them all?"

Alex knew he had neglected his duty in that regard and replied with chagrin. "I am sorry to say I have not. I have left them in the hands of my steward and have dealt only with him thus far."

What he did not add was that it was easy to pretend that portion of the estate did not exist because the tenant houses were on the far end of the fields. He could ride most of his land without necessarily meeting any of them. In fact, that was precisely what he had done, because he hadn't known what he would say.

"I am sure they will be glad to meet you," Christine said. "Any tenant would wish to greet the new owner of the estate and see what sort of a man he is."

He glanced at his betrothed, encouraged by her contribution to the conversation. "I will take your word for it. Perhaps we might visit them together."

She smiled and nodded. The tea tray was brought in then, and he enjoyed watching Christine prepare the tea and serve everyone. The tray was charmingly arranged, which he suspected was her doing rather than the cook's. And the lemon cake he bit into was so delicious, it almost brought tears to his eyes. His life was about to change in more ways than one.

Christine watched him as he ate, smiling at the expression on his face. "You like lemon cakes."

"I am convinced I will like everything you serve," he said truthfully, which only made her smile grow broader.

"How many servants do you have?" she asked, serving him a second cake.

Of course she would wish to know, since they would be her servants, too, many of them under her direction.

"My cook, a kitchen maid, a scullery maid, a maid-of-all-work, in addition to the head maid," he said, listing them with his fingers, "two footmen, two stable hands, a butler, and a groom. Oh, and a gardener."

She nodded as though satisfied, and he added, "I will need a housekeeper but the head maid has been handling the task so admirably I haven't seen a pressing need."

"She might very well do for the role then," Christine said. "I would like to meet her."

"I hope you will. Come any time. Come tomorrow," he said, then briefly closed his eyes at his impetuous, schoolboy-sounding phrase. Although he had become adept at social niceties and could successfully mask whatever insecurity he might feel, he had never been at his best when he was around a woman he admired.

After a surprised moment, she said, "I will."

A loud clatter erupted outside, and she whirled around at the noise then turned back to them with knit brows. "Please, stay seated. I will see what has happened, if you'll excuse me."

She hurried out of the room toward the source of the noise, and Honoria set down her cup. "Sir Alexander—"

"Alex, please."

"Very well," Honoria replied with a smile as she clasped her hands on her lap. "Alex. I wish to speak to you about something while Christine is not here."

Her slight hesitation that followed this pronouncement threw Alex's mind into all sorts of confusion. Was there a big confession? Some deep secret he needed to know about his future wife? The way Honoria bit her lip and sent him a speculative glance seemed to confirm his worst fears.

"Please go on."

"I have seen the parts of your house that are fit for company, and I would not be so brassy as to bring this up if it were not for the fact that you have openly admitted that you have no taste for decorating..." Honoria began.

At her pause, he relaxed, now fairly certain she wasn't going to reveal something terrible about his bride-to-be.

"It is true. What are you proposing?"

"Well, I was wondering if your bedroom has been properly

made up, and if...if the adjoining bedroom which will belong to your wife has been given any attention."

She stopped, as he stared at her with dawning horror—a look which caused her eyes to crinkle kindly.

"Have no fear, Alex. This is precisely why I asked. As Christine's closest friend, please allow me to take charge of her room in the month that is left to us. I will let Arabella oversee the wedding breakfast, for she is closer to her confinement than I am, and I know she will not accept having nothing to do."

The relief he felt was touched with some guilt. "I would gratefully accept, but are you sure you are in a state to be doing anything of the like? I am not sure your husband would agree."

"I promise not to overexert myself. If you will allow me to direct some of your servants, I will merely oversee the project," she promised him.

Footsteps coming from the kitchen forewarned Christine's return, and he had only time to murmur his thanks before the discussion was cut short.

"I hope you will forgive me," Christine said, rushing in, "but I must leave you both. And Alex, I might be obliged to put off my meeting your servants tomorrow. Part of the greenhouse has collapsed on my winter garden and I will have to oversee its repair and the removal of the plants."

"Of course," he assured her, hiding both his disappointment and the sense of injustice that it must be she who oversaw the project. He would have liked to have asked whether her brother would be equally tied up with the project but could not do so. When she was his wife, he would ensure that she did not bear the entirety of an estate's maintenance on her slim shoulders.

They bid Christine farewell and walked outdoors together. Honoria assured him that her groom would bring her home and told him to expect her at Gracefield the next day.

CHAPTER TWENTY-ONE

T rue to her word, Honoria arrived the following afternoon, bringing one of her own footmen who she claimed was skilled in renovations. When Alex brought her to see the bedchamber, she did not seem dismayed by its state. Emboldened by her lack of judgment over his future wife's bedroom, he invited her and the footman to see the master bedroom as well. He had done nothing at all to the room, but at least its somber appearance was more appropriate for the masculine sex.

Honoria had no hesitation in going over to examine his mattress with a simple "do you mind?" although she did not wait for an answer.

After she had gone through everything in his room as well, she turned to face him. "If you will permit, I'll give your servants instructions on how to replace your mattress since they are not from Horncastle and might not know. You may as well do yours at the same time as the other bedchamber, although this one is in better shape."

He nodded and trailed her back into what was to be Christine's bedroom, where Honoria went over to look through the window at the view.

"The windows will only need to be cleaned to bring more

light into the room." She stood looking out for a moment with a satisfied expression. "I think Christine will be happy with a view."

She went on to recommend where to order the sheets and counterpanes and suggested the cheerful colors of pale blue and white for decoration, conferring with her footman and Alex's servant, who had joined them, on where to start.

He gratefully agreed to all of Honoria's suggestions. It was a relief to have somebody take charge of the colossal task, and he hoped Christine would be happy with the results. A dreadful image filled his mind as he pictured his wife discovering her room in this morbid, unfinished state on their wedding night. Without Honoria's intervention, he was not sure he would have thought about fixing the room in time to have much done before the wedding.

He instructed the servants to obey Mrs. Townsend in everything. And after offering his help, but having neither the proper clothes, nor the skill to carry it out, Honoria finally begged him with a laugh to go and ride and leave it to her. He gratefully acquiesced, then declared an interest in seeing Philip—an idea she heartily endorsed.

Before he took his leave of her, Alex could not resist asking about his betrothed since Honoria had offered no news about her since she arrived.

"I hope Christine will not be too burdened by the greenhouse that collapsed. Do you know how she views the upcoming wedding preparations? Is she...at ease?"

Honoria sent him a cheerful smile, stopping to help remove the wall hanging that the servant seemed to have trouble with.

"Since Arabella and I are handling many of the wedding details, such as the breakfast, her biggest project will be to sew the dress that you will see her in on the day she walks down the aisle to meet you." The thought sent a frisson of nerves through him—and one of delight.

"Her only disappointment," Honoria went on, "is that she is unable to find similar beads to what she used for the gown that was meant for the Stuff Ball, which was carried away in the flood. She had hoped to create something equally as fine for the wedding."

She stepped aside as his footman carried a ladder into the room. "I must say that her gown was truly magnificent with the way she had adorned it with those tiny glass beads. I've never seen anything like it. Somehow, the way the beads shone, it looked like a night sky of glittering constellations."

"I see," Alex replied, trying to envision what she meant.

With a self-conscious laugh, Honoria waved it off. "I don't quite know how to explain it, but the effect was very pretty. She discovered them in the haberdasher's shop in Grantham, and it must have been a rare find, since she did not see them the next time she went. They were very small beads that had a shimmer to them."

"I am sorry to hear it," Alex replied, a little lost amid the talk about dresses and beads. "I am confident, however, that she will not need the embellishment in order to be a beautiful bride."

Honoria smiled up at him brightly. "I am in perfect agreement with you."

Alex turned to go, and she called out after him. "Let us keep my involvement in Christine's room between us, shall we? What I mean to say is, I will not tell her of it, and I hope you will not either, so it might be a surprise." Alex gave his word, then bowed before taking his leave.

A short while later, as Alex rode up to Boden House, the Townsends' groom was leading a Thoroughbred horse to Philip, who stood in front of the door.

"You're the last person I expected to see," Philip said upon spotting Alex. His smile was quickly replaced with a look of alarm. "Honoria is not hurt?"

"Heavens, no! I did not think how my visit might be perceived, but she is perfectly well. In fact, she practically pushed me out of my home by suggesting I go and ride." Alex grinned. "When I said I wished to come and see you, she approved the plan so quickly I could see I was quite in the way."

Philip chuckled. "Sounds like she is doing what she loves best. She will be in fine fettle there. I was just on my way to visit the spa."

"As a matter of fact, that is the reason I've come," Alex replied. "Might I accompany you there? I've been wishing to see it since I first heard it mentioned."

Philip's cheeks were already flushed in the cold air, and he climbed onto the saddle. "You won't find me dissuading a person from visiting my spa."

Alex turned his horse, and they rode in the direction of the public road. "Do you remember the steam pump that I told you about?" Philip made a noise of assent, and Alex lifted his eyes upward where a flock of geese flew in a V-formation in search of a warmer destination.

"I have not had much time to oversee my project in Boston and should not be thinking of adding another. However, when I learned of your thermal baths, it occurred to me that perhaps a steam-powered excavator might dig through the rock to expand it, and that a steam shovel might remove the earth."

Philip absorbed this, then said, "Go on."

"You might have an excavator for hire, but I have been working on a prototype for the steam shovel that could be used in tight spaces. I have not yet had a chance to try it out and thought perhaps we might do so at the thermal baths by way of an experiment."

When Alex saw Philip's look of excitement, he felt it necessary to set expectations and added, "It would not be a project to enter into right away, but I do like the idea of being able to test my steam shovel closer to home."

"Your wedding must be the first priority—I understand," Philip said. "But I would be glad to attempt it. I must confess that when you'd mentioned the pump at the Mercers' dinner, I speculated whether it might be of use to me." He gave a dry laugh. "It would have been of great value when I flooded my field, and the public road, with an irrigation project gone awry. It took weeks to rectify."

"I can imagine." Alex smiled in sympathy. He was proud of his steam prototypes and knew they were the thing of the future. Steam machines would help reduce time and labor for just such projects as these.

They exchanged more conversation on the subject but decided to leave the rest until they reached the spa and Alex could see it for himself. He went on to praise Honoria's help with his bride's bedchamber, admitting with chagrin what a sorry state the house was in.

"I do apologize for taking up your wife's time," he said, "especially in her delicate state. I've begged her not to exert herself in any way. However, I cannot bring myself to refuse help so freely offered, for I could not accomplish even a quarter of it on my own."

"Do not feel the need to apologize," Philip assured him. "My house was in a terrible state, and it was not until I married Honoria that everything began to be set to rights."

This eased some of the guilt Alex had been carrying. "I would hate for Christine to have been shown to such a room on her wedding day. To have that be her first introduction to married life." He shook his head with a dry chuckle. "With everything I have on my mind, I can't say it would have occurred to me to do something about the room until her trunks were brought, and the impossibility of her staying in it was forced upon me. I am truly indebted to your wife."

"Think no more of it," Philip said. "I don't think I could stop Honoria, even if I tried. Fortunately, her first pregnancy went very smoothly, except for a little sickness at the beginning, and this one is looking to be the same. You see before you a relaxed man, now that I've had proof she will not actually break if she stays occupied. In any case, it is what she likes to do."

"You relieve my mind."

"Besides," Philip said, "I've known Christine since I was a boy. Honoria is not the only one who wishes to see her happily settled."

GUS ENTERED THE SITTING ROOM, and Christine lay aside the dress she was working on. She needed to rest her eyes anyway. He moved with the same restless energy he'd had lately, but it was not the despondent restlessness he'd shown when he and Sarah were estranged. Rather, it was a nervous energy, as if he were on the brink of making some permanent change in his life. It did not take a scholar to imagine what that might be.

"How is Sarah?" she asked, picking the dress up again and pretending to examine it. She felt his surprised gaze on her.

"How do you know I was visiting Sarah?"

"I can tell. You are always like this when you return from meeting her. She stirs something in you."

Christine stopped herself from saying more and glanced at her brother. She wanted to tease him and say that she wondered whether it was a good thing, considering how much they argued, but did not want to plant seeds of discouragement. Sarah was good for him—Christine was now convinced of this—and the fewer obstacles that came in Gus's way the better. After all, anyone who was still a bachelor after so many years was not a man who could easily come to the point.

"I am of a mind to visit Gracefield," he said, taking the conversation in an unexpected direction. "Why don't we go together?"

Christine darted a glance at him, then tried to keep her heartbeat steady at his suggestion. She had not dared to go, even when her greenhouse had been repaired.

"Why do you wish to go to Gracefield?"

What she would not admit was that the idea had taken hold of her to have Alex's mother's portrait more suitably framed. If she could bring a tape measure and find a way to measure it without being observed, she could make a frame in secret and offer it to him as a wedding gift. It was the least she could do after hurting him over the portrait. Even back when she wasn't sure she even liked him, she knew her comment had been in extremely poor taste.

Besides this objective was the longing to see the house again. Never before had such an exciting prospect lain before her. Working room by room, she would be able to bring each into beautiful harmony and order. The idea was tantalizing.

Any wish to see Alex apart from this, she brutally pushed down. He seemed to be showing signs of softening toward her, but she must not display her longing openly and allow herself to get hurt. After all, he would not have chosen her if he had been able to help it.

But a house could not hurt her. Having her own home to care for could bring no disappointment—what more could she want in her life?

By the time Gus answered her question, she had almost forgotten she had asked one. "I've heard that Alex has horses in his stables worth visiting. Let us ride there. We can bring Hunter and Artemis with us for exercise."

"A fine idea," she said, folding the cloth of her dress in two.

It came as no surprise that Gus had taken to the dogs. She had always known he would. Guinea was snoring on the couch next to her, but when she stood, the pug looked up at her with sorrowful eyes.

"I won't be gone for long, Guinsey," she crooned, leaning down to kiss him. She had forgotten to ask Alex if she could bring her animals when she moved there, but somehow she was not worried he might refuse.

Christine had forgotten how much she liked to ride. She tended to walk places more than anything else, but riding gave her a fresh view of the countryside. There was frost along the far border of the trees that was untouched by the midday sun, and the dogs raced across the meadow toward it, their coats gleaming in the sunlight.

At Gracefield, Gus fell immediately into conversation with the groom and left Christine to find her own way to the house. She knew that if she waited for him, he would forget all about her. So much time would pass, she might not even see Alex. She would not allow that to happen.

A footman came to answer her knock and showed her into the drawing room, where Alex stood waiting for her. He walked forward to greet her, taking both of her hands in his. It was a much warmer, more affectionate greeting than she'd expected from him, even in her imagination, and she smiled up at him.

"Do not think I am here on my own. I left Gus in the stables with your groom, where I could not pull him away. It was his suggestion we come."

"I am very glad you did," Alex said. "You need no invitation. What would you like to do? Shall I have tea brought?"

She shook her head. How was she going to get into the breakfast room and measure the frame without Alex suspecting anything? She had to find a way.

"Would you take me on a tour again of the rooms on this floor?"

He looked momentarily surprised but answered, "Why, of course."

Instead of leading her across the drawing room, as he had the first time she was here, he brought her into the corridor, now empty of servants, and pointed to the stairwell farther in the distance.

"But first, you must see…"

His words trailed away, and she followed his eyes to where his collection of engravings was perfectly positioned on the wall of the stairwell. It brightened the wall and made the stairwell look modern and lived in.

"You took my suggestion," she said, smiling. She climbed three of the steps to get a better view of the engravings there.

He followed to the step below hers and waited while she took her time examining them. The effect was just what she had thought it would be. "I must tell you how very happy I am at the prospect of transforming Gracefield into a home for you," she said.

She turned and found him exactly eye level. When she saw

his expression, she was immediately abashed. How forward of her to speak of making changes in his home when he was only marrying her because he had been forced to.

She looked away and bit her lip. "That is, I hadn't meant..."

Before she even knew he had moved, his arms were around her. He pulled her into him and kissed her on the lips. The gesture was so unexpected, she did not immediately react. She remained frozen as he laid a soft kiss on her lips, then pulled back a few inches to look at her, his arms about her still.

Then the sensation and comfort of his embrace finally pierced the surprise of it, and she lifted her eyes upward before settling her gaze on his mouth. His expression was earnest— almost as though he were in love, although such a thing could hardly be true. The intensity of his regard melted something inside of her. Somewhere in the recesses of her mind, she knew it was the armor she kept firmly in place around her heart.

This—his look—and the fact that he stayed in place without breaking his gaze, pulled her into him again, and she kissed him back. His passionate response almost made her knees buckle, and she clutched the back of his coat so she wouldn't fall.

The sound of a door opening in the distance made him release her and step back. His cheeks were a dull red, and his eyes searched hers as he gave her a shy grin. "I hope you did not mind that liberty I just took."

She shook her head, her lips lifting, and caught a flash of something exultant in his grin

The footman was approaching, and Alex gestured forward, saying in a more audible voice, "Let us now visit the study, for I did not get a chance to show it to you the last time you came with Mrs. Townsend."

Inside Alex's study, which was large and like a small library in itself, she could see that some renovations had been attempted, and she mostly listened as he described what he hoped to achieve in this room. They spent little time in the library, which needed dusting more than anything else, before retracing their steps back through the drawing room.

She did not feel any desire to linger in this largest of projects and allowed him to lead her into the parlor, the dining room, and at last to the breakfast room. The engravings were no longer on the sideboard, of course, but the paintings were all still stacked on the floor. His mother's portrait, however, was no longer there. She hoped it had merely been relocated to another place in the pile.

"Would you mind ordering some tea for me after all?" She looked at him anxiously. "I know it is forward of me to ask you for it, but I thought to look over these paintings and see if the frames are ready for hanging. It would be nice to have refreshment, and I am quite certain that Gus will be wishing for some tea as well."

Only the desire to get her hands on his mother's painting could force these reluctant words out of her. It was a bold thing to ask, even from one who was his betrothed, and it embarrassed her.

But Alex only looked pleased. "I would like nothing better than to send for tea. After all, as your husband, it will be my object to care for you in this manner and in others like it."

Christine brought her stunned look to him. *He* planned to care for *her*? She did not resist the impulse to lift her hand and lay it affectionately against his cheek. The intimacy of this gesture was not difficult, not when they'd already kissed. Not when they were to be married. And certainly not when he was eager to see to her comfort. He smiled more broadly and leaned his cheek into her hand for a brief moment.

As soon as he left the room, explaining that the bell pull was still broken—a fact for which she sent up a whispered thanks—Christine dropped to her knees and began searching through the paintings. She leaned the first stack against her chest and pulled one back after the other as she quickly flipped through them in search of his mother's portrait.

She found it toward the back of one of the piles, but her initial exultation at having discovered it gave way to a pang of dismay when she realized the implication of its concealment. He had put it in the back of the pile because of her disparaging remark—because she had said it had no value.

She covered her face with her hands. *I have to be careful. So careful.* A wife's words could just as easily wound a husband as they could build him up.

Her eyes pricked with tears, and she rubbed them. But she had no time to waste, so she pulled out the measuring tape and little pencil and paper from her reticule. She quickly took the painting's measurements, then leaned it gently back before going over to the other pile, so he might not suspect her true object when he came. She began examining these frames and was thus engaged when he returned.

"You did not wait to have your tea before beginning the task," he said in mild reproach. "Why don't we stop and have some first, and then you can look at these paintings to your heart's content. Except I will be the one to hold them for you." He regarded her with affection. "I am sorry for this, but the frames seem to have dirtied your gown."

"Oh no, have they?" Christine leaned the stack of frames back against the wall and stood. "Very well. Let us have tea, although perhaps a footman might be sent to fetch Gus? I know he will not want to miss it."

"I will send someone straight away."

They retraced their steps to the drawing room, and when they reached it, they heard a knocking at the entrance. "It seems as though we will not have to fetch Gus after all." Alex glanced at her with a creased brow, adding, "I am afraid he will not be pleased with me when he sees the state you are in."

The sounds of the front door opening, followed by muffled voices, reached them. Christine shook her head with a smile. "You must not worry. Gus is accustomed to seeing me in this state when engaged in a project."

"Oh, it is not only that." Alex reached into his waistcoat pocket and pulled out a handkerchief. "It is just that you have managed to get dirt on your face. I was hesitant to say something, but if you will allow me..."

He brought the handkerchief up to her face as the door opened. And just as he bent down and brushed the dirt off her face in light strokes, Christine heard the stringent voice of a visitor who was not Gus.

"Alex, what in the devil do you mean by this letter you sent? I came as soon as I could. Surely it is not too late to back out of an improvident match."

Christine had been hidden from view with Alex's back to the visitor, but she now stepped to the side and saw Mr. Thorne, Alex's brother. He, too, stopped and stared at her, his initial shock turning to a look of incredulity. At this glaring sign of disapproval, she turned a hesitant, fearful face toward her betrothed. His brother was unhappy with Alex's choice. It was as clear from his expression as it had been from his words.

"Leonard, this does not concern you." Alex turned and stepped partially in front of her so that his shoulder served as a barrier between his brother and her.

But she could not bear the critical scrutiny coming from his closest family member, and she touched Alex on the arm.

"Gus is still in the stables. I will explain that you had an unexpected visitor and that it is not a convenient time for a visit." Before Alex could reply to her, she slipped out of the room and into the corridor, anxious to put distance between Mr. Thorne and herself as quickly as she could.

CHAPTER TWENTY-TWO

Alex turned furious eyes to Leonard as Christine fled the room, before he ran into the corridor after her to take her arm. "No, wait."

She turned to him with pleading eyes. "You will come and see me at a more opportune time, I hope. I beg you will let me go now."

After a brief internal struggle he knew he needed to let her go. He lifted his head and signaled for Davies to come, saying, "Please accompany Miss Grey to the stables where her brother is and deliver her safely into his hands."

Although this was a task more suited to a footman, Davies nodded and went to open the door. "After you, Miss Grey."

The door was closed behind them, and Alex reentered the drawing room, fully intending to give his brother a piece of his mind. Leonard forestalled him.

"I had to leave my affairs at the mill to come here and clean up after your mess! What were you thinking? Have you no family loyalty?"

"Whom I marry is my own affair—" Alex began, but Leonard cut him off again.

"I would agree with you if we had not clearly shared an understanding *for years* that I would carry on the work at the mill, including your part, and that you would promise to see to our standing in London society. I have high hopes for my daughters, and Martha does as well."

Alex swallowed, knowing his brother spoke the truth. When drafting his letter, he had considered explaining what led to his sudden decision—that all this had been due to circumstances out of his control—but had decided it was better to keep the reasons for their engagement a secret to protect Christine.

To protect her, but it was also because he was coming to believe she would make him the ideal wife, never mind that it might require being less involved in Parliament—or not involved at all. Such a thing would be a sacrifice, for the thought of giving up his mark on the country's future caused a twinge of regret. But she was worth the price, and he was willing to give even that up for her.

His posture was stiff from the burden of keeping all of this from Leonard. "If you need me to pay you back for anything you've put into the mill on my behalf, I will certainly do so."

"There is no price on the work I've put into the mill to make it profitable," his brother retorted. "I cannot calculate such a thing. And besides, a man of honor keeps his word."

When Alex did not respond to this, his brother shot a glance toward the open door where Christine had fled.

"And just what do you see in her? Did you not notice that she was covered head to toe in dirt? Let me assure you that *my* wife would never allow herself to be seen that way. Martha will be appalled when she learns of your decision to throw everything away. She was visiting her mother when I received your news, but you may be sure I left a letter informing her of this development."

An impartial observer would have agreed that Christine had not looked her best and was indeed covered in dirt. However, considering the fact that the dirt came from sorting through the frames in *his* house to see which ones were ready to hang, he found nothing wrong with it. Besides, the little streaks of grime on her face had been charming, especially when they gave him another excuse to get close so he might wipe it off, though he had not fully succeeded in this agreeable pursuit before Leonard had interrupted them.

The memory of her leaning into him and kissing him back raised in him every protective instinct on her behalf.

"Leonard, you are six years my senior, and I have always looked up to you. I've always done what you asked. The fact that I was given the education instead of you did not change me. You cannot accuse me of ever having looked down on you as a result of it." Alex challenged his brother with a stare, who finally returned a reluctant nod.

He went on. "I was willing to agree to your idea of marriage when my heart was not engaged. But you are simply going to have to accept the fact that this is my choice, little though you like it. I will make whatever other amends you ask of me, but I will not rescind an offer of marriage to a woman who has accepted it. Surely you cannot imagine I could do such a thing."

Leonard's face portrayed a variety of expressions as he wrestled with his thoughts, but he finally said begrudgingly, "No, I suppose you cannot back out now. Her brother would sue you for breach of contract."

Alex suggested stopping for refreshments. He had ordered a tea tray for Christine, but taking some with Leonard would allow his brother to calm down and see things in a more rational light. Soon, a maid and footman brought the tray into the drawing room, and he made sure Leonard's plate was full.

It seemed to have worked, for by the time he had had something to eat and drink, his brother was still annoyed but no longer unreasonable. Alex decided to take his chances while Leonard was in a malleable mood.

"I think you owe Miss Grey an apology. The words you uttered in her hearing will not easily be forgotten and I should not like for there to be a rift between our two families because of it."

Leonard folded his arms on his chest. "I will not say that I owe her an apology. No, I will not say it. The facts are the facts.

But I suppose I had better see where she lives and what sort of family you are marrying into."

This sparked Alex's own internal wrestling as he tried to decide if it was worth pushing Leonard to realize that of course he must apologize—and wishing to show off just what sort of family he would be joining. Although the Farlow estate was not as large as Gracefield, it was a respectable one. It was also set on the edge of town with the tenant lands connected to it by a narrow tract of land behind it rather than the traditional arrangement of having the house in the center. But these were small matters, after all. And after one glance at the tastefully decorated home and the artful tray that Christine set out, Leonard would not be able to accuse her of being anything less than a lady.

"I will send word to Miss Grey and ask if she will receive us tomorrow." Alex leveled his brother with a stare. "I wish you would apologize, but if you will not do so, then I am in every expectation that you will treat her with the courtesy my future wife deserves."

Leonard grumbled a noncommittal reply, and Alex rang to have the maid make up a room for his brother.

The next day, Leonard's mood was not much improved, and they rode to Farlow mostly in silence. They drew near, and Leonard cast his gaze along the broad, tree-lined path that led to the manor and the stone wall just beyond. When they reached the iron gate with the house beyond it, he made a noise in his throat that sounded like approval. Alex brought his carriage into the courtyard and on to the stables, where he handed the reins over to the head groom.

"He has a respectable stable," Leonard observed, indicating the stalls full of purebred horses.

The foxhounds that had accompanied Christine on their first meeting left their bed on the straw and came yapping over to Alex, greeting him with affection. The memory of his first meeting with Christine brought a smile to his face.

"Gus has a passion for horses and hunting." He stood and

brushed the straw from his hands, then directed his brother toward the house.

"That is something you have in common then," Leonard said.

Alex could not be sure if his brother was jealous about the fact that he'd never learned to ride for pleasure or follow a hunt. This was one advantage Alex's school education and connections had given him.

"It is one thing we have in common, although we have not spoken much of it," he replied.

They were admitted into the drawing room, and Leonard looked about him in surprise.

"Why, despite how big the house is, there is no entryway. Here you are, right in the sitting room. This is a rather informal set up for a genteel house."

"It is," Alex replied without attempting to explain that it did not follow that the house must therefore have less value. He willed his brother to notice the spacious room, the artwork and beautiful vases, and the pristine condition of everything in it that showed the owner's superior taste.

Gus entered the room from the corridor, and came over to shake their hands. He apparently knew nothing about the insults his sister had received the day before. His demeanor was perfectly pleasant as he asked about Leonard's journey and what he thought of the upcoming wedding. For once, Leonard did not say exactly what he thought.

It was some time before Christine joined them, and Alex speculated that she had held back out of hurt, a fact which bothered him. She could not be blamed for it, but he wished he had been able to protect her from it.

When at last she arrived, Christine curtsied before Leonard, all traces of openness carefully concealed.

"Welcome to our house, Mr. Thorne. Won't you be seated?" She glanced at Alex, and he tried to reassure her with a smile that she could count on him for his support. She returned the smile fleetingly.

Within minutes, a tray was brought in by a footman, and a

maid followed with the teapot, everything done with perfect decorum. His fiancée was making efforts to leave off her delight in doing, Alex noticed, and prove to Leonard that nothing was lacking in her education as a lady.

She prepared the tea to everyone's liking and served it in beautiful china cups with monogramed silver spoons. Although Leonard would not likely admit it, there was nothing to criticize in Christine's bearing. And as much as Alex was fond of Martha, his sister-in-law was not half so gracious.

Leonard took his first bite of the cake and grunted in satisfaction. "You have a good cook," he said.

Gus was sprawled back in his chair, and he crossed one leg over the other and balanced the plate on his lap. "Those cakes are done by Christine's hand. I'll miss them when she leaves."

"You bake, and you clean..." Leonard's tone was not admiring, and he left the rest unsaid. Alex felt the veins pulse in his neck. Leonard would not be invited to his wedding if this continued. If he kept on, he would not retain the possession of all of his teeth.

A knock came on the door, and Christine, whose cheeks were tinged pink, remained seated as a footman went from the back of the room to answer it. She was doing everything she could to portray the image she assumed his brother must require in a wife, and Alex's irritation mounted. Why should she have to prove herself to Leonard?

"I believe you've mistaken the door," the footman was saying to somebody outside. "The tradesmen's entrance is around to the left."

The visitor popped his head inside and peered into the drawing room, not at all abashed.

"No, I've nothing to sell. Name's Duncan. I'd told the mistress I might stop by. Since I happens to be in Horncastle, I took t'occasion to make sure that Mr. and Miss Grey arrived home all right."

By degrees, Alex came into the understanding of what was happening. Gus stood, looking at the man in confusion. By instinct, Alex stood as well. Perhaps he ought to push Duncan back out of the door before he could do any harm. Gus fore-stalled him by walking over to the visitor.

"I'm sorry, who are you?" he asked.

"Duncan's the name. I came only to pay my respects to Mr. and Miss Grey."

In one hand he held a Hessian sack, and with the other he indicated Alex and Christine. "I've brought 'em a cackler. 'Tis a gift since they didn't stop to eat with me."

"You mean to say Sir Alexander and Miss Grey?" Gus asked, looking back and forth between the visitor and his sister.

Christine finally stood and went to the door. "It is very kind of you to see to our welfare and bring us a gift. Unfortunately you have caught us at a time when we are entertaining. Might I take this from you with our thanks?"

"How does he know you?" Gus asked, perplexed.

"She and her brother"—Duncan indicated Christine and Alex with his head—"stayed in my home when they 'ere flooded out."

"Brother?" Gus and Leonard uttered at the same time.

Gus shook his head. "You mean to say Sir Alexander. This is my sister's fiancé."

As soon as the words were out of his mouth, he must have realized what lie his sister had told Duncan in order to keep her reputation safe. It was too late, though, because the words were out. Leonard was not very far behind in comprehension.

"You were forced to marry her," he said slowly as under-standing dawned. He brought his eyes from Alex to Christine, then back again.

"You decided you had to marry her when this whole thing could simply have remained a dalliance. Why? If you said you were brother and sister and nothing came of it, why must you go through with this farce of a marriage? That'll ruin everything you have planned for your future. What of those political dinners you spoke of hosting? How is *she* to do it?"

Gus listened to Leonard's insults with growing outrage, and Alex wasn't sure whether he would be called to hold Gus back, or whether he would be the one to plant Leonard a facer. To his surprise, neither happened. With a restraint Alex had not known Gus possessed, he walked over to Duncan and placed a hand on his shoulder.

"I thank you for your hospitality in allowing my sister and her betrothed to seek shelter in your house. And we thank you for the pheasant. Allow me to offer you a gift for your troubles."

He pulled out his coin purse as he drew the trapper out of doors. Duncan's muted response did not seem as though the offer would be refused. Alex, however, had not forgotten his brother's words.

"Let me set one thing straight," he said, reproving his brother with gritted teeth. "Miss Grey's carriage was flooded and carried away by the river current. Thanks to her strength and courage, she was able to escape the carriage and climb out of danger to higher ground. After walking a great distance and nearly freezing to death, she *by chance* landed in the same hut where I was taking shelter. This was no dalliance." His last words were laced with icy rage, but he was not finished.

"And yes, we agreed to marry to calm the gossip that threatened—not only her reputation, but also my political career. However, make no mistake. I am marrying Miss Grey because she is the only woman I wish to have for my wife." His breathing was controlled from the effort of keeping his fists at his side rather than raising them to his brother's face.

Christine had kept her eyes firmly fixed ahead at some distant point, but at these words she at last brought her regard to Alex. The look of warmth in it only fueled his feeling. She was not beholden to him in any way. He was marrying her because he wished to.

Gus stepped back into the room and seemed to assess the mood in it. Alex was fairly certain he had heard at least a part of what he'd said. The footman had come to close the door, but this effort was blocked by the arm of another visitor seeking entrance. He opened the door wider, and Martin Pasley stepped through it. He dispensed with the formalities.

"Grey, I'd like a word with you."

Gus pulled his attention from the scene he had partially witnessed and faced Martin. He broadened his stance and folded his arms defensively. "What is it?"

"Perhaps we should find somewhere more private," Mr. Pasley suggested, but from the look on Gus's face, he was too excited to think logically. Christine stepped forward, but Gus threw out a hand to stop her.

"What you have to say, you can say here."

"Very well," Mr. Pasley said, eyeing Gus with resolve. "Although your sister's reputation has been restored by her engagement to Sir Alexander, I have come to tell you that I have not changed my mind about *my* sister's marrying into this family. In fact, I object to it."

Alex threw Christine a questioning glance. Her brother had proposed to Sarah Pasley? He supposed it had not been long in coming, but it was hard to think of any wedding but his own.

When he had envisioned this visit, he had not gone beyond hoping for an apology from Leonard—and a vague desire that everything would be restored to harmony. The last thing he'd expected was for an objection regarding marriage to come from another quarter. Well, perhaps that was not the last thing he'd expected. That honor had to go to the trapper's surprise appearance.

"You see," Leonard whispered to him in a loud aside. "I'm not the only one who objects to the idea of marrying into this family."

Alex was not sure that Gus had heard him, but the reply he made to Mr. Pasley served to answer Leonard as well.

"That's rich. You are objecting to Sarah marrying into our family, and yet I am a gentleman, and my sister is a gentleman's daughter. What are you? What is your standing in society? *You* are a mere apothecary who must work for his living. I hardly think you the appropriate one to protest a match on the grounds of lack of suitability."

At his side, Leonard was growing red around the collar. Although Alex was thankful his brother could hear Gus's retort that set Christine back in the place of honor she deserved, he was less thankful when his brother entered into a discussion that was not his own.

"It is just like a gentleman to think that your honorific makes a man," Leonard said. "There are other reasons why marrying into a family might not be desirable. A match in the wrong family might hinder you from achieving the position you seek. Or the family might be inferior in wealth, which I suspect is the case with you, Mr. Grey."

Mr. Pasley was not slow to join in. "Or you might object because of the character of the man your sister wishes to marry."

He squared up to Gus with a puffed-up chest, like a cock about to fight. "Sarah will spend her days bludgeoned by your lack of sensibility and will likely be dragged all over the country-side on one of your precious hunts. You care more about them than you ever will her."

"Enough." Christine broke her silence with the command. Alex had never heard her speak like that, and he turned to her in admiration.

"Martin, although your relationship with your sister is none of my business, I do know she is of age. And I am sorry to be the one to tell you this, for brothers are very often the last person to understand their sisters, but Sarah is perfectly suited to Gus, despite what you had hoped for her. They might not be the most orthodox couple, but they will be very happy together as they share the same passions."

She then turned to Leonard. "Mr. Thorne, I am very sorry I do not meet with your approval as a candidate for your brother's hand. But your brother and I are also of age, and we have decided to marry. The reasons going into it do not matter. All that does is our own happiness, and such a thing is the business of the two of us alone."

Alex stepped forward and grabbed her hand to kiss it, his bold little fiancée. That she had echoed the very thing he had said to himself only increased his conviction that they were right for each other. The fact that she did not tremble to make her voice heard when she knew what was right made him want to sweep her outdoors into some private corner and kiss her on the spot. No matter what his brother thought, she was the wife for him.

They were perfectly suited and would be happy. They would be most happy, indeed.

CHAPTER TWENTY-THREE

Alex and Leonard's ride home was carried on in a cautious truce, where Leonard gave his word not to utter another critical word about Miss Grey, and Alex promised to continue to make every effort to advance the success of his two nieces in their London debut. Shortly after they arrived back at Gracefield, they sat down to an early dinner, where they struggled through a stilted conversation.

Only the first course had been served when the distant sounds of a carriage approaching reached their ears. Alex was not expecting any visitors and only hoped, due to the unusual hour, that the visit was not to herald bad news.

They continued to eat as if there had been no interruption, while the butler went to investigate. There were the muffled sounds of the visitor's arrival, and shortly thereafter the dining room door opened again. Davies entered.

"A Mrs. Martha Thorne, a Miss Anna Thorne, a Miss Clara Thorne."

"Why, what is this?" Leonard exclaimed, nearly knocking over his chair in his haste to go and greet his wife and daughters. It was a distance of three large rooms to reach the main hallway, and Leonard was nearly jogging to get there. Alex was not far behind.

"Martha," Leonard exclaimed as soon as he saw her. "I am all astonishment to find you here. You did not apprise me of your coming."

"You gave me no chance to," his wife replied calmly, allowing him to kiss her cheek. "You left before I was able to tell you I also wished to meet my future sister-in-law."

This surprising revelation silenced Leonard, and Alex was able to go forward and bow over his sister-in-law's hand. There was something sympathetic in her demeanor and reply that encouraged him to risk kissing her on the cheek, which he had never done before. He was beginning to suspect he would have an ally in Martha.

He then bowed over both of his nieces' hands in greeting, who returned embarrassed curtsies.

"Please join us in the dining room, where we have been sitting down to an early dinner," Alex urged his sister-in-law. "I am confident my cook will be able to come up with more dishes, and I hope you will accept my simple fare."

"I am not overly particular," Martha assured him.

Alex delivered the orders to his butler. "Have the footman add three places to the table. And tell Mrs. Mulhouse that we have additional guests. If there is any of the white soup left from yesterday's meal, she might bring some. And tell the maid..."

He stopped short, distressed at the idea that he would need to find three more rooms to put his newest guests, when he knew none were serviceable. He turned to Martha with a look of hesitation on his face.

"I fear I will not be able to welcome you in the way I would have liked. Gracefield House has been vacant for over a decade and is in a deplorable state still. It will be some time before my wife and I can hope to offer you the accommodations you deserve."

Martha smiled and shook her head. "I beg you will not distress yourself over this. I will happily share Leonard's room for the sake of convenience, and the girls can also share a room. And—I am hoping this does not offend you—but I did bring enough linens for our family, as well as a few other comforts, for I had given you no notice of our arrival."

Alex thanked her, grateful for her gracious manner and her practicality. "I am glad you did. Please follow me," he called over his shoulder as he led the way back into the dining room.

Leonard walked at her side with their two girls following behind, and Alex listened to his brother's nervous questions about the comfort and safety of their journey.

Alex had never come to know his sister-in-law well. While his father was alive, he had always stayed with him at their family home, and therefore only met Martha occasionally over a family dinner. After their father died, Leonard did not go out of his way to invite Alex to stay at their house, but rather sought opportunities to visit Alex instead. He never knew why this was but suspected his brother saw no point in increasing the familiarity between a wife, whose relationship was of a sentimental nature, and a brother whose was of a practical one. He wondered if that was about to change despite Leonard.

The footman added the place settings, and they all took their seats in the dining room. Several extra dishes including the white soup were quickly brought up, which showed that Mrs. Mulhouse—bless her—was capable of dealing with the unexpected.

"I hope you will tell me more about this wife you have chosen," Martha said as she dipped the large silver spoon into her soup and sipped it noiselessly. "I do not have a sister and have always thought it must be nice to have one. I am looking forward to meeting her."

She could not have said anything that would have delighted Alex more. "I am sure she will be equally pleased to make your acquaintance. I will send word to see if she might come and visit us tomorrow."

Although his two nieces said nothing during the dinner, and Leonard was more quiet than usual—Alex guessed he was abashed to have so misread his wife's thoughts on the matter of the upcoming marriage—Alex grew in appreciation for his sister-

238

in-law. She was full of surprises and showed such kindness and good-natured behavior, he was ready to call her a friend by the time everyone bid each other goodnight.

The next day, Alex received a reply from his betrothed saying that she would come, and that they might expect her at two o'clock. Right on the hour, the sound of the knocker brought Alex to his feet, and he went into the corridor to greet Christine himself after Davies opened the door. She entered and began untying her bonnet, smiling shyly up at him.

"I was pleased to receive your note, for we left things rather unsettled," she said.

That was much more than he deserved, considering the insults his brother had continued to deliver ever since he had arrived, and which she'd finally had to put to rest herself.

Alex slipped his hand under her arm and pulled her close. "After my brother's display yesterday, for which I heartily apologize, we received the unexpected arrival of my sister-in-law and two nieces."

"Yes, your note told me as much." She tilted her head up, and he saw her look of caution. He rushed to reassure her.

"I made a very pleasant discovery in my sister-in-law last night. I do not think you will suffer the same fate at her hands, for she seems very keen to meet you." They were at the door, and he leaned in to whisper. "I had always assumed she was even more snobbish than my brother, but it appears I was wrong."

They entered the drawing room, where the introductions were made. Leonard was now perfectly civil, which did not surprise Alex, for he thought Martha would have something to say to it if he was not. His sister-in-law greeted his Christine with warmth. And she, in turn, asked Martha about their journey, before turning to the two girls.

"Anna, if I were to guess, I would say that you are thirteen years old. How close am I?"

"Yes, ma'am. You are exactly right." The girl blushed and Christine smiled at her before turning to her sister.

"And Clara, I would guess your age at twelve?"

"Eleven, ma'am."

"Eleven," Christine repeated. "You look older. Do either of you like animals?"

His youngest niece lifted her face with a radiant smile that he had never himself been witness to.

"I adore them. A cat had five kittens in our stable. The groom allowed us to play with them until they had to be given away because there were too many to keep." Her lips turned down in disappointment at the recollection of their absence.

Christine gave an understanding smile. "I adore cats, too. I have three."

When both girls turned to her with expressions of envy, she sent them a conspiratorial look before her eyes flitted to Alex. "I have been dreading to ask your uncle if I might bring my three cats and my little pug, Guinea, to his house after we are married. Do you think he might allow it?"

Her eyes were on him when she asked this, though the smile still hovered on her lips.

"Oh, but of course you must, uncle," Anna exclaimed, with Clara adding her voice.

"Why, yes I must," he assured his nieces, pretending to think about it. "After all, the house is big enough that we might shut them in an empty wing and never have to see them."

His two nieces protested this idea loudly, but he was pleased to see Christine chuckle.

They sat down to tea, and Christine displayed a gift of pulling not only Martha, but also both of his nieces, into the discussion. He would never have guessed her to be so skilled in the art of conversation, but he was beginning to suspect she only made the effort when she considered her contribution necessary.

Alex also guessed that the warm attention she was giving to the women in Leonard's family had gone a long way to mollifying his brother. As the visit came to an end, he watched her and Martha near the doorway, sharing a quiet confidence. His nieces seemed like a puzzle box that had finally been opened. They had become more voluble and chattered with their father like two magpies in a way he had never imagined them to do. It also allowed him to see Leonard in his best light—as a truly doting father.

When Christine at last took her leave—he accompanied her down the steps to her carriage but could not steal a kiss because her groom and his footman were both there—Alex rejoined Leonard and his family in the drawing room. Martha suggested in a voice not to be countermanded that her daughters go to their room and work at their cross-stitch.

"She is delightful," Martha affirmed, once the three of them were alone. "I could not have hoped for a better sister-in-law, and I am sure she will make you an excellent wife, Alex."

Leonard was not one to give up a battle easily. "I hope you may be right, Martha. But let us not forget that she will not bring our daughters into the cream of London society, for she does not know anyone there."

Alex could not refrain from taking up his fiancée's defense. "Leonard, I told you that I will happily launch your daughters for their season when the time comes, and although I have not yet had the chance to speak to Christine about it, I am sure she will be happy to do so as well."

"You must see it is not the same as having connections, though," his brother argued.

Martha sat and carefully arranged her skirts. "Our girls are shy, and we will need to bring them to the local balls when they are of age so they might practice before they have their season. I have always thought that London society might be a bit intimidating for our girls to attempt directly."

Leonard prepared himself to launch into a protest, but she went on without allowing him to begin.

"I am convinced that a woman like Miss Grey will be able to draw them out of their shells and set them to the best advantage in London society when the time comes." She dimpled at her husband and patted his arm. "Although I know how hard it is when you set your mind on a thing."

Alex had to work hard to bite back a smile.

The next days were more pleasant than he could have contemplated an extended visit with his brother could be. Leonard and his family were to stay until the wedding, and he would conduct his operations by correspondence. And Martha was introduced to Honoria when she next came to see how the renovations were coming along for the bride's chamber. The two women took to one another straight away, and Martha approved the changes that were being made with as much enthusiasm as her natural temperament allowed.

When Alex was certain that his brother's family was comfortably settled at Gracefield, he excused himself for a two-day trip that he had been planning and could no longer put off.

Before Leonard's surprise visit, he had made plans to go to Grantham. He'd had an idea in mind of something to give to Christine, ever since Honoria mentioned the beaded gown that Christine had been disappointed to lose in the flood. He did not know the first thing about buying her a gown, but he thought he might find beads similar to the ones she lost. He was willing to bet his two days' travel to Grantham that he would find them there, even when she had not had success on her last trip.

The beads might serve as a wedding gift—a token gift, at least, since it was such short notice. There were other things he wanted to give her, such as jewelry, but he had a lifetime for that.

The miles seemed to pass quickly as he journeyed onward, and he spent them in pleasant reflection. He thought about the day he would finally marry Christine—for whom he was beginning to feel the buddings of love. He imagined the look of pleasure on her face when he handed her the beads. She would know the strength of his attachment then. She would see how far he was willing to go to get them for her.

Unfortunately, the idyllic picture he had conjured ended at Grantham, for his search in the haberdashery there turned up empty-handed. It was naïve of him, perhaps, but he had been optimistic that the mere desire to offer her this gift of sentiment would be enough to ensure a successful mission. He looked around for something else that might serve as a gift but found nothing special—nothing that could not be had in any town.

The next day when he neared home, he decided on a whim to continue on beyond his house and go to Horncastle to look there. He could not imagine declaring defeat so soon and remembered that there was a haberdasher's shop in town. Perhaps there were even two. He had deposited his carriage in the mews and was on his way to the shop on foot when he crossed paths with Mrs. Reid and Mrs. Pickering.

He continued on, expecting them to ignore him, or whisper about him, as they had done and was therefore surprised when they called out his name. He almost did not acknowledge them, but held his antipathy firmly in check and stopped to hear what they wished to say.

"Sir Alexander, we hear you are to be married. Allow us to congratulate you," Mrs. Reid said. "I have not seen you in the creamery as of late. Perhaps Mr. Reid and I might extend an invitation to dinner, for we are in the habit of dining with the same families in Horncastle as you are."

Mrs. Pickering stood at Mrs. Reid's side, with a benign smile as though nothing unpleasant had ever occurred between them.

He thought of all he might say and dismissed it before asking in a carefully neutral voice, "Have you then gone to apologize to Miss Grey?"

"Apologize?" Mrs. Pickering answered, claiming her share in the conversation. "But why should we? All *I* did was to merely state the conditions in which she had been discovered, which was nothing less than the truth."

He cocked his head, still refraining from showing his dislike, though it was difficult to suppress.

"Come, come, Mrs. Pickering. You are not a naïve woman," he said. "You knew when you disclosed to the world at large that you had seen us together what the implications would be—as well as what the damage would be to her character."

He paused to let that sink in, adding, "I would think a woman who serves as housekeeper to a man of the cloth would

243

be careful not to engage in gossip—or the first to cast stones on her fellow parishioners."

She made no reply to this, but he could see in her heightened color that it was rather hurt pride than hurt conscience that reigned supreme within her. He turned to Mrs. Reid.

"And I know you have been busy on our behalf as well, for the woman who works in your shop was very free in sharing her opinion of my character when I went there. She would not do so if you had not allowed it."

Mrs. Reid gave no answer to this, and he said, "I shall be delighted to return to the creamery when you have apologized to my betrothed." He gave them a cold bow. "As for the dinner invitation, I will leave that for her to decide."

Alex walked on and heard Mrs. Pickering mutter something about his slim chances of election to the parliamentary seat if he was to be so high in the instep, but he paid it no heed. Right now, he had won something more valuable. He had defended Christine's honor, and she deserved nothing less. For that, he was triumphant.

His first look into the haberdashery on High Street turned up nothing, but the shop owner reluctantly admitted that he had a competitor who had his shop on Church Lane. Alex thanked him, promising future patronage, then went out to seek out the second place. This shop was much less fit for genteel society, with its hodgepodge of boxes and heaps of ribbons strewn about in no particular order. He entered and greeted the man behind the counter.

"Good day. I am looking for beads to sew onto a dress. They must be very small in nature, but not necessarily uniform in size. It is most important that they be made of glass and have a shimmer to them."

"What color?" the man asked, turning to the shelves behind him that held an impossible number of boxes. Alex was lost for a moment as he had not thought to ask, nor had he told Honoria what he planned to do.

"I do not know, but I suppose clear would do."

The man had been rummaging through the boxes, and he turned around with one box in his hand. "Don't have any clear ones. Appear to 'ave only these yellow ones. Otherwise, they're what ye want."

Alex took the box and poured some of the beads into his hand and carried them over to the window. When in the sunlight, they did seem to glitter like stars. Little though he knew of such things, he thought it must be what Christine had been looking for. He was elated over his unexpected success and turned back to the shopkeeper.

"I'll take the lot of them."

CHAPTER TWENTY-FOUR

C hristine put the finishing touches on the frame she had
made to hold Alex's mother's portrait. She had
eschewed the traditional gold paint because it did not
match the colors in the painting; the frame had needed to be
much simpler.

Since she was not a skilled woodcarver, she made the frame
by applying *papier-mâché* columns to a simple wood frame and
formed vines and leaves to add to it. Once the glue was dry, she
painted it a light green color she hoped would be in perfect
harmony with the greenery in the portrait—that was, if she had
remembered it correctly. Apart from the time spent sewing her
gown for the wedding, she invested her remaining waking hours
on the frame, working until she was satisfied.

On the day she and Martha had first been introduced, they'd
arranged for Martha to send her a signal when Alex was away
from the house. With any luck, she would have enough time to
frame the portrait, and perhaps even hang it in a place of honor,
while he was gone. When Martha sent word at last, Christine
learned she would be more than lucky. He would be gone for *two*
days.

This first piece of good news was chased by a second, less

happy one. Alex had not informed her that he would be leaving town. She would have liked for him to have told her and tried not to think about what it meant for their future that he didn't. Would he leave town frequently without apprising her of it?

She did not finish the frame until the second day of his absence, and as soon as she was able, she brought it to Grace-field. Martha received her at the entrance, and together they went to the breakfast room where Christine unearthed the painting. She carefully removed it from its elaborate gilded frame and set it in the lighter one she had made. Once the portrait was secure, she turned it over and looked at it.

"Oh," she breathed and stopped for a moment to admire the effect. Although the faux Grecian background could not be helped, the painting now showed to advantage, for the colors of the new frame brought out his mother's lovely green eyes and the dress she wore.

"It is much improved," Martha agreed. They brought it to the drawing room, where they discussed the best place to hang it.

"I believe we should place it here," Christine said, pointing to an empty recess between two windows that was bare of furnishing. "I know the room has not yet been redone, and the portrait will not necessarily be set to advantage with this old wall color. But I do want for Alex to see it when he returns."

"An excellent idea. The wall there is missing something of this size," Martha agreed. "Allow me to fetch the footman so he might hang it for us."

"Oh no, that is not necessary. I know how to do it myself." Christine had carried a small bag containing a hammer and nails in the event that the tools would not be found when needed. She could not be sure of how prepared Alex's servants were.

She stood on a chair to hang it, with Martha hovering anxiously by, then stepped back to admire her work. The portrait and frame were the perfect size for the alcove. And even though the color in the room was not what it should be, the portrait already brightened this section of the wall. She stared at the painting, content, and offered a quiet thanks to the woman who had given birth to Alex.

The door opened behind them, and Mr. Thorne stepped in. He walked over to them and stopped short when he saw the painting.

"Why, that is a nice painting of my mother." He peered at it. "Perhaps it belongs in our house instead. The one we have of Mother has a more traditional look and must be better suited to this house. I will propose to Alex that we exchange them."

Martha put her hand on her husband's arm. "No, Leonard. This is Alex's painting, and Christine has just made a most beautiful frame to go with it. It is her wedding gift to him. I forbid you to take it from them."

"Ah, very well," he grumbled. "I suppose I am used to the other picture at the mill."

The front door opened again, and they heard the sounds of the butler greeting his master. Christine's heart began to thump frantically.

So this is what it's like to fall in love with somebody, she thought. It seemed one's emotions were destined to fly all over the place. She kept her eyes on the door until it opened.

Alex stepped into the drawing room. "Davies said you were here."

His glance soared past Martha and her husband and came to rest on Christine. Smiling, he came and took both of her hands in his and placed a kiss on them.

"I did not expect to have the felicity of seeing you so soon upon my return. I have been away, you see," he explained.

She returned his smile, willing him to lift his eyes above her. At her back was the painting, perfectly in his line of vision. She saw the minute his eyes fell on it, because his mouth dropped open. He let go of her hands and walked over to it.

"Why, you bought a frame for it," he exclaimed in wonder.

"She *made* a frame for it," Martha corrected.

"It is..." He could not finish his sentence and seemed to be holding in emotion.

Christine came to stand at his side and tucked her arm under his. Behind them, Martha told Leonard that she had been wishing to show him one of the books she had found in the library and successfully steered him from the room. It was now just the two of them, and they turned to face each other.

"Christine." His voice was full of affection. He began to lift his hand to her face but stopped and took her hands instead. "I dare not kiss you, for I am covered in dirt. But I do indeed thank you for this gift. I will treasure it."

She swallowed the lump in her throat. "Please forgive me for the unkind comment I made about your mother's portrait."

"I do forgive you. And now you have improved it beyond everything," he answered, shaking his head. "I am proud to show it. When I think of the hours you spent... This is perhaps the kindest thing anyone has ever done for me."

She smiled up at him then, her eyes flooding with moisture that she blinked away. "I hope there will be many more instances to do kind things for you. I shall certainly seek them out."

His answering smile fell and his look grew hesitant. "We have never spoken about our future and the time we will spend between Lincolnshire and London, and we must do so at some point. I have not yet told you this, but I have long promised my brother I would launch his daughters in London society. We will be required to see to their care for two seasons at least, and it is not something I can do without your assistance."

As Christine contemplated this, he added, "Of course, we can discuss this after our wedding."

She set her hand on his arm and looked at him. "I dearly love Lincolnshire and could happily spend all my days here." Alex nodded—he knew that.

She paused, choosing her words before looking up at him. "However, as much as I want to continue our life here, which makes me happy, I have an equally strong desire as your wife to follow you in the life that makes you happy. I want to accompany you in the things you aspire to. And if that means learning to host parties in London—even in the years when you are not required to launch your nieces—then I am ready to do so."

Alex pulled away to study her face, his brows knit. "I did not expect as much—did not hope for as much. I was going to suggest that you stay here in the months I must spend in London, except perhaps to beg you to come for a visit so I will not miss you too much."

She smiled at him. "We will have many more occasions to discuss this at the right time, but I have drawn a similar conclusion. I am beginning to fear I will grow so used to you that I will miss you, as well. These are things I must take into consideration when determining where to spend those months during Parliament."

At these words, Alex pulled Christine into his arms and kissed her, seeming to forget all about his earlier reticence at having just returned from traveling. It was impetuous and romantic at first, as though he acted on impulse and wished only to continue their conversation in a way that did not require words. As she kissed him back, her lips reveling in the novelty of exploring his, the kiss grew softer and more intimate. She leaned into him, wanting more, until noises from somewhere in the house recalled them both to their surroundings.

He pulled away and looked at her. "My dear Christine. A little more than two weeks and you will become my wife." She beamed up at him. It seemed she had lost her words as well.

Alex looked as though he remembered something, and he began feeling in his waistcoat pockets. "I went to Grantham, because Honoria told me about the beads you had sewn onto your dress for the Stuff Ball that you were sad to lose. I wanted to find more for you, even though I was going merely on description."

Christine looked at him fondly. "I could have saved you the trouble. I knew that they were no longer there, for I had searched for more in Grantham even before I finished the gown."

"You were right; they were out." Alex pulled the parcel out of his coat and smiled. "However, I took a chance by looking at the shops here in Horncastle. Not the one on High Street, but the smaller one on Church Lane."

Wordlessly, he handed her the package wrapped in brown paper. Her mouth formed a little circle as she unwrapped the parcel. Inside were beautiful yellow beads that were indeed what she had been looking for, and very similar to what she had lost, except for the color.

"It might be too late for it," Alex said, "but I had thought you might sew them onto your wedding dress—that is, if you wish to."

"Oh, Alex," she said softly, smiling at his thoughtfulness. "I love them and will certainly find a use for them." She met his gaze, her smile turning uncertain on her lips. "However, the dress I am sewing for our wedding is green."

She laughed, watching his face as comprehension finally dawned on him. "These beads will not do at all for the wedding then, will they?" he said.

"Not a bit." She stood on her tiptoes and kissed him softly on his lips. "But I will find the perfect use for them, you will see. Thank you."

"You are most welcome," he replied. "I look forward to giving you more gifts in hopes I might do better in the future."

Christine thought this earned him another kiss and stood on tiptoe to pay the reckoning.

THE REMAINING days until the wedding flew by, bringing with them many tasks and two surprises. The first was the determined knock on their door that Christine was forced to answer since her maid was upstairs with the entirety of Christine's wardrobe stacked in neat piles, and the footman was bringing up the trunks.

She opened the door, and on the other side of it stood Mrs.

Reid, looking defiant. The short woman pulled her stout frame upright. Christine could not imagine what had brought her to their door.

"Well, Miss Grey, as you can see, I have come."

Christine looked behind her as though the empty courtyard could solve the mystery of why Mrs. Reid had decided to do so now. She put her hand on the door. "I see."

"Are you going to invite me in?" Mrs. Reid asked even more belligerently, angling her sturdy frame as though to lend strength to her words.

"I am not immediately of a mind to," Christine answered carefully. "I would have been very glad of your visit in the days following my near escape from death."

She used a strong image in her speech to purpose, although she did not often allow herself to contemplate the danger she'd faced on that day.

"Well." Mrs. Reid looked at her uncomfortably. "I don't doubt you would have liked that, but a person cannot be too careful, you see."

"Good day, Mrs. Reid," she said, closing the door.

"Wait!"

Christine did not know what stopped her from shutting the door firmly in the woman's face, but it might have been the pleading sound in her voice. She opened the door again and waited.

"You are right. I should have come after your rescue to see for myself that it was not an assignation between you and Sir Alexander. It's just that the evidence was difficult to refute."

Christine exhaled and thought how best to answer this. There was nothing to say on the matter to convince a person of something who would not be convinced, but she said it anyway.

"To the pure, all things are pure, Mrs. Reid. I would have liked to have you believe in my innocence, despite the evidence you thought you had, simply based on your knowledge of my character."

At once, Mrs. Reid lost her bravado. "Yes, yes. I should have. After all, I knew your parents, God rest their souls."

This touching display caused Christine to soften towards her and she gently touched her on her arm. But Mrs. Reid had not finished.

"And now I have fewer patrons coming into my shop, and it is most distressing."

This caused fat tears to fall down Mrs. Reid's face and Christine's mouth to slacken as the woman's words sank in. She was just wondering what she was going to do with her when her saving grace came in the form of Sarah Pasley, who ran toward her from the stables.

"Christine, come! Brown Birch is about to foal. Gus said you will want to see this. Oh. Good day, Mrs. Reid."

Christine knew she would not be as interested a spectator as either Gus or Sarah to the event, but it saved her from wondering how to rid herself of her visitor.

"I will come directly," she told Sarah.

"Do say you will forgive me," Mrs. Reid said. "I will admit my fault to anyone who asks."

"I forgive you," Christine said promptly. "Thank you for your visit. I know you will understand if I must go now."

"Oh yes, of course." Mrs. Reid looked relieved. "I hope to see you soon at the creamery. You can tell everyone we are perfectly reconciled."

Christine nodded, offering her a polite smile. "I will certainly do so just as soon as Sir Alexander and I have returned from our honeymoon."

She had no idea if there was to be a honeymoon, but she would rather stay locked up in a cellar at Gracefield Park than let anyone think a honeymoon had not been planned.

Mrs. Reid turned to go back to town, pleased with the success of her mission, and Sarah waited while Christine slipped on her coat and fell into step beside her as they walked toward the stables.

"That woman," Sarah exclaimed, wrinkling her nose. "I

253

assume she came to apologize? I would not have forgiven her so easily. Why did you?"

"Because..." Christine hardly knew. She did forgive her, although she was not likely ever to trust herself to Mrs. Reid again. "Because I suppose we all make mistakes and need forgiveness."

"I am not so convinced she was in search of forgiveness," Sarah answered drily. "She is worried that no one will receive her anymore or buy her goods. Did you know that many of the townspeople have stopped purchasing her butter, although it is the best in the area?"

She hadn't known. Christine had not been deceived about Mrs. Reid's motivations, either, but she would not have changed her response.

"Perhaps she did apologize for the wrong reasons, but either my forgiveness will soften her and she will be changed by it, or"—she shrugged—"she will remain exactly the same. But there is nothing I can do about *that*. Besides," she added, "the town is too small to have enemies."

"True. We must not make an enemy out of Mrs. Reid," Sarah agreed.

Then, with a wicked grin, she added, "We will simply be *exceedingly* cordial."

CHRISTINE'S other surprise came on the day her trunks were brought to Gracefield Park. It was three days before their wedding, and although Alex had intimated on one of his visits that he was hesitant to let her see her room before the wedding, she asked him to make allowances for her. It would ease her mind if she could unpack her own trunk and grow used to the room that was to be hers. She assured him that she would not utter a single complaint about it, even though there was much work yet to be done.

Alex detained her in the drawing room while his footman and hers both carried up the trunks to the bedchamber that would be hers. Only once they had finished did he lead her upstairs. He opened the door to her bedchamber and stepped back to let her see it.

To her astonishment, the room was completely redone. It was newly painted, with a fresh mattress and new curtains that were pulled back to show the view beyond the sparkling paned-glass windows. Her trunks sat against the wall, but there was still plenty of space to walk around them. She could even have a sewing table placed on one side of the room if she wished.

"Alex, it is simply amazing," she cried out, stepping in and turning about to take everything in.

"I am so glad you think so," he said with a contented look. He grabbed her hand and brought her over to see the sizeable dressing room in one corner and then pointed to the door that adjoined her room with his. "And this is where I sleep, but I'll show you that another time. My room has not been touched, but that does not matter."

"We will do yours soon," she promised, smiling up at him.

"But not too soon," he replied. "Do not forget there is the honeymoon."

"*Will* there be one?" She clasped her hands in front of her. "I hadn't dared to ask."

His look was one of mock outrage. "Of *course* there will be a honeymoon. I shall overlook this additional evidence of your lack of faith in me."

When this bit of teasing caused her to look uncertain, he tugged her until she was close enough to put his arms around her.

"I will not trade the weeks that should be devoted to learning about my new wife for anything else. As for the honeymoon, we are to do a tour of Lincolnshire. I hope that meets with your approval?"

She nodded, grinning up at him, and he added, "After all, this is your favorite shire in all of England. I think it's only fair to visit every corner of it on our honeymoon if I am going to ask you to sacrifice some of your time to London in the years that follow."

"I suppose so," she said, beaming at him in happiness. She had never grinned so much in her life. She was turning into the silliest of creatures, betrothed to this man.

THE DAY of the wedding arrived, and Christine was fully dressed in her pale green silk dress that had been embroidered around the neckline with dark green thread. She was looking in the mirror at the effect this produced on her and turned when Gus entered.

He was looking handsome, having trimmed his hair and wearing the new suit he'd had made—which he told her was more for his own wedding, but he may as well have it done in time for hers. If she harbored some doubt that he would actually remember her wedding, now that he was caught up in the plans for his own, she was happy to be wrong when he came to escort her to the church.

Honoria and Arabella were waiting outside the church in fur-trimmed cloaks, and they both came over to her with broad smiles when she stepped out of the carriage.

"We could not go in until we had a glimpse of you," Honoria said. "There is a very nervous groom waiting at the front of the church. He will know you have arrived when he sees us go back in and take our seats."

"Go then, go!" Christine said, laughing, before recalling her words. "No, do not rush. You are both in the family way, and there is nothing that cannot wait, after all."

Arabella gave a little wave, and they both hurried into the church without heeding her appeal for caution.

Breathless, Christine licked her lips, then gave her brother a smile. "This is it, Gus. A new life for us both."

"That it is." He put his arm around her shoulders and pulled her in for a hug. "Who would have thought it would all end so happily for us?"

Christine cocked her head and considered this. "I suppose I had always hoped it would deep down, even if I tried to protect my heart by convincing myself otherwise. But hope is a presumptuous thing, don't you think?" she asked Gus with a bright smile. "It cannot be tamed."

EPILOGUE

Two Years Later

Gracefield Park had been fully decorated for Christmas, with both the drawing room and dining table resplendent with evergreens and cheerful red berries, white candles, and red and green bows.

The guests had finished feasting on a Christmas supper and were now gathered around the armchairs and sofas in the drawing room, where the intention had been to play a game of charades. For the moment, however, everyone was too comfortable and full from the meal to wish to begin.

Christine let her eyes stray to her husband's and he came over to her side, putting his hand on her lower back and letting the warmth and comfort of it settle there. Across the room, Arabella and Honoria sat on the lower sofa allowing their children, Amelia and Henry, the pair close in age, to sit at their feet while they played with wooden rings.

Arabella's older son, David, was following the tabby under the chairs, followed by an admiring Matthew who cheered him on. But Ichabod always managed to twitch his tail and elude his pursuer at the last minute. Theo and Philip stood on the side of the room in conversation, each with a glass of port in their hands. They called out occasional admonishments to their sons not to knock anything over.

It was a domestic scene, made no less so by Sarah Grey and Barbara Bassett discussing in earnest tones the importance of supplying babies with charms to wear to counter the drastic effects of teething. After an initial period of infertility, Barbara had delivered herself of a healthy boy over the summer and had become an expert on all things related to infanthood. Meanwhile, Gus and Samuel attempted to out-boast the other with their individual exploits during last year's hunt, which was considered superior to this year's.

Roger Garrick and his wife stood near the chimney, in which blazed a cheerful fire. Mary caught Christine's eye, and she linked her arm through her husband's to bring him over. Roger and Alex stepped aside to begin a discussion.

"You have made much progress in the house since we last visited," Mary said with an encouraging smile. "And everything is decorated just splendidly. This has been a happy Christmas, has it not?"

She didn't wait for an answer but let her gaze roam around the room. "You have the most delightful connections. There is so much goodness in the friends and family gathered here."

Christine thanked her for the compliment and agreed. There truly was.

She glanced at Gus and Samuel, who had grown flushed as they began to argue, and thought that there was also a great deal of foolishness as well. But after all, what was family for if not to honor the goodness and bear with the foolishness?

She turned to Mary. "I must thank you for your promise to help when we arrive in London this February. I know I shall be quite lost, and I do hope to be an asset to Alex's political career."

They had decided to purchase a London house in a slightly less fashionable—although perfectly respectable—district so they might have a larger house with a small ballroom. Christine was nervous about settling in London for her first season but decided she would not back down from the challenge.

"You may rely on me," Mary assured her. "I was raised in politics, with both my father and older brother in Parliament, and I will be there to guide you. Alex has already proven himself by gaining the seat for South Lindsey, and I am sure you will only shine at his side."

Mary was a vivacious, petite woman with red hair and an inviting smile. She and Christine were similar in height, and although Christine preferred domestic duties to socializing—the perfect foil to Mary—they found much to share in common and had struck up a regular correspondence.

"You will have to see the thermal baths for yourself," Alex was telling Roger at her side. "Once the excavator did its part, all I needed to do was to find a way for my shovel to scoop out the rock and earth so the additional cavern might fill with water—"

"Pooh. Engineering," Mary said, turning back with a pouting smile. "Poor Roger is always so happy to see Alex. He is the only one who shares his interest."

Christine laughed and linked her arm through Mary's, bringing her over to Honoria and Arabella and taking the two remaining chairs there. Guinea left off sniffing at the toddlers and came over to Christine to be picked up. Honoria and Arabella turned to include the women in their discussion.

"Were Alex's brother and his family not able to come?" Honoria asked.

"Unfortunately not," Christine replied. "Martha's mother has fallen ill. Although I do not think it is serious, they preferred to travel and see her instead. I wanted his girls to meet the Garricks, who are sure to help me launch them in society when the day comes," she added with a smile for Mary.

"We have time for that," Mary said. "The oldest won't have her come-out for two more years."

The conversation moved easily from one light topic to another, and Christine knew she needed to deliver the news she had been holding on to but, now that it was time, found it difficult to begin. It must be done, however, before the moment was lost with the four women she most wanted to talk to sitting all in one place.

She seized a brief lull to say, "I have an announcement to make."

Unfortunately, her voice carried, and everyone but Gus and Samuel in the corner ceased to talk as they brought their attention to her. Christine felt her face grow crimson. She glanced at Alex, who shook his head and laughed at her with a knowing smile. He walked across the room to stand behind her and put his hand on her shoulder.

"You might as well tell them since everyone is listening," he said. Christine had intended to tell only the women, but now it seemed they would have no choice but to announce the news to the room at large.

"*Hum.*" She pinched her lips shut and smiled. It was impossible to know how to begin. She'd hoped Alex would help her, but when she glanced up at him, his embarrassed grin revealed his own discomfort.

"You are in the family way," Honoria announced practically. When Christine did not contradict her, she got up and went over to kiss Christine's cheek. "I am so happy for you."

The congratulations flooded in then, with even Gus and Samuel coming over to see what the fuss was about. When Gus was finally made to understand, he said, "I'm to be an uncle and you did not even tell me first."

"Perfectly understandable," Samuel said. "Honoria has never thought to tell me first."

"I am increasing again, Sam," Honoria said. She met Philip's gaze with dancing eyes. "And now you are the first to know."

"For heaven's sake, Honoria," her affectionate brother replied, after he had closed his dropping jaw. "Are you trying to pad Wellington's army? There's no need. Napoleon has abdicated the throne."

Christine joined in the laughter, not at all bothered that the attention was now off of her. Her anonymity was all too brief, though, because Gus piped up again.

"This is everything you women dream of. Think of all the arranged marriages you can plan! Amelia with Henry, Tom and Jane..."

He brought his eyes to her, adding, "Christine and Honoria, if you don't manage to pop out babies of the same sex, you can plan another match, too, while they are still in the cradle."

"No more arranged marriages for me, thank you very much," Christine said, without thinking about the import of her words.

The general roasting that ensued, while causing a deep blush to consume her, showed that no one present was in any doubt about the fact that hers and Alex's was a love match, even if it had not started that way.

"My wife, my heart," Alex protested theatrically, making her laugh and get to her feet.

"My dear one, I have no cause to regret *our* match, but I very much hope our children might choose for themselves."

She allowed Alex to slip his arm around her. Rather than giving her an answer, he called out for the servants to bring everyone a glass, so that he might make a toast. When this was accomplished, he raised his glass as everyone stood and followed suit.

"As for myself, I cannot have anything to say against arranged marriages. Although the bride I was given was the very last one I would have thought to choose, the gracious workings of Providence had a better idea."

Alex tipped his head to look down at Christine, his expression growing tender. "And that is the most fortunate thing to have happened to me." He looked up and raised his glass high.

"To happy endings," he cried out and emptied his glass.

"To happy endings," the guests shouted and did the same.

Alex brought his regard to Christine, waiting until she met his gaze and smiled. "Happy?" he asked her.

She nodded, smiling. "Until the end."

A FEW WORDS ON THE SERIES...

It is with much regret that I bring to a close this glimpse into the lives of our Lincolnshire families. I have grown attached to them, all of them—yes, even Gus. Honoria has always been capable and loyal, but she grew from a green girl, who could not understand her own heart, to a mature woman with a good understanding of human nature. Arabella was able to escape her emotionally impoverished childhood and early adult years and come into her own as a woman loved by family and friends, and ready to stand up and defend those she loves. Christine had to admit that the longings of her heart were valid, and have the courage to go after them, and her reward when she finally did so was great. Our heroes did not have quite such an evolution of character, for the stories were less about them, but let us just say that they were much improved overall by the women they chose as partners in their lives.

A few historical discrepancies in this book that I must mention: the tilbury was not invented until 1815, about a year after this book takes place, but I needed an open carriage pulled by one horse that could be brought on a short overnight journey. Regarding the engineering aspect, which is not my strongest suit, the steam engine was developed in the late 1600s so I have our hero tweaking the engine's performance. The steam excavator was invented in 1796 and the steam shovel in 1836, and let us say Alex's prototypes are the precursor for that later invention. This is fiction, after all.

I am not the biggest fan of epilogues, but I do feel one is needed when it comes to closing a series. I hope the many names that appear (a town's worth) did not cause too much confusion. But now you have an idea of what is in store for all of them. And yes, there is a bit of foolishness (I'm thinking of you, Gus—and Samuel, and sometimes Barbara), but there is a great deal of goodness as well.

My biggest thanks goes out to Rod Stormes, who—as you likely know from earlier acknowledgements—gave me the idea to set a series in Lincolnshire, and then supplied me with a wealth of details, in addition to reading my sloppy first complete draft to catch implausibilities for the time and place.

A huge thanks to Emma Le Noan, my other English reader and dear friend for giving me her input as well. I cannot leave out my critique partner, author Jess Heileman, without whom I might still be wandering in the morass of the muddling middle. And finally, a big thank you to my editors, Jolene Perry of Waypoint Academy for the developmental edit, and Theresa Schultz of Marginalia Editing for her keen eye for commas and word misusage. You guys always make me look good. The illustrations for this series are by the talented Sally Dunne, and I hope to be lucky enough to have her illustrate more for me in the future.

And now, it is time to move on to other series and to other stories. I hope we might meet again there.

ABOUT THE AUTHOR

Jennie Goutet is an American-born Anglophile who lives with her French husband and their three children in a small town outside of Paris. Her imagination resides in Regency England, where her best-selling proper Regency romances are set. She is also author of the award-winning memoir *Stars Upside Down,* two contemporary romances, and a smattering of other published works. A Christian, a cook, and an inveterate klutz, Jennie sometimes writes about faith, food, and life—even the clumsy moments—on her blog, aladyinfrance.com. But if you really want to learn more about Jennie and her books, sign up for her newsletter, on her author website: jenniegoutet.com.

* Photo Credit : Caroline Aoustin

Printed in Great Britain
by Amazon